INVISIBLE

SARAH BOURNE

First published in 2021 by Bloodhound Books.

www.bloodhoundbooks.com

Print ISBN 978-1-914614-39-2

To my family, near and far.

ALSO BY SARAH BOURNE

The Train

~

Ella's War

PART I

1

July 2005

You think I am a terrorist or a deluded fanatic, some burqa-wearing jihadist intent on destroying this country, our way of life, the peace we enjoy. I tell you I am not.

I will set down the truth – no frills, no embellishments. I am not proud of all that I did, nor what was done to me, but I will tell my story honestly. Perhaps you will believe me and nightmares will cease trespassing on my sleep.

My name is Laila Farida Seaver. My given names come from Northern Pakistan and belonged to my father's mother. I believe Laila means beloved, and I certainly felt loved, although not by my namesake. Neither she nor my father knew I existed. It was my mother, Lynette Seaver, and her parents who gave me cuddles and treats, who made me feel loved and precious.

My name has always been important to me, although for different reasons at different times. As a child, I loved that it rhymed with sailor. My mother used to read me a book about

Popeye the Sailor who had adventures all over the world, and I wanted to be like him. My best friend at primary school was called Kaye. I used to call her Kayla to make our names rhyme and we'd pretend we were twins even though we couldn't have looked more different, her with her red hair, and mine black as a raven's wing.

As a teenager, I longed to be called Ann, or Susan, or any name that made me the same as everyone else. Kaye-Kayla had moved away and suddenly I was at high school and everyone looked at me as if I was an alien. Even kids who'd known me all my life suddenly seemed to notice, with the help of strangers' gazes, that I was not the same as them, not quite. I tried to stand up to the bullies, look them in the eye and maintain my dignity, but after suffering stolen lunches, defaced books and gobs of spit, I slid into the corners and stayed out of sight. My gaze no longer met theirs. For years, until I didn't care anymore what they thought of me, I made sure my grades didn't set me apart. I became an expert in ways of being invisible.

After school I left my small Yorkshire town and lived in London, where I began to cherish my name as I made friends with Dimitris and Prakashes, Ivanas and Siobhans, and also found out more about my heritage.

I'm not very good at this, I'm digressing already. I will try to stick to the facts.

On 24 July 2005, I was arrested. Or perhaps detained would be more accurate, as I was never charged with any crime, and for a long time, not even told why I was being held in Solitary Confinement. I capitalise the words because that is how I think of them. Those two words contain all the isolation, the fear and panic I felt. The very same things that a terrorist is meant to make you feel, yet I was the one being terrorised.

Faisal and I were in bed when they came. We hadn't made love, although there was the anticipation of it between us. I remember wishing that we had, that it formed part of that last memory of him.

I think there were seven or eight of them. Perhaps they were expecting trouble, but we offered them none, unless our confusion gave them cause for concern. It may have done – having no idea what they were there for, we weren't very quick to obey their orders, and asked a lot of questions. Or the same question over and over again. We fumbled with clothing and I couldn't find my left shoe. It was wedged under the bed, goodness knows how. I may also have screamed. There was certainly a scream in my head, but I am not sure it made it out into the room. In any case, no one responded.

I wanted to talk to Faisal, to find out what he thought was going on, but we were taken away separately. I wasn't allowed to talk to him or anyone else, not even a solicitor. I thought everyone had that right at least.

I didn't know what crime I was meant to have committed. I kept telling the police that I was innocent of whatever it was that they thought I'd done. Not that I have lived a blameless life – there have been many things that I regret, both in the doing and the not doing. But I am not a criminal.

They – whoever 'they' were – obviously thought I was though. They took me away in a closed van, handcuffed to the bench I sat on. A guard stayed with me, but would not answer any of my questions – why have I been arrested, where are you taking me, what am I supposed to have done? He was stony-faced, wouldn't look at me, and as the journey went on, sweat rings grew under his arms and the van filled with the smell of him and his power.

We stopped eventually, and as the door opened, I caught a glimpse of razor wire and a watchtower before I was marched into a white room and told to strip. A camera moved on its bracket in the corner of the room watching every move, as did the two female guards. I was too scared to do anything but comply, even as I reddened in embarrassment and anger. Why were they making me do this? What was going on? I wanted to cry and had to bite my lip hard to stop the tears from flowing. It seemed important to appear strong.

2

Solitary Confinement

'Open your mouth,' ordered one of the guards. She shone a torch in my mouth.

'Arms up.' I put my arms above my head but brought them down again abruptly when the guard reached for me.

'I said arms up,' she barked. She patted my torso down.

'Bend over.' Hands parted my buttocks in case – what, I'd hidden something there?

I jumped and received a blow on the back for my reaction. The tears started then. Tears of shame and rage.

'Get up on the bed. Lie on your back, bend your knees and let them drop out to the sides.' The guard squirted lubricant onto her gloved hand.

'Why are you doing this?' My knees were firmly together.

'Just do as I say and it'll be over soon. It's procedure.'

The second guard, a brick shithouse of a woman, moved closer, hands on her hips.

All my clothes and possessions were taken away and I was given a white T-shirt, navy jumpsuit, a pair of tracksuit bottoms, knickers too large, a bra with no under-wiring, and told to shower and dress.

I was handcuffed and with one guard on each arm, half dragged through doors and along corridors that all looked the same, until we came to a hallway where I was handed to another pair of guards who pushed me into a small cell, undid the handcuffs and banged the door shut behind me.

On my own, I slid to the floor and sobbed. I was scared, humiliated and confused. It was impossible to know what to do because there was no sense to anything that was happening, and anyway, I was unable to pull myself together enough to produce a coherent thought.

For hours I was too frightened to feel anything else. I cowered in the corner, knees bent up to my chest, staring around the cell for clues as to why I was there. The first time the slot in the door opened I uncoiled in fright, banging my head on the wall, but it was only a meal being pushed through.

When anger replaced fear, I shouted at the camera in the corner, demanded answers, gave those who were watching me the finger. It made no difference to my treatment, and instead of making me feel powerful and strong, my performance made me feel pathetic and small, so I stopped.

Soon I had no idea how long I'd been there already, but guessed it was a couple of days. Nor did I have any idea how long I would be here. There was no one to ask. There was no one who would answer. I asked my questions to the camera that watched my every move. I was afforded no rights, not even a phone call.

Apart from having no information, the worst part of it was the aloneness. I saw no one, heard no one except for a hand when my food was pushed through a slot in the door three times a day.

There was something unspeakably sad about eating on my own. As a child, my mother was always there. Even if she wasn't eating with me, she was there talking, asking about my day, telling me about hers. And when I left home, I shared a house with three other girls, and we always ate together – meals of dubious quality were made bearable by the company. Food is meant to be shared, talked over. How often have my friends and I put the world to rights over bangers and mash, picked over the shards of a broken relationship as we pick over the crumbs of a blueberry cheesecake? Food is for comfort, for sharing, even for easing over the awkwardness of a first date. It is not for eating alone.

My cell was small, spartan, a study in deprivation. Everything was off-white: a plinth with a plastic mattress on it for my bed, concrete shelves. In one corner a stainless steel toilet with basin attached. No hooks to hang anything from. There was no window. No natural light. The door was thick and either it was well soundproofed, or I was the only inhabitant of that place. That prison.

I had little to do but think, make up stories, daydream, but I was scared to let my mind wander in case it took me to places I didn't want to go. Faisal, Mum and Gran. What were they thinking, what did they know about where I was and why? When would I be out of there?

Time was an enemy. The only sign of its passing were the meals poked through the door slot. Porridge for breakfast, a stale sandwich for lunch, meat and veg for dinner. Plain, tasteless. Nothing to enjoy, to stimulate the tastebuds. Nothing to look forward to. The only good thing about them was that they marked out the hours. I knew I had survived the time since the last meal without resorting to beating my head against the wall, or crouching in a corner rocking and burbling. Both these alternatives were tempting at times.

I tried to impose some sense of a routine on my days. At first, I always woke before the Porridge Hour, and did some yoga-like stretches. I hesitate to call it real yoga because I hadn't been doing classes long, and couldn't remember the finer points of the poses, but I did what I could. It took the stiffness out of my back and limbs from lying all night on the thin mattress. I didn't sleep much, or not in long bouts, anyway. The overhead light was on all the time, a long neon strip, and try as I did to block it out, I was still aware of it. The first night I wrapped my T-shirt around my head, but I was shouted at through the slot to take it off. They probably thought I was trying to suffocate myself. So I lay awake, tossing and turning, trying to find a position in which my hip was not being ground into the concrete plinth, and I tried not to think. Or to think about my blessings, as Gran always used to encourage me to. I did not feel blessed there though, so inevitably I ended up unable to focus on the nice memories and ruminated on the negative, on why the hell I was there, on what was going to happen to me. I woke up shouting. I had so many questions and no one to answer them, so I yelled and shrieked and hammered the mattress with my fists and heels. Nobody came. Maybe there was no one out there. Perhaps the guards went home after dinner and watched the scenes in my cell in the comfort of their own homes. Or maybe they were punishing me with their silence.

After my stretches came porridge. I tried to eat it slowly, to make it last longer. It was always cold, lumpy, made with water not milk. There was no sugar. It was barely even nourishing. I washed my thick plastic bowl and spoon in the sink. Breakfast and doing the dishes took maybe ten minutes. Fifteen at most.

Then I paced. Round and round. My cell was three short paces by five. The bed took up the end wall away from the door, there were two shelves as wide as the bed above the foot end. The desk (another concrete plinth) was set next to the bed, the stool bolted to the floor. The toilet and sink were next to the door. I have a rug at home that is bigger than that cell.

After pacing, I sat and read. The books were chosen by the guards. Either they had a warped sense of humour, or it was another form of punishment. They gave me *Great Expectations* by Charles Dickens, and an awful romance called *A Million Miles Away*, with a half-clad woman in the arms of a buff hero on the front, published the year I was born. After a few days they added a magazine to my library. It was almost as old as the books – a *National Geographic* with several pages missing, so that none of the articles were complete and some of the pictures were torn in half. I was not allowed to see a newspaper. I was not allowed to send or receive letters.

When I'd had as much as I could take of pathetic, simpering women and strong heroes or Pip and his obsession with Estella, I walked again until the slot opened declaring Lunch Hour and I handed back my breakfast tray and received my sandwich and watered down juice. The bread curled at the edges, the cheese sweated, the meat was hard and dry where it escaped the bread. The margarine was pale and sparse. It's amazing, though, how long you can make a sandwich last. Tiny mouthfuls chewed a hundred times each. It filled time, gave me something to focus on. If I'd still had my watch I would have set up a competition with myself to see if I could make it last longer every day, but it had been taken away with everything else.

After lunch I washed my paper plate and cup, letting them begin to disintegrate into the sink. It was something to do.

The first couple of days I tried to engage the guard in conversation. All I saw was a hand. It was even difficult sometimes to tell if it belonged to a male or a female; it was there and gone so fast. There was a dark jacket cuff, no other hint as to its owner. A hand only, disembodied. Different hands. Coarse, male hands, one with a wart on the index finger, female hands that had perhaps been softened with creams and lotions.

Silence was all I had. When I was at college I used to think that it would be heaven to have time to myself, uninterrupted, unpeopled. Now I know it's a form of torture. I was aware that I was watched. After my adolescent antics for the camera, I behaved myself because, although I saw no one, they saw me constantly, and the people who watched were the people who decided my fate.

I used to love attention. Being an only child, I had plenty of it from Mum, Gran and Granddad. I knew I was loved. They guided me, protected me and cheered for me as appropriate. The people who watched me in prison did none of that.

Afternoons were writing time. I'd been given a notebook and stubby pencil. I was never much of a writer before. I wasn't the kind of teenager who kept a journal. I have always been good at watching though. The irony was that when I had the time to note my observations down, there was nothing to see. So I wrote about the past, for something to do and so that I remembered what I had outside that place. It was good to write about my family, but painful. I had no idea when I might see them again.

I was brought up in a small town in North Yorkshire. My grandparents owned a shop and a tea room next door to each other on the square, in the centre of which was a stone clock tower, greening with lichen. Mum and I lived in the flat above the café and Gran and Granddad lived over the shop. Granddad had been born there too. His family have always lived in Thirsk. Gran had come from all the way over in Felixkirk, three miles away. They'd met at a church picnic in 1948 and started 'walking out' when they could. Which meant when Granddad walked over after church on Sundays if his father didn't want to be read to. Great Granddad was blinded in the First World War. He lied about his age so he was only sixteen when he joined up and nineteen when shrapnel deprived him once and for all of his sight. When he came home his parents removed most of the furniture from the house so that he didn't fall over it. He never worked again, but he'd sit in the shop and talk to the customers while his parents served them. And he did marry, a local girl who'd been his sweetheart before the war, and who'd waited for him. She died early of some mystery illness, so there was only Granddad to look after his father then.

Great Granddad died the month before I was born. Gran once said that it was a good thing that he didn't know about my birth. I can't have been more than four at the time – I hadn't yet started school. We were out shopping, and we'd bumped into Mrs Rob from the post office. I wondered what she meant, but I wasn't allowed to say anything when she was talking to her friends, because it was rude. I noticed Mrs Rob giving me an odd look, though – an appraising stare, really, as if she'd never seen me before and was assessing whether my great grandfather would have approved. She shook her head, poked a piece of hair back under her hat, and lowered her voice.

'He'd have had a right turn if he'd known, and that's a fact.'

Later that night, I asked Mum why Great Granddad would have had a turn if he'd known about me. She went a bit red, found the mending she was doing suddenly more absorbing, and changed the subject.

It was like that with a lot of my questions when I was little.

No one seemed to want to answer them. Perhaps it was training for being in prison. Maybe they all knew that one day I would be held alone in a cell with no answers.

It was easy to get paranoid in prison, to imagine things and to make strange connections like that one. Of course, I knew that my grandparents and my mother weren't preparing me for a particular future, but with so much time the mind does odd things. I had a lot of weird ideas in Solitary.

The slot opened again at the Dinner Hour, and some sort of meat and vegetables were pushed through plus an unrecognisable dessert, another juice or some water. What would I have given for a decent coffee? Or even an indecent one? Instant, weak, sugarless, but coffee at least? Or a cup of tea?

There was a great café round the corner from my house in London. Saturdays, me, Bhindi, Jeanette and Sooz would go there for breakfast. Well, brunch really. Eggs Benedict with wilted spinach and garlic mushrooms and a large cappuccino. I could almost smell it when I thought about it, and my stomach rumbled. It was torture. In prison I never knew what day it was, but often wondered if my friends were at that café, talking about me, wondering where I'd got to.

I wondered almost constantly what had happened to Faisal. Was he also somewhere in a featureless cell? Why wouldn't anyone tell me anything? As I paced I kicked the walls, glared at the camera. 'I've done nothing. I want to see a lawyer. You have to let me go.' I turned away when tears threatened. My feet hurt, my toes were swollen.

At door-slot-open time I told the guard. From their vantage point in the control room she had, of course, seen the kicks, the punches, the rant at the camera. She passed through my meal and sounded sympathetic when she said that she could understand my frustration, but could tell me nothing. She had a pleasant voice but spoke with an accent I couldn't place. Being told she could tell me nothing was even more frustrating than not being spoken to at all, but I thanked her anyway. A human interaction was worth something.

Some days after I was detained, stretches and bland breakfast over, I was ordered to stand facing the door and place my hands through the slot. I didn't understand what was happening, why I had to give them my hands. I felt an old familiar heat rise in me. Mum always called it the Flame of Righteous Indignation. I've always had a bit of a temper. I get angry and bolshy when I'm scared. I know that at times I can be my own worst enemy. I felt handcuffs being locked onto my wrists.

'What the hell are you doing?'

'Now stand away from the door.' The order was barked.

'What are you doing, where are you taking me?'

'Stand back or your shoulders'll get dislocated. It's very painful. I wouldn't recommend it.'

I stood back. They were going to open the door!

For the briefest of moments, I thought I was going to be released and my heart sped up. There were two male guards outside. One had a face like a potato, all pudgy and mottled. The face of a drinker. He told me to kneel on a chair beside the door, facing the wall. The other one, thinner with hair yellow and straight like straw, clamped cuffs round my ankles, apologising in case he'd hurt me. Then he fitted a thick belt round my waist, and fed a chain through a link and locked that to my handcuffs. I searched their uniforms for name badges. Just to be able to call someone by name would have been a novelty. To speak, to have a conversation. There were no name badges. I made up my own names for them. Silly, cartoonish names to degrade them as they degraded me.

'Am I being released?' It seemed somehow unlikely given the chains, but I had to ask.

Derisive laughter, Spud scratched his crotch. I shuddered.

'Why are you doing this? What have I done? When am I getting out? What am I charged with? I want a lawyer, when can I see a lawyer?' My questions tumbled out without pause. Spud and Straw ignored them. Maybe they hadn't heard. Perhaps I'd only asked them in my head. I asked them again, louder, making sure that I could hear the words outside of me, that they would have to hear them too.

'Walk,' grunted Spud, and yanked on my chain.

'Where are you taking me?'

I felt panic. Was I going to be interrogated? Tortured?

'Shower,' said Spud, tugging harder. I almost fell over, but Straw caught me, fingers tight around my arm. When he'd righted me, instead of letting go, he kept holding me and muttered 'sorry' under his breath. The muscles in Spud's jaw tightened. He'd heard, and he hated me, hated whatever he thought I was. But I was going to have a shower. I'd never gone so long without a decent shower before, and the washes I'd had in my cell had been cursory, as I knew that I was being watched and I didn't want to give the guards anything to excite them.

I shuffled across the empty white hall. Seven steel doors including mine opened onto it. There was a circular office in the centre, like a panopticon, glassed in, another guard in there watching every move from behind banks of computer screens. On one of them was the interior of my cell, no doubt being monitored even when I wasn't there.

Spud turned and nodded at a third guard, and a door silently slid open; a room, bare except for two showerheads sticking out of the wall and two grates in the floor. The door closed behind us.

'Nice warm shower. You have ten minutes,' said Straw, unlocking my leg irons and handcuffs.

'Go on then, take your clothes off.' Spud stood in front of the now closed door, feet apart, hands in front of his groin, as if he was a footballer in a penalty wall. He looked me up and down, a lecherous smile on his face. Straw had the decency to look away, examining the overhead light fitting.

'What – with you here? You must be kidding.' It felt unsafe. Spud was still staring.

'Take them off or shower with them on. Makes no difference to us,' he said. Straw started whistling.

The water trickled out of the showerheads. My time was ticking away, but I wasn't going to undress in front of those two goons, so I stood under the lukewarm water fully clothed, keeping an eye on my guards. There was no soap or shampoo, and when I asked for some, Spud just laughed. So I rubbed water through the length of my hair, rinsed my face, massaged the water through my jumpsuit so that at least I was wet all over, pulled my sleeves and trouser legs up and washed as well as I could.

When the water stopped, Straw handed me a small towel.

'Dry yourself off now, girl.'

It wasn't easy drying myself. I tried wringing the water out of my clothing, but it was still sopping wet when Spud demanded the towel back. I was chained again, and led the ten or so metres back to my cell, sloshing with every step. The jumpsuit was heavy with water, my hair still dripping. Outside my cell I knelt on the chair again while Straw undid the leg chains and I was pushed back into my little box, still handcuffed. The door slid closed behind me, but the door slot opened.

'Hands.'

I offered them my hands, the cuffs were removed, the door slot banged shut, nearly taking my fingers off. I'd have to be quicker in future.

I looked around, almost glad to be back in my cell until I realised what had been going on in my absence. My notebook had been moved, and if it had been moved, there was no doubt in my mind it had also been read. I felt a rage then that made me want to punch the walls.

I had been so naïve – I should have known that nothing was secret. I was searched, my cell was searched, my notes read.

'You bastards,' I yelled, staring straight into the camera. 'What do you think I've got in here? What were you looking for? How dare you invade my space like that. I've got nothing. I hate you all.'

I thought I heard a snicker, but I was probably imagining it.

I was cold in my wet clothes so I started doing star jumps to warm up, but quickly got tired. I folded my mattress over so as not to wet it, and sat on the concrete of my bed staring at the pools of water on the floor. Soon I was shivering. I think they'd turned the heating down. In the end I dried myself with my T-shirt, hoping that it would be dry enough to sleep in when the time came.

I cried then. I hadn't allowed myself to in the last couple of days, but I felt so powerless, so angry. I curled myself into a little ball and sobbed.

After that interlude, the day was the same as the others. I'd been out of my cell for maybe twenty minutes, asked a few unanswered questions, seen two of my warders, heard them speak a handful of words. It had been a deeply humiliating experience, and yet, much as I hated them, I found myself wanting more. Straw at least seemed human. Spud, not so. But just seeing another face, however unfriendly, was better than nothing. Having them all but ignore me was better than having no one to even hear me. Maybe next time they'd be more talkative. If I asked fewer questions and kept the talk to inconsequential chatter, maybe they'd respond. I almost started to look forward to my next shower, whenever that might be. And I hated myself for my neediness.

After a while the days slid into each other. Day drifted into night into day. The only way I could gauge time was by which meal was shoved at me. My routine slipped. I slept when I was tired and never knew how long I'd been out. My eyes hurt from the constant light. It's possible that my 'days' were four hours long, my 'nights' an hour or two, that my diurnal cycle had been upended. I was woken for meals, sometimes breakfast, sometimes lunch or dinner. Other times I was awake waiting for food as if it was the highlight of the day. Sadly, it often was.

Everything I did, they could see. They watched as I drew, which I started doing instead of writing, as I ate, as I exercised, as I went to the toilet. It was like being in a zoo. I will never go to one again.

I had learned to gain some privacy when I was on the toilet by spreading some spare clothing over my lap, but sometime after shower day, my period started. I banged on the door until someone came. The door slot was opened, and I was ready, kneeling on the floor, looking through. I did that those days, to look at a human being occasionally, even though they may as well be made of stone. I could only see the mid-section of uniform, no face or anything, but it was better than just a hand. Anyway, I think it was Straw. I could tell because he was the thinnest of the guards I'd seen. I asked him for some tampons and pads. He said that he'd see what he could do, and shut the slot. I waited. I counted to three thousand slowly before I gave up. Eventually, he opened the slot, gave me one tampon and whispered 'there you go, love,' before he closed it again. As if it wasn't humiliating enough asking for feminine hygiene products, and having to change them while being watched, I had to ask every time I needed a tampon. They probably thought I'd hang myself with them if they gave me more – tie the little strings together until I had a noose to hang from – what? There was nothing. Or perhaps they thought they'd miss out on the opportunity of humiliating me further if they gave me more.

But he had spoken a few words to me. I imagined Straw's life outside of here – a wife, children, neighbours. He was the most human of the guards, and I fantasised about being his friend, of having chats as he slid my meal through the slot. In my mind, the only reason he wasn't even nicer to me was the other guards watching, making sure no one treated me like a human being. That place brutalised people, staff and inmates alike.

Sometimes the heating was turned right up so that I sweated like a pig, and then turned off until I was freezing and trying to wrap myself in my mattress to get warm again. This happened several times, so I knew it was being done on purpose. I don't know why they did it, except perhaps to remind me that they could do whatever they wanted.

I had a strange experience. I looked up from drawing in my notebook and there was a spider on my wall. I backed away. Spiders are the only insects I don't like. Arachnid, not insect. Anyway, it stayed very still, having been seen, and I watched it, like Straw and Spud and the others watch me. After a while, it must have realised that I wasn't going to hurt it, so it started scuttling round in circles, round and round with no purpose. I didn't take my eyes off it until the door slot opened and dinner was pushed through. In the time it took me to collect my tray and return to my seat, it had turned into a black mark on the wall. I got up close. It was still just a black mark. No sign of a spider. And although I don't like spiders, I felt bereft, because at least I thought it had been another living thing.

How many days? It was too exhausting to be angry. It got me nowhere.

I dreamed of Faisal when I was awake. He deserted me in sleep. I wondered where he was being held. He might have been next door for all I knew. Or at the other end of the world.

We'd met at the party of a mutual friend. Kamila had asked everyone she knew, I think. The place was heaving. Sweaty bodies crushed against each other, it was impossible to hear anyone speak over the doof, doof of the music. I hate parties like that, so I was trying to make a getaway, but I couldn't find where she'd put my coat. Finally, in a bedroom I found the bed piled high with coats and jackets, and there he was. He started when I walked in, as if guilty of something, and then held up a scarf triumphantly and smiled. It was the kind of smile that demands the same in return, and I'm sure sterner people than me had found themselves beaming back at him.

'Arriving or leaving?' he asked.

'Leaving,' I said guiltily.

'Let me help you find your coat then.' He started picking up one garment after another, holding them up for my perusal, eventually turning up my old and much abused red woollen coat.

He held it for me as I slid my arms into the sleeves, and let his fingers linger on my shoulder like a whisper so soft that I wasn't sure if it had really been.

'I'm Faisal, by the way. Loud parties aren't my thing, really. Would you like to go somewhere quieter for a drink?'

'Laila,' I said, 'and yes, I'd like that.'

We slunk out of the house like two thieves. Kamila didn't like people leaving her parties before dawn at the earliest, and it wasn't even eleven.

We settled ourselves into the corner of a nearby pub and talked until we were thrown out. He was an orthopaedic surgeon working at The London Hospital. He'd trained in Karachi, where he came from, but had also worked in Northern Pakistan patching up the Afghan refugees who streamed over the border with their limbs in tatters from stepping on landmines. Mines that first the Russians, then the Taliban and more recently the Americans had so recklessly strewn around. My life seemed so pale in comparison, and yet he listened as I told him about my job in the primary school, and the children I taught, as if I was a Nobel Laureate expounding my ideas for world peace.

He walked me home in the wee small hours, and asked for my number. He ran his hand along the sleeve of my coat like a promise of more, and walked into the night.

My lips tingled from the expectation of a kiss, and I let my own fingers brush them lightly in consolation.

It was so hard to concentrate in prison. There was so much time, so little noise, that the smallest of tasks could be delayed so that there was the anticipation of something to look forward to. Even the idea of washing out underwear could be a treat. But then something would happen – a meal, a shower – and the thing was forgotten.

My mind went foggy too. When I woke up, I never felt rested.

For a while, I could think clearly, but soon thoughts began to jumble, to hop over each other, to hide from me.

I had to remember to walk in both directions round my cell. I'd undo the top of my jumpsuit and tie the arms round my waist and walk so that I could touch the walls, the rough paint reminding me that I was alive, that I felt. I'd look at the skin on my upper arm, and my shoulder, which were raw from the rubbing. The grazing, the tiny spots of blood, were satisfying. Next time, anti-clockwise.

I 'met' some new guard – until then it had just been Spud and Straw. A female who looked like a ferret, and another man who had a lazy eye. But one time, it was a woman who looked like Jabba the Hutt, with a wide mouth and bulging eyes, and a man almost as big with hands like bunches of bananas who escorted me to the shower. Jabba and Banana were as silent as Straw and Spud, but at least Banana looked the other way when we were in the shower cell, and so I undressed. Jabba stared and went a bit pink, pulled at her uniform as if she was suddenly too hot.

I fantasised about masturbating in front of the camera. I didn't know where that came from, but I think I wanted to shock them. I am usually a private person.

A month must have gone by and still I hadn't been charged with anything or told what I was meant to have done. I was treated like a criminal with none of the rights of one. I wished someone would tell me what they thought I'd done, so that I could refute it. As it was, I sat, walked, read, drew, shat, slept, ate, always thinking about what could possibly have landed me there. Sometimes I thought someone was playing a big joke, that Spud was suddenly going to break into a huge grin and say 'April Fool!' I never thought that for long though. No one hated me enough to do that to me. And yet, they did – it seemed that at least some of the guards who are meant to be protectors of the innocent had decided already that I was guilty of something and deserved no kindness.

I begged them to talk to me. Tell me. WHAT HAVE I DONE? WHY DO YOU HATE ME?

If my great grandfather would have been displeased at my birth, what would he have thought then, if he could have heard from his grave? His great granddaughter held in solitary confinement for... fill in the gap. He'd no doubt roll his unseeing eyes and say 'Aye, that's what you get for mingling with them darkies. And a bastard, too.'

Because that, I found out later, was what my grandmother and Mrs Rob had been referring to in the street that day. I was a hybrid. Father unknown, but definitely not white. My mother knew who he was, of course, but she never did tell her parents. Or me, until much later. As if I didn't need to know. Actually, as a child, I didn't. I was happy as I was and no one made me feel different. I grew up with children who had blond, brown or red hair. Mine was black. So what? I was just me, they were just them. It was the adults who cared, who whispered and who, some of them anyway, didn't allow their children to 'mix' with me, as if being a half-caste was catching. As if I would be encouraging their precious offspring to have children with foreigners of colour. But I was oblivious to all that at the time. I had my friends, plenty of them, some of them also with no father at home, and the colour of our hair mattered not a jot. It wasn't until high school that I was made aware of my difference, and the fact that, for some reason, I had to pay for it. The Anns and the Susans ignored me. The Davids and Peters called me Paki. My mother wondered why I stopped bringing friends home. I rolled my eyes at her and told her that we didn't do that sort of thing at our age, that we hung out in town after school. But what would she know, she was always at work. I stayed in my room a lot. As I got older and the bullies lost interest in me, my grades went from safely average to pretty good because I had nothing to do except study, and my fate as the school outcast was sealed. Different and brainy were worse in combination than either on their own.

I worried about my mother. Had they told her where I was? She would be missing my weekly calls, the texts I sent if something happened worth mentioning between times. Gran hadn't been well last time I'd spoken to her. Granddad had been gone a while then, and she got lonely in spite of her active social life, church and voluntary work. She was always doing something for someone. I hadn't been to church in years, but I thought I'd like to go while I was in prison, have a chat with God and see if He knew why I was there. I tried to remember a prayer before I went to sleep one night.

The next day I was put into hand and leg cuffs. The cold metal hurt my skin. I hated that ritual. What did they think I was going to do? How far would I have got if I ran?

I thought I was going to have a shower even though I didn't think it had been five days, but instead, I was taken to a different door that led into a corridor, through another door and into a room twice the size of my cell with a table and two chairs in it.

I smiled to myself, thinking that prayers do get answered. Here I was, out of my cell, and it looked like someone was going to tell me why I was here.

I was told to sit. Ferret and Straw took up their station by the door and I watched the camera in the corner rotate on its fixture. The guard in the control box was obviously making sure that he could see every corner of the room. The camera came to rest on me and the table and the chair opposite. Ferret sucked in her lips. Straw scratched his stubbly face. We all waited. My heart was racing. I didn't know who was coming, but maybe they'd be interested in hearing my side of whatever story they'd concocted about me.

A tall, balding man was let in, the door sliding shut with a firm clunk behind him. He sat opposite me, put a briefcase on the table and looked at me. There was a hint of pink lipstick on his collar, which made him human, a man with a life outside that place.

He smiled. I smiled.

'So, Laila, tell me what you've been up to?'

I thought he meant there, in the prison.

'Nothing. There's nothing to do. It's hell.'

His smile started fading.

'I mean' – he opened his briefcase and pulled out a laptop. My laptop.

'What the' – I tried to get up but Ferret moved fast, grabbed my clothing and held me in my seat.

'I mean,' repeated the man, who hadn't introduced himself, 'why the recent interest in Pakistan? We've been through this' – he tapped my laptop – 'and it's very interesting. Research on Al-Qaeda and other terror organisations, searches for their training camps, women and Islam, taking the veil. Thinking of doing that yourself are you? Wanting to make a political statement here by covering yourself up? Seems you were thinking of a trip to Pakistan. Want to tell me about that?'

I couldn't speak. I wanted to snatch my computer from him. I wanted to be anywhere else but that room.

'Well?'

My insides lurched. What else had he found? I had nothing to hide in terms of my Pakistan research. I'd been looking for my father, but had been completely unsuccessful on that front. I knew a fair bit about the country, and how to apply for a visa should I need one, but that was all. And whose computer these days didn't show up searches on terrorism? I would bet that every person in the whole of England had read something about Al-Qaeda, the Taliban, Hezb-i-Islami or another group. It was a way of trying to make sense of this new world order. I could remember looking up at planes flying overhead after 9/11 and wondering if they were suddenly going to explode. The world hadn't felt safe from that day on.

And apart from all that, there was all sorts of private stuff in there. Photos, emails, addresses, class presentations and lesson plans. What else had they found? I took a deep breath and bit my lip.

He didn't seem to like that. The smile was gone. He took a folder out, opened it and read for a while. I tried to read it upside down, which I'm actually quite good at, being a teacher and often having to try and see what the children are writing to each other rather than doing the work I've set them, but he shielded it from me with his hand.

Eventually he held up a photo.

'Know this man?'

Of course I knew him. It was Usman, Faisal's cousin who often stayed with him.

'No.' I don't know why I said that, except that this man didn't seem to want to help me, so I didn't see why I should help him. I knew I should quell the Flame of Righteous Indignation, but I couldn't.

'How about him?'

He showed me a grainy picture of a middle-aged man in

what looked like beige pyjamas, a cap of some sort on his head. He was just coming out of a brick house and looked like he hadn't known he was being photographed.

'Haven't a clue.'

The man looked pissed off.

'Do you know what's happening to me? These guards' – I spat the word – 'stare at me in the shower, turn the heating off in my cell, keep the lights on twenty-four hours a day.'

It was as if he hadn't heard me.

'Him?' He held up another photo.

Faisal. I wanted to grab the photo, hold it to my lips and kiss it, whisper that whatever he was meant to have done, I would never say anything. I pressed my hands together between my legs instead.

The man stared at me, eyes narrowed.

'You do realise what a serious situation you're in, I suppose?'

'I'm being tortured. Don't you think that's serious?' I shouted.

He ignored it. 'You were found at this man's flat. In bed with him if I'm not mistaken.' His voice had become cold, hard.

He wasn't here to help me. He was here to get information out of me. If I wanted him to take me seriously, I'd have to comply. I took a deep breath.

'His name is Faisal.'

'And?'

'And what? I don't know what you want me to say.'

'Hmph.' He looked at Ferret. There was tension in his jaw. 'You can take her back to her cell. She's obviously not ready to talk.'

I thumped the table with my chained hands. The cuffs bit into my skin and I tried not to wince.

'I am ready to talk – I have lots to say. Like, why the hell am I here? Why are you letting these bastards finger me? When are you going to let me go? What am I meant to have done? Why don't I get to see a lawyer? Who are you? You didn't even introduce yourself. You know who I am, how come I'm not allowed to know who you are?' I was shouting, spit flying. He ducked out of range and the smile returned to his lips.

'You can call me Mr Smith. And I suggest you have a think about how best you might help yourself here. You will talk, eventually. Everyone does.' He smiled and left without another word.

Ferret was not happy with me. I had bruises on my arms later from the grip she held me in on the way back to my cell. Straw quietly suggested that maybe I should have a think about what I could tell them. Perhaps I could prove my innocence. Good cop, bad cop, or did he really believe I might be innocent?

Maybe it had been wrong to say nothing? If Faisal or Usman were being questioned and shown photos of me, would they have done the same? Were the three of us meant to have done something together? Had I been stupid? I was certainly no clearer about why I was there or how long it would be for. It did seem, however, that in saying nothing, I had committed myself to longer in this place.

And my original opinion about prayers had been confirmed. God doesn't listen.

I couldn't sleep. I kept thinking about the interview. When I might get a chance for another one? What I would say. I honestly didn't know the man in pyjamas, but they knew that I knew Faisal and probably Usman. What good did it do any of us not to admit it? I felt stupid, adolescent. I'd behaved like a teenager caught doing something and refusing to admit it. It used to frustrate my mother no end. She caught me smoking once, in a field just out of town. I was with Frankie and Mona, the two other people in the year that no one talked to – Frankie, because he had mild cerebral palsy and talked funny, and Mona who everyone had decided was a slut. Maybe she did sleep around, but what business was that of theirs? Anyway, Mum somehow managed to be right there before we saw her. No chance to hide the evidence, but I swore blind that I wasn't smoking, even as I blew smoke into her face. Her fists had clenched, but she wasn't a hitter – however angry she got, she never struck out. Frankie and Mona ditched me – ran off leaving the fags and the matches in plain view, and still, cigarette in hand, I said it wasn't me. She didn't know what to do, so in the end she just left and never said anything about it again, and I lost interest in smoking soon after. Mr Smith had done the same, hadn't he? He'd left me to think how stupid I'd been and was waiting for me to change.

Faisal. I wanted that photo so much. I couldn't get him out of my head. His eyes followed me round the cell. His amber-gold eyes that I loved so much. I used to want to submerge myself in the warmth of his eyes. He laughed when I told him that, but said that I'd make a great poet. I wanted to wrap myself in his laughter, let it buoy me up, hold me gently until the nightmare was over.

He had rung me the day after Kamila's party and asked me out for dinner. We went to a little bistro in Bayswater, far more expensive than anywhere I would normally have gone. Thank God he insisted on paying.

I don't remember what we ate, although at the time I thought I should take notes so that I never forgot a moment of our time together. We shared a bottle of wine and talked and talked. At the end of the night he escorted me home again, and this time he kissed me, a light touch of the lips that left mine aching for more.

The walls of my cell started melting. I didn't know how they did it, or if the guards had some sort of gadget that they shone in to make it appear so, but I could be sitting staring at whiteness, and all of a sudden it was like a giant vanilla ice cream melting in a hot sun. When I reached out to taste it, the walls solidified again and I could hear the guards laugh.

I was tormented.

The sliding of my hatch one morning brought a wedding ring. Not for me, of course. A new ring, or a new hand. It looked female, smaller than Jabba's, and black. It was a shiny ring, probably new. People don't tend to buy wedding rings second-hand. Although it could have been a family heirloom, passed on from a dead mother or grandmother and polished up for the occasion. I spent almost the whole time between breakfast and lunch thinking about that. At lunchtime, my attention was diverted. A fly must have got in through the hatch with my tray. It certainly wasn't here before. I called it Henry, I don't know why, and watched him buzz around and land, buzz and land. My lunch sandwich was hard and stale before I got round to eating it.

I observed that flies seemed to be clean creatures. When he landed, Henry rubbed his spindly legs together as if he was drying or clapping tiny hands in anticipation of a feast. All he got was my crumbs, but I suppose that is a feast for a fly.

Just before dinner was poked through the slot, I got bored of his buzzing and annoyed with the way he flew around my face all the time, so I swatted him with my pillow and then all I had was a permanent reminder of him on the wall and something else to look at other than the mark that I had thought was a spider. I felt sad and guilty about Henry all evening. I don't know what made me do it.

It changes you, being alone all the time. It changes your values. On the outside I would never have killed Henry. I was the kid who rescued beetles, the teenager who studied earthworms, the adult who donated to campaigns to save habitats of endangered insects. Well, someone had to. I was the teacher who taught the value of life, all life, however small and seemingly insignificant. And Henry was just an interesting blot on my wall.

As the weeks went on I became convinced that something was wrong with my eyes. The edge of my vision blurred all the time as if a cloud of smoke was closing in on me. Maybe my mother had sent it as revenge for the smoking, all these years later. I know that was paranoid, and I didn't really believe it, but it was spooky that it started happening just after I remembered that incident. I kept shaking my head to try and get rid of it, but it clung. I was terrified of going blind, I always have been. I used to keep myself awake at night wondering how Great Granddad managed to get through life without being able to see. The sadness of never looking at your own child, the indignity and frustration of having to rely on others to do things for you. The tricks that might be played by cruel or unthinking youngsters. I know what children can be like. I really would be paranoid if I couldn't see. I would expect the worst of everybody, and they would come to hate me for being suspicious of them, as much as I was fearful of their potential pranks. I've always hated games like blind man's bluff and those trust exercises where you are blindfolded and someone else talks you through an obstacle course. I worried that the guards knew that and would devise ways to persecute me. I thought, sometimes, that they could read my mind. When I thought that, I would spend my time counting so that there was nothing interesting for them, and they would stop.

They searched my cell each time I left it. I don't know what they expected to find given that I was watched all the time, allowed no visitors, had been sent nothing. Did they think that I could magic things out of the air? That they would suddenly come across the plans for a bank heist, the plotting of a murder? Connections to a drug ring? That I had admitted to some crime in the doodles in my notebook?

I started talking out loud. I needed to hear the sound of my own voice in the absence of anyone else's. I commented on what I was doing, I asked myself questions and answered them. I sang sometimes. Jabba, in a rare moment of humour, told me that they turned the volume down in the control room when I was singing. It was the first full sentence she'd said to me, and the facial expression that accompanied it was, I think, meant to be a smile. We were on our way to the shower. I was in my chains, barely able to stand the noise of their clanking as I walked. Spud was with us.

Shower day had become such a routine to me by now that as soon as the cuffs were removed, even before the door was fully closed, I started undressing. I had got used to the indignity of always being watched, of every move being observed.

I stood under the water, eyes closed, running my hands up and down my thinning body, enjoying the warmth. And then it dawned on me that mine were not the only hands touching me. I swallowed the bile that rose in my throat, opened my eyes. Jabba was staring right back at me, rubbing her naked body against mine.

Where was Spud? They always worked in pairs – where was he? My heart pounded.

'No one here but you and me,' cooed Jabba into my ear. 'Perks of the job, you sometimes get time alone with the inmates.' She looked up at the camera. 'It's off too.'

I backed up, tried to duck away from her, but she was bigger, stronger, and pinned me to the wall. I felt her fingers slide into my vagina and she started swaying and groaning as her erect nipples brushed my skin. I became a statue. The shower had never seemed longer.

'Come on, honey, lick me,' she said, pushing my head down, making me kneel in front of her.

I gagged. The water finally stopped but tears of rage and fear still coursed down my cheeks. She released me and I fell on to my side on the cold hard floor. She threw a towel at me and started drying herself.

'I'm sure you'll do better next time,' she said.

On the way back to my cell I shook their hands off me. I couldn't bear to be touched by these vile excuses for human beings. Did Spud know what had happened? He must, surely, to have allowed her to be in there alone with me. What about the guard in the control room – had he been in on it? Had he really switched the camera off, or did they all watch the video later over a few drinks?

I sat on my bed for hours, reliving the scene. I had been raped. Violated. Was this some scheme to make me talk? To humiliate me to the point where I would do or say anything to get out of here? I stood facing the camera and yelled, shouted and screamed until I had no voice left, and then I made obscene gestures until I was exhausted, my body heavy and sore.

I heard the door slot opening. There was laughter.

'No dinner. You don't deserve it after that display.'

I spat, but the saliva didn't even make it as far as the door.

The only power I had was the power to protest, and they'd just reminded me that even that had consequences.

Eventually I slept but woke up shaking wildly. I couldn't stop. Terrified, I thought that on top of everything else, Parkinson's or some other neurological illness had overtaken me. I lay there, writhing, trying to work out how to kill myself.

3

'Please give this to Mr Smith,' I said as I shoved a note through the door slot with my return breakfast tray.

I had torn a page out of my notebook to write to him. I wanted him to acknowledge what was happening, that crimes were being committed in this prison by the very people who were meant to be guarding us. Me. I still had no idea if there were any others here.

'Of course,' came the reply. The voice was deep, the laughter that accompanied it turned into a hacking cough. Spud.

After he had gone I banged on the door and walls until my hands were bruised. They weren't going to give the letter to anyone. It would probably just provide a few minutes' mirth to the guards before being thrown in the bin. What had I been thinking? Why would they tell anyone in authority what they did? What a fool. Worse than a fool. Now I was worried that they would make things a whole lot worse for me, the pathetic little woman in Cell 4.

Jabba and Straw came into my cell and ordered me to pile everything, including my mattress, pillow and spare clothes into a box that Straw placed at my feet. A bucket, a mop and a cloth were also thrown to the floor. I was so relieved that Jabba wasn't alone that I almost smiled. I managed to catch myself in time, though, and didn't make eye contact with either of them. Then they left.

I've never enjoyed cleaning. It's always been one of those chores that lack purpose. You finish, everything looks great for about three minutes, and then starts the slow, inexorable journey to grime and disorder again. It was the only thing we used to argue about, Bhindi, Jeanette, Sooz and me. Jeanette was a clean-freak. She used to go ballistic if one of us so much as left a spoon in the sink. Well, she did when it was her time of the month, anyway. Bhindi had grown up in India with servants and had no idea of tidying up. She left clothes, food, plates, books, her phone, nail polish, her watch – everything – lying around and always seemed slightly bemused that they didn't find their way to her room. Sooz was the peacekeeper. She liked things clean, but she wasn't as bad as Jeanette. I did do my share, though. I'm not a complete slob, and the thought of pissing my friends off was usually enough to motivate me. But there were some times when it all fell apart; busy times at work, hectic social life and laziness clashed head-on with Jeanette and her PMS. It wasn't pretty. Angry words and accusations flew. Tears fell. Feet stamped. And then it was over. We'd all pull together and clean until the house sparkled and promise that we'd never let it get like that again.

Cleaning my cell for the first time in what must have been the six or seven weeks since I'd been there was at least a diversion. I didn't know how long I was going to have the mop and bucket, but I decided I'd start with the walls. Henry the Fly and my 'spider' went quite easily. I'm embarrassed now to think I didn't see that it was only dirt. Some other marks were harder though, and when I got in close with the cloth, I saw that they were blood. Mine from my walks against the wall, or someone else's? I had no idea, but was vaguely repulsed. I didn't like to think that there have been others in that cell. It was mine.

That was an odd thought. That I'd be possessive over a cell. But what else did I have?

When I'd finished, it worried me that there were chips of paint coming off the edges of the shelves showing the dark concrete underneath. It wasn't perfect. Had I done that? I'd have to be more careful.

I had another round with Mr Smith. This time he didn't even smile when he walked in. I was already sitting at the table like last time, and Spud and a guard I'd never seen before, with a port wine stain covering half her face, stood by the door. I spent the time waiting for Mr Smith trying surreptitiously to map that birthmark. It looked like Ireland. There were darker bits, really deep purple, dotted in the redder whole. She wore a wedding ring, and I wondered about the man who woke up and looked at her birthmark every morning, and loved her.

I probably should have been thinking about what I was going to say to Mr Smith, but I couldn't concentrate on that when confronted with the map of Ireland on the woman's cheek. Maybe I'm shallow.

Anyway, Mr Smith started by showing me the picture of Usman again.

'We know that you know this man. Who is he?'

'Usman.'

'Usman what?'

'I don't know. I only ever knew him as Usman. At least he didn't rape me.'

Mr Smith tutted.

'Your vicious allegations won't help.' He paused, looked at the photo and then back at me. 'Where does he live?'

I wanted to be angry, to refuse to answer his questions, but I only felt stomach-churning defeat. There was no help to be had. Maybe if I answered him I'd get out of this awful place.

'I don't know. I only ever saw him at Faisal's flat. He came and went.'

'He didn't live there?'

'No. He stayed when he was in London.'

'So he didn't live in London?'

'I don't know, but I don't think so, otherwise he wouldn't have needed to stay.'

'Tell me about Faisal Abbas Choudhry.'

The way he said his name made it sound hard, alien. I knew that it shouldn't sound like that, that it was a strong but beautiful name. I repeated it to myself in my head, letting it work its way into my mind. Faisal Abbas Choudhry. The man I loved.

'He's a doctor. A surgeon.'

'And?'

'And what? Surely you know all this. I don't know why you're asking me. What's he meant to have done? What am I meant to have done? I'm trying to help you now – but I don't know what any of us is meant to have done!' I leant forward, begging for an answer, but also dreading what I might hear.

It may seem strange to those who have never been in that situation, but sometimes the strain of getting through each day makes you forget why you're actually there. Waking up and knowing that there are hours to fill before you can escape into sleep again for a while becomes the only thing you can think about. Not friends, not family, not what might be happening on the outside in the real world, that's too painful. Just getting through the hours without going mad. Concentrating on anything more becomes impossible. There is the constant fear that you are going mad anyway without realising it. Who would tell you? There is no one you can check out your thoughts and ideas with. So I hadn't thought much in the last few days about what I was doing in prison. I'd been focusing instead on getting by without smashing my head against the wall.

Mr Smith, as usual, ignored what I said anyway.

'Asim Malik, you're going to tell me you don't know him either?'

'I do know a family called Malik, Asim is the eldest.' My heart was pounding. Were they going to question Kamila's family? Had I just dumped them in the shit? But how did they know about Asim, the older brother who was always so standoffish to me, but whom Kamila idolised?

'What do you want to tell me about him?'

'I've only met him once or twice.'

Once again Mr Smith looked at me like I was some sort of shit on the bottom of his shoe and carried on.

'What's your connection with these men?'

He showed me pictures of four men with scraggly beards.

'They're the London bombers, everyone knows them, they were plastered all over the front pages for days.' Light began to dawn, finally. My eyes nearly popped out of my head as I stared at him.

'What was the purpose of your trip to Leeds last February?'

He thought I was a terrorist! I couldn't stifle my laughter. He honestly thought that Faisal and Usman were terrorists? And me?

'You think it's funny.' His eye was twitching. He rubbed it.

'Actually, yes I do, and if you knew Faisal, you'd think so too. He's one of the gentlest people I've ever met. He doesn't blow people up, he puts them together again.'

'Tell me about Abu Hafs al-Hasri.'

'What?' I'd never heard of him, had no idea what he was talking about.

'It's an organisation.' He stared at me for a moment. 'What about Usman Wakim Khawaja? What does he do?'

'Is that Faisal's cousin?'

Mr Smith nodded.

'No idea. He didn't talk much when he stayed, not to me, anyway. He read a lot.'

'Oh yes? What did he like to read?'

'I don't know. I sort of got the impression that he was a scholarly type.'

'How long have you known them?'

'A couple of years.'

'What were you doing on 7th July this year?'

'What? Oh, come on – you can't possibly think I was involved in that! I was watching news reports of some fundamentalist arseholes blowing trains and buses up, like everyone else in England, and probably around the world. We were all glued to the telly in the staffroom when we weren't with the kids. It was awful. One of the children asked if his daddy was okay because he got the Tube to work, and that started all of them off. We were in damage control all day.'

'What about the day before?' He asked about my whereabouts on specific dates, but how was I meant to know? Without my phone or my diary, I had little memory of much at all. 'I don't know', and, 'I can't remember', became my answer to all his questions.

'I ask again, your trip to Leeds?'

'I went for a wedding – one of my friends was having her hen night at a club there and the wedding was a couple of days later so a bunch of us went up together and stayed.'

'Name? Which club? What hotel did you stay at? What else did you do while you were there?'

'Sandra Kearns, The Space, Novotel, and we had a massage, hung out chatting, drinking, eating, having a look at Leeds.'

'I'll need the names of the people you were with.'

He kept asking questions, fast, so that I had no time to think. Had I met Shehzad Tanweer? What was my knowledge of Hasib Hussain? Mohammad Siddique Khan? They were the London bombers. Had any of them visited Faisal's house? On and on. His voice was hoarse by the time he called it a day. He'd been shouting and banging his fists on the table a lot because I couldn't tell him anything about anything after the questions about Sandra's wedding. He clearly thought that I wouldn't tell him.

He didn't ask many questions about me, it was all about them. They thought that I had information that I didn't have, and that I was a terrorist. I had no idea how to convince them otherwise. I could only keep asserting my innocence and hope that eventually I was believed. I was screaming inside. I had no power, no voice, no credibility amongst these people. They saw what they wanted to see and would not be diverted.

And I didn't get to see the photo of Faisal again. If anything, seeing him would have made the experience worthwhile. I ached for him. I was beginning to forget what he looked like; the drape of his hair across his forehead when he bent to kiss me, the feel of his lips.

I thought about the guards a lot. Did they like their work, or did they just do it to pay the bills, because there were no other jobs in the area? Jabba and Spud were cruel. They took delight in letting me know that they thought I was guilty, that I was less than human in their eyes. Ferret was influenced by them, but her heart wasn't in it. She played at being hard but hadn't yet sold her soul. I imagined her going home and playing with children, taking them to the park, out for an ice cream. Straw reminded me of Kaye's dad, my friend from primary school. If there was anyone there who tried to keep an open mind, it was him. I spent hours wondering if he had a family, what he did when he wasn't watching me. The days when he was on were better than the others – once he even stood outside my door with the slot open and we had a chat. He told me that he'd just become a granddad, and I congratulated him. I could hear the pride in his voice.

I woke up the next morning thinking about Kaye, my 'twin'. We were practically inseparable. We started school on the same day, and were in the same class for five and a half years. On the rare occasions when another kid – usually someone new – was being horrible to me because I looked a bit different to them, i.e. darker, she would literally fly at them, fists at the ready, and get them to take back their words and apologise. With her wild red hair and her eyes narrowed to slits, she was pretty scary. I've always had a temper, but she could really fly off the handle. And then one day, when we were ten, she wasn't there anymore. Her father died of a heart attack, and within days, her mother had moved to York to be with her family. I never saw Kaye again, even though she'd only moved twenty or so miles away. That's how it was. I never questioned it, although I grieved for my friend, as I'm sure she did for me. Funny I should think of her now. Perhaps because I feel I need a defender.

We must have made a funny pair, her all red and freckly, me dark and exotic, or so people said. Although I'm not dark-skinned. More dusky.

Laila Farida was, as I've said, my paternal grandmother's name, and it was all my mother had to give me of that side of my family. Mum discovered that she was pregnant with me after my father returned to Pakistan. She never saw him again.

She had been living in Nottingham, but moved back to Thirsk when I was born. I suspect Gran and Granddad were extremely angry with her for getting herself 'in the family way', but by the time I can remember anything, they were okay with it. In fact, they were a bit overprotective of both of us. Mum used to get really pissed off that they wanted to know all that we did, and living next door, in a small town, it was difficult to keep anything from them anyway. I could hear what they watched on telly.

~

In prison I began to pace even more, I couldn't settle. There were people talking about me. I heard them whisper, but when I turned to confront them, they hid.

One day I saw the sky for the first time in – how long? I was shackled, but I'd had a shower and Jabba's special treatment the day before, so I thought I was to see Mr Smith again. I didn't even care that Jabba used me by then. I did not do what she wanted me to – I fantasised about bashing her head in with a brick while she rubbed herself against me, fingered me, tried to prise my mouth open with her tongue. I am not normally a violent person. These fantasies concerned me. I was frustrating for her. She sometimes hit me those days. There was violence in her and I was at her mercy. I should have been scared, maybe I was, but I couldn't feel it. When she touched me it was as if I left my body and went elsewhere.

The sky was a ragged selection of greys which bled into the high concrete walls of the enclosure. I couldn't see the ground outside, only a few square metres of sky, but I sat against the wall and stared. My bum got cold, so I got up and walked round and round, still looking up. I was meant to be exercising. There was a ball in the corner and I thought about throwing it at the walls and catching it, but I have never been one for sports. I wasn't picked for the school teams, and in games lessons, I was amongst the last chosen for the friendlies we played against each other.

I got a crick in my neck, a painful muscle spasm that locked my head in its upward position. Instead of trying to ease it, I was grateful that my body was supporting my desire to look to the heavens.

Drizzle started falling. I opened my mouth and my arms to welcome it, spinning slowly, eyes closed.

The Map of Ireland called me in, shackled me again and led me back to my cell. I was supposed to be outside for an hour, but rain stopped play. At least she apologised, as if it was her fault that it was raining.

The sky occupied my mind. It was the same sky that my mother looked at each morning when she opened her curtains and looked out the window to decide what to wear for the day. The sky that stretches over my house, the school where I work, my friends, the streets I used to walk, the buses full of commuters, the shops I used to browse, the pubs I drank in. If Faisal could see it, it was his sky too.

Faisal.

I couldn't allow myself to think of him. It was too easy to lose myself in pain. If I was to see the sky again as a free woman, I had to be strong, and submerging myself in painful memories or fantasies of the future was not the way to do that. I had to live each moment as it came. Watch for opportunity. Mind my temper and my words.

After that first time I was allowed into the exercise yard daily. Perhaps I have been a good girl, or maybe I was being softened up, made to feel grateful so that I'd co-operate. Either way, it was a welcome change.

The sky was blue the next day, with a few puffy clouds. They were moving quite fast, so it must have been windy, but in the concrete box, the air was still and dank. I never saw the sun. I suspect it didn't shine over that place.

The yard was about double the size of my cell. Like two of them had been joined longways. There was a drain in the centre with green mould round it. The walls were smooth and must have been twenty feet high. There were circular marks dotting its surface. I noticed that there was a metal grille over the top. I wondered how I didn't notice it the day before. The sky was divided into small squares. I was not even allowed an uninterrupted view of freedom.

I walked round and round and round and round then kicked the ball, which I noted had been moved. Maybe someone else exercised here. Maybe someone threw the ball at the wall to dot it, to prove that they were there, that they existed. I picked up the ball, rolled it in the drain mould and smeared it on the wall. A signal to another soul, although I doubted I would ever know who they were or if they'd seen my sign.

At the end of my hour I was tired and distressed at how much I ached. I had let my body waste and made a resolution to look after myself better from then on. I'd start doing the stretches again, and star jumps and push-ups, squats, whatever exercises I could think of. I would eat the meals that lately I'd only been picking at. And yet, I didn't want to make myself more attractive to Jabba. I had been starving myself because I sensed that her appetite was for big women whose flesh she could sink herself into, grab great handfuls of, lose her fist or her tongue in a cavernous vagina.

~

Mr Smith visited again. He got less friendly every time I saw him.

This time he threw a copy of the Qur'an on the table as he walked in.

'Yours, I believe,' he said as he pulled a chair out and sat down.

'Where did you get that? Have you searched my house? How dare you!' I actually screeched. My insides roiled.

'So you don't deny it's yours then?'

'No, but if you've been through all my stuff, you'll know that I also have the Bible, the Bhagavad Gita, several books by the Dalai Lama...'

'Yeah, yeah, yeah. You're a veritable religious freak, aren't you?'

'No, but I have children from many countries and religions in my class, so I've read what I can.'

He ignored that, opened the book and turned it so that I could see. Not that I needed to, of course.

I'd bought it in a second-hand bookshop. The books on Islam were on the bottom shelves, so I was kneeling on the floor, flicking through a paperback copy of the Qur'an, wondering whether to buy it. Really I wanted a more beautiful copy to reflect the writing. Tooled leather with gold calligraphy perhaps. When I closed the book, I heard a sound, a bit like a snort or a grunt, and looked up to see a man staring down at me.

'What are you looking at that filth for?' he asked, his eyes shifting to the book.

I thought I must have heard him wrongly, or that he had mistaken the Qur'an for some other book. Erotica or something.

'What?' I asked.

'Scum, Muslims, the lot of them.' And he spat.

I managed to pull the book out of the way so his saliva

landed on my knee, leaving a splotch of white bubbles that my jeans slowly absorbed.

'I beg your pardon?' I couldn't believe what I was hearing. This man wasn't a skinhead, didn't look like a yokel. He wore a suit, there was a briefcase at his feet.

I looked up at him, the Qur'an still in my hand. I could feel his spit moistening my skin through the denim of my jeans.

'You lot, you're all the same. Fly a couple of planes into the Twin Towers, kill a few thousand people, and think we'll give you whatever you want. Well, we won't. Bloody terrorists, the lot of you.'

It took a moment for me to register what he had said, that he had included me in his racist slur. That he had made the assumption that because of the way I looked and the book in my hand, that I was a terrorist. I was stunned. All the Muslims I knew were outraged at the things that were being done in the name of Allah. All had been shocked and scared, like every other reasonable, sane human being.

I got to my feet and held the Qur'an up to his face. He leapt back as if I was trying to burn him.

'There is nothing in this book that promotes violence,' I said. 'Do not judge over a billion people who base their lives on the teaching of this book on the actions of a few nutters who say they are killing in the name of Allah. They are not. They are fundamentalist jerks.' My breath was coming fast.

The man turned to go, and I thought I had won that little encounter; Laila 1, Racist Moron 0. But no – as he walked away he turned and said,

'You should go back to where you came from. We don't want you here.'

'What, Yorkshire you mean? That's where I'm from.'

But he didn't hear. The bells on the door jingled as it closed behind him.

I was still angry, but I became aware of several other shoppers looking at me, and anger gave way to embarrassment. I shrugged, gave them a weak smile, muttered something about people with uninformed opinions, and took the book to the counter. Having defended it so hotly, I felt I had to buy it. Maybe I'd get a beautiful copy as well one day, or maybe this one was the one I was meant to have, its plain black cover hiding the beauty within from ignoramuses like that man.

I went straight to Faisal's from the bookshop, fighting my way through the commuter crowds on the Tube, emerging at West Hampstead to twilight drizzle. On the train, standing with my nose in another woman's armpit, I had calmed down. I was left with a feeling of pride for having stood up to that idiot. I felt good and stood tall and confident as I rang Faisal's doorbell.

Usman opened the door. Faisal's younger cousin with his calm, serious eyes and his studious demeanour always made me feel shallow and frivolous. As hard as I tried to prove myself otherwise, I always felt I managed to deepen his impression of my superficiality and unconsidered opinions. I suppose it is often like that when you try too hard.

'Hi, Usman,' I said, smiling goofily.

'Good evening,' he said in his heavily accented English. He didn't look directly at me. I don't think that in all the times we'd met he ever had. Rather, he looked just over my left shoulder.

'Is Faisal in?' I asked, knowing he was because I could hear him singing along to 'White Flag' by Dido, his current favourite.

'Yes, he is here.' Usman stepped back to let me in, backing against the wall as if he was afraid I'd touch him.

'Thanks,' I said as I rushed past him into the kitchen and Faisal's waiting arms.

Later, over dinner, I told him about the encounter in the bookshop.

'Are you all right?' he asked, his brow furrowed as his eyes swept my body.

'I'm fine,' I said, reaching across the table to take his hand. 'I was quite proud of myself really.'

He smiled. 'Quite the activist!'

'Oh, no. Not me. I've never felt strongly enough about anything to be an activist. I was just trying to put the jerk in his place.'

'There's a first time for everything, you know. Anyway, well done.' He lifted my hand to his lips and kissed each finger.

When we took the plates into the kitchen, Usman was in there. He never ate with us. Faisal told him about the bookshop incident as he assembled fruit and ice cream and poured microwaved fudge sauce over the whole lot.

'So you see, Usman, she's one of us!'

Usman didn't look convinced, and I felt deflated. I didn't want to be 'one of them', whatever that meant, but I wanted to be the one to make the decision, not him.

He took an apple from the fruit bowl and left the room.

'He doesn't like me.'

Faisal pulled me to him. 'It's not that he doesn't like you, it's that he doesn't approve of us.

'Because I'm not a Muslim?'

'That, and also because I don't practise. He is devout, and to him, I am fallen. He prays for me. I know he is worried about my soul.'

'What about you – are you worried?' I asked.

He let me go and leant back against the kitchen bench and folded his arms.

'I am not worried about my soul, but–'

'But what? Is there something the matter?'

He smiled and shook his head slowly.

'I wasn't going to tell you, but I want no secrets from you. I had a phone call from my parents.'

'And?' I held my breath.

'And they are disappointed that I have not accepted any of their candidates for a wife. They have been quite worried in that regard. I think they suspect that I'm gay!'

I laughed. Faisal took my hand.

'I told them that I had found the woman I want to spend my life with, and asked them to accept you as their daughter.'

'Their daughter – are you proposing?'

'You know I want to be with you forever.'

We kissed then, and I thought no more about his parents or Usman until the following morning when I found my copy of the Qur'an on the kitchen table. Usman had inscribed something in the front of the book. I hadn't been able to read it – it was in an Arabic script. I was touched that maybe this was the beginning of him accepting me. And then Faisal translated it for me, and I felt a chill creep through me. I gasped. Surely not. Usman wouldn't have written anything like that. He was gentle, quiet.

Mr Smith cleared his throat, his face inches from mine.

'Well? How about this inscription?'

'I don't know what you want me to say. Yes, I have a copy of the Qur'an. Yes, it has an inscription in the front. I have no idea what it says. It was there when I bought it in a second-hand bookshop. I thought nothing of it.'

He slipped a piece of paper over to me.

'That's a translation of what's written in your copy of the book.'

Wherever you may be, death will overtake you, even if you should be within towers of lofty construction.

'So, you still reckon you don't know who wrote that, or what it said?'

'Absolutely.' I'm sure he read the lie on my face.

'You thought nothing of it, even though it says that we're all going to die in lofty towers. Remind you of anything?'

'Of course it did – does. But I didn't have anything to do with it – are you accusing me of organising 9/11?'

'So you do know what it says.'

'You just told me. And anyway, that is only a part of the verse, and taken completely out of context.'

'Yes, but that's what people like you do, isn't it? Take things out of context and blow up innocent people.'

I tried to get up, to stand face to face with him, but my chains got caught on the chair, and I fell sideways, hitting my head on the table. Even so, I shouted at him from that undignified position.

'I am not a terrorist. No one I know is a terrorist. When are you going to believe me and let me out of here?'

Mr Smith chuckled, and Spud, standing by the door, allowed himself a quiet snort. Great joke I was.

On the way back to my cell, he whispered 'good show in there,' as his fingers bruised my arm.

So I was a terrorist because I owned a copy of the Qur'an and slept with a non-practising Muslim from Pakistan. I wondered how many more of us were locked up who fit that bill. And then I remembered that I was also seen as one of them because of an accident of parentage. I had the look therefore I must be one of them. Never mind about all the other things that make me Me. Ignore those, look only at the colour of my skin, and judge me for that. I know myself to be the sum of my genes and the thousands of experiences, events, memories, fantasies and stories that I have lived or heard. A compassionate person, a good friend, a loyal, if sometimes challenging, daughter, a committed teacher, a loving partner. They knew me as a hate-filled terrorist, a foreigner, not fit for their world. What if I was becoming the person they believe me to be? In not telling them that Usman wrote the inscription that so bothered me, was I complicit in something? Was Usman a terrorist? Surely not. There was intelligence not fanaticism in his eyes.

My skin began to tingle and my muscles twitched. My body felt energised and my mind agitated. Mr Smith. Mr Fucking Smith. I grabbed my pillow by the throat and pummelled it with a right hook, a jab, an uppercut. I headbutted it, and then went in for the kill, biting, smashing him against the wall; blood flowed, it was all over my hands and still I carried on. I wanted nothing to be left of him. I beat him until I fell back exhausted and sweaty. A warm glow of satisfaction overwhelmed me and I laughed. I was so happy I'd killed Mr Smith. Later, when it was time to try and sleep, I wondered what had happened to my pillow. It had gone lumpy and limp as if someone had attacked it.

I thought about my father, the man who gave me my colouring. If he were in England would he have been arrested? Surely they hadn't incarcerated every single person of Asian or Middle Eastern appearance?

Mum never said much about my father as I was growing up. I knew other kids with no dad, so I wasn't an oddity. I know Mum loved him. When she decided that it was time for me to know a little about him, some arbitrary day when I was about thirteen, I remember her face softening as she spoke about him.

'Sit down, Laila, there's something I've been meaning to tell you.'

I'd just got in from school and was starving. But the look on Mum's face made me do as she said. I remember my heart fluttering, and being convinced she was going to tell me that she had cancer and was going to die. I felt the blood drain from my face, and I held myself very still.

'You're a big girl now, and it's time you knew – what's the matter, pet, why are you crying?'

Fat tears followed each other down my cheeks. I couldn't stop them, and I couldn't talk through them.

Mum hugged me close.

'It's all right, pet, nothing awful's going to happen. Did you think I was going to tell you some bad news?'

I nodded.

'Oh, darling, no. I thought it was time to tell you about your father, that's all. If you want to know, that is. Do you?'

I nodded again, wiping my face, feeling embarrassed. I couldn't look at her, so I traced the patterns in the carpet with my eyes. She could have told me anything then, and it would have been better than what I had expected.

'All right, well, he was a student from Pakistan. Near India.'

'I know where Pakistan is,' I said. 'We did it in geography.'

'Okay. Right then. His name was Janan Faridun Afridi and he came from near Peshawar in the North-West Frontier, near the border with Afghanistan. He was here on a scholarship studying agriculture. The first things that made me notice him were his eyes – they were the greenest green – and his unassuming manner. I was working in one of the university cafés and he used to come in for his lunch sometimes. Not many of the students talked to us waitresses, they were too up themselves, but he was always polite and asked how I was, thanked me when I served him, that sort of thing. Anyway, over the weeks we got chatting, and eventually I asked him on a date. I think he was so surprised that he agreed before he realised what he was saying, but he didn't back out. He said his word was his word, it was a matter of honour. It wasn't an auspicious beginning really. I ended up feeling like I'd tricked him into the date. Anyway, we went for a picnic and spent the afternoon talking a bit awkwardly, but the next time, we went to see a film – *Annie Hall* it was. His English was good, but afterwards he asked if we could go for a coffee so that I could explain the humour to him. And that's how it started. He was the most considerate man I'd ever met. You know, respectful, kind, sensitive. And a great lover.'

'Mum! That's disgusting.'

'Oh, sorry.' She had a faraway, dreamy look in her eyes, and I think she'd almost forgotten I was there. 'So, where was I?'

'Being revolting,' I reminded her.

She smiled. 'It's a beautiful thing, making love with a man you adore,' she said. 'But you'll have to take my word for that for a few years. Quite a few years.' She gave me one of her mock-stern stares, and we laughed.

'So, what happened to him? If you loved each other so much, why isn't he here now?'

Mum's face changed. It looked suddenly heavier, older and all the light went out of her eyes.

'Sorry–'

'It's all right, pet, it's all right. Pakistan went through some political trouble. The military took over and suspended the constitution. I didn't really understand it all, but Janan was worried about his family. He called his father to make sure they were all okay, and to see if he should come home, but his father assured him that they were well, and that he should finish his studies. Apparently in Pakistani families, the father's word is the law, so although he continued to worry, he stayed. I know it was selfish, but I was so pleased. And it did seem as if things were settling down in Pakistan, even if not everyone agreed with what had happened. So for us, the only thing that changed was that Janan kept in touch more closely with his family.

'Then, just over a year later, he got word that his father had died of a heart attack as he was on his way to the mosque.' Mum stopped and looked into the distance as if she could see it happening. She bit her lip and took a deep breath. I held her hand and said nothing. I wanted to comfort her but I didn't know how.

'Janan took it very badly. He idolised his father. And he was the eldest son, which meant he was now head of the family and had to go home immediately to take up his new responsibilities. It was all so fast. He was gone within three days. We didn't even get to say goodbye properly.'

'Did he come back?'

She shook her head. 'No, pet, he didn't.'

'So... did he know about me?'

She looked at me, examining my features as if for the first time, taking in my eyes, my nose, my mouth. She looked so sad.

'No. I didn't know I was pregnant until after he'd gone, and he had so many responsibilities in Pakistan that I didn't feel it was fair to burden him with another when I found out.'

'Burden him?' I felt the words like a kick in the guts. 'Is that what I am – a burden?'

She looked aghast. 'No, no, pet, of course not. Never. Not to me. But I thought at the time that it might be to him. With family comes responsibility, and he already had so much on his shoulders.'

I took some deep breaths but barely felt any calmer. There was anger in my voice when I asked, 'So did you ever think of, you know, getting rid of me?'

Mum looked like I'd slapped her. Her hands flew to her face, her mouth shaped like a big O.

'Never. Not for one second. I wanted you right from the

moment I knew I was pregnant. And I've never regretted my decision. Ever. I love you, Laila, more than I've ever loved anyone, or ever will.'

I smiled at her. 'Good. Glad to hear it!'

We laughed, then, all tension gone.

'Want something to eat?' she asked.

'Thought you'd never ask,' I said.

If I'd known that she would put the lid on all discussion of my father again, I might have put my hunger to one side and asked more questions, but I thought that now she'd started the ball rolling, there'd be more information forthcoming. As it was, if I asked her anything about him after that, she either gave vague, unsatisfactory answers, or pretended she hadn't heard. After some initial frustration, I assumed in my selfish, adolescent way, that there was nothing more to know.

Some years later, in the break between my first and second year of university, I was home for the summer to work in the shop and make some money for moving out of college. My mission for the holidays, though, was to find out more about my father and his family. In London, mainly through Kamila and her family, I'd met more and more Pakistanis, both British and those who were visiting or studying. Without exception, they asked me about my family. Her mother was the first to interrogate me, and set the template for all the others.

'So, Laila, who are your parents?' asked Mrs Malik the first time Kamila invited me to her house.

'I was brought up by my mother and grandparents,' I said.

'And they are from where?'

'Yorkshire. Thirsk. It's quite near York.'

'How long have they lived there?'

'Oh, my family's been there for generations.'

'Mum, they're not from Pakistan,' Kamila said.

'Oh, not from Pakistan, is it? So...'

'My father was. Is. Maybe. They don't live together.'

Mrs Malik looked relieved. She was getting to the bottom of the puzzle. 'Yes, of course. What about your father's family? Who is he, who are they?'

'I don't actually know much. His name is Janan Afridi and he comes from Peshawar. That's about it.'

Mrs Malik was visibly shocked, but Kamila gave her a death stare, and she didn't ask any more. Not then, anyway.

Soon, everyone was asking. Everywhere I went, every Pakistani person I met, young and old, asked about my family. At first I offered polite excuses, these people were, after all, new friends. But they didn't let up, and after a while I found their questions offensive. What did it matter who my father and his family were – they hadn't shown any interest in me, why should I be interested in them? As I rebuffed their questions, or argued that it wasn't important, that I was comfortable with who I was, I found myself angry with them, and also with a father whom I'd never met. A man who had left my mother and let her struggle to bring me up on her own.

It was Kamila I turned to at such times. It was she who reminded me that for many Pakistanis, Partition had meant that they never saw uncles, aunts, cousins, sometimes even parents, again, and that migration to England, while a choice, also disrupted family and community. In a culture in which family was important to begin with, it almost became enshrined when families were so thinly spread. If a relative was discovered, however distant, they were treated as a long lost brother or sister.

'Yes, the questions are annoying, but they are trying to find out if you are blood- related. Anyway,' she'd said, tucking her long hair behind her ears, 'they're not going to stop, so you might as well get used to it. Think of it as a form of flattery – they like you enough to want to see if you're family.'

Looking at it that way, it was flattering, and I found myself sounding regretful rather than disinterested when I said that I didn't know anything about my father and his family.

It was exciting getting to know all these new people with their different ways – Kamila's family treated me as one of their own but I wasn't ready to be fully a part of it. I was comfortable where I was, accepted but not expected to know anything, do anything different. I could observe without participating, and although a part of me was uneasy in the role of observer, it was as much as I could handle. And anyway, it would feel like a betrayal of Mum and all she'd given me to suddenly embrace a culture so different.

That summer university holiday, Mum and I spent a lot of time together, but it wasn't until toward the end of my stay that I asked her about my father, as if knowing I was going to be returning to all the questions in London made it imperative that I have more information.

At first she was reluctant to talk, said she'd told me all she knew about him, but I wouldn't put up with her denials any longer. I had a right to know.

'He was a gentle man,' she said, a wistful look on her face. 'He wanted to learn as much as he could to make his country a better place. We didn't mean to fall in love. He was always going to go home, but we thought we had more time. I suppose at one time I had visions of marrying him and going back with him, but I think that was love talking. If he'd asked me, I would have gone, but I think I would have hated it. His life there sounded harsh, farming land that was rock and dust in a climate that burned crops to a crisp or buried them under early snow. But he loved it. He used to talk of Pakistan as if it was the woman of his dreams, the love of his life. When he talked of the mountains and the valleys I'd imagine him gently stroking them with his strong hands, rather than gazing at them through his eyes. I didn't really stand a chance. And he would never have gone against his family's wishes and brought home a foreign wife.'

I took her hand. She was struggling not to cry. This was a side of Mum I hadn't seen – the dreamer, the romantic.

'When he went back, did you know you'd never see him again?'

The breath caught in Mum's throat like I'd just dug my fingers into a raw wound.

'I'm sorry, Mum. I didn't realise you still felt this way about him. It explains why there's never been anyone else.'

'Oh, there have been others, but none of them lasted because they didn't match up to him. Even though over the years I realised that it couldn't have worked, it's still him I love. Silly, isn't it?'

That was a shock. 'Oh, Mum, I'm sorry. That's so sad.' I squeezed her hand. Her eyes held the light of a long ago love.

She shook her head, dislodging the feelings, and smiled absently.

'But there were others, over the years?' I asked quietly. 'I never knew.'

'Yes, a few. I'm not a nun, you know. I never brought them home though, because I didn't want you to meet them unless they were going to stick around, and none of them did.'

'I'm sorry, Mum.'

'It's not your fault, pet, how could it be?'

'But you've been lonely.'

'I've got you and Gran, my friends. I've got less than some, but a lot more than most.' She blew her nose. 'Anyway, what else do you want to know about your father?'

I felt guilty asking now that I knew she still missed him so much, but I was also worried that this might be my only opportunity. 'What did he look like?'

'Tall, dark and handsome. To me, anyway. You've got his

eyes, not only the colour, but the look – like you see more than just what's there in front of you, that you read people. He was proud of his country, but humble about himself, although he had a good brain and read and spoke English fluently, unlike the rest of his family. He had always wanted to travel, to study, and was the first in his family to go to university, first in Islamabad, and then here in England.'

'Did he say much about where he was actually from, what it was like?'

'Peshawar's in northern Pakistan. Up near the mountains, a rough, rugged place. Now there are thousands of Afghani refugees there. When he was growing up it was part of the hippie trail, and Westerners used to hang out smoking dope and wanting to make love not war. That's how he put it, anyway. It was those hippies that he learned English from in fact, running errands for them when he was a boy, finding them rooms, helping them when their passports were stolen, that sort of thing.'

Tears gathered at the corners of my eyes. I imagined him, a young boy wanting to better himself, and Mum and he torn apart through no fault of their own.

Mum put her hand over mine.

'I'm so sorry, pet, I should have told you all this a long time ago. I just wasn't ready. It was selfish of me, I suppose. And now you're nearly the same age as I was when I met him.' She got up and went out. I heard her rifling through drawers. She came back clutching a dog-eared photo.

'This is your dad. It's the only picture I've got of him,' she said, holding it out to me.

A young man stared straight into the camera, a serious look on his face, as if he was uncomfortable having his photo taken. He was standing upright and rigid. It was like looking in a strange mirror that changed the gender of the viewer. My features were softer, rounder, but there was no doubt that we were related. My father. I was looking at my father. Mum had said, 'your dad', and suddenly, that's who he was. Not a random stranger who was out there somewhere in the world getting on with his life, but my dad.

Mum and I got very drunk together that night, something we'd never done before. She was trying to bury the painful longings for my father that my questions had dredged up for her. I was trying to drown the pain of never having known him.

The next morning I heard Mum leaving for work. God knows how she did it. I had a hangover the size of Britain. I went back to sleep and woke again at lunchtime with a splitting headache and a promise to myself that I would never, ever drink again. After a cup of tea and some paracetamol, I sat at my computer and typed Janan Faridun Afridi into the search engine. Dozens of Afridis came up: shops, restaurants, individuals, some even in Peshawar, but not a Janan Faridun Afridi. I looked at some of the other Afridi profiles, followed several links, but kept coming up with blanks.

Frustrated, I started researching Peshawar instead. I found pictures, news articles, maps. The old city looked medieval, while the more modern suburbs sprawled in all directions. And in the background, the mighty Hindu Kush. That was the real beginning of my interest in Pakistan, although I had studied what I could before then, in atlases and geography textbooks at school.

~

I was going mad in Solitary, although it was intermittent. I had periods of lucidity, phases of madness, paranoia. Although when I was in them, they were real. It was only when I regained my sanity that I knew I had been mad. The walls would melt and spots appeared on them. I knew I was meant to interpret them, but couldn't. I traced the pattern with my fingers, my heart racing. If only I could understand what it meant, maybe I'd know who was trying to communicate with me. Was it Faisal?

I was getting close, the meaning was becoming clearer, but then I heard people talking, shouting things about me.

'She's a slut, sleeps with anyone and everyone.'

'Abusive to the kids she was meant to teach, to protect.'

'Whore.'

'I'm not those things,' I yelled, 'none of them. Stop telling those lies.'

'She betrayed her best friend.'

'She's selfish.'

'Her mother never wanted her.'

'Shut the fuck up!' I covered my ears, but I could still hear. They were in my head.

My food was poisoned, so I couldn't eat it. I knew because I had a visitor during the night. She had to bribe the guards to get in, but she knew them. She was once an inmate here. She told me that they put mind control drugs in the food. I thought she was right, that I'd already known it. She said that the evening meal was usually okay because they don't interrogate you at night, but not to eat breakfast or lunch.

Her name was Carol, and she'd been in prison for murder. I thought she was lying about that, though, because she didn't seem like a murderer, she was trying to help me, wasn't she?

She wasn't real. A figment of my imagination. Gone as soon as she arrived. But she made me realise that maybe anyone could kill. I could kill. I indulged in violent fantasies of murdering the guards, smearing their blood over the walls of this place, throwing their entrails to huge tusked pigs that waited in the yard.

One shower day, Jabba wasn't there. Spud was on his own. I

cringed away from him, knowing what was coming, but he was bigger than me. He grabbed me, held me with one huge hand as his other stroked my body. At first he was gentle, even murmured a few words of kindness as his eyes roamed over me.

'You're very beautiful, your skin is almost luminous.'

I almost believed him.

'Shame you're a fucking traitorous little bitch.' His grip tightened.

Words formed in my head but humiliation drowned them. I'd been so desperate for kindness I'd let my guard down. I turned my head away.

'Just got to do a little search. You know the drill.' His breath was on me. I could feel his erection against my hip. I tried to move away but he rammed me against the wall.

He licked his index finger and ran it down my breast bone, my abdomen, forced it into me, searching my orifices. He maintained the lie that he was looking for contraband even as he sucked on my nipples and I felt the sticky wetness of his excitement.

I sank to my knees when he released me, shaking, revolted by my own body, which had responded to his in a way that my head did not.

Touch is a powerful weapon.

The next day, when he pushed my lunch through the door slot, I gave him an example of what was up my arse. As he wiped the shit off his sleeve I couldn't stop laughing. Until I was hog-tied and left naked in a chair in the middle of my cell for hours on end. I forgot sometimes that I was the one with no power.

4

When I walked back into my cell after what must have been a few hours with Mr Smith one time, I noticed that it smelled bad. Had someone else done that, or was that the smell of me? It could have been. There is no ventilation. The only new air that gets in is through the door slot three times a day, and occasionally when the door is open for a few moments. It bothered me for hours. And then I couldn't smell it anymore.

Straw passed through my breakfast and asked me if I was okay. Such kindness. I told him that he was the only one who cared about me, who didn't play tricks on me. He asked how it had gone with Mr Smith the day before.

'I didn't see him yesterday,' I said.

'Yes you did – it was Tuesday – he comes every Tuesday and Friday – has done for weeks.'

I went cold. I had no memory of it. Was he lying? Had I been wrong to trust him, to like him? Twice a week for weeks? Surely not. Such gaps in my memory. What did I say to Mr Smith those times? What did they want from me?

I became obsessed with the idea that they were drugging me, and ate and drank as little as possible. I had to know what was happening, what they were asking, what I was saying.

When I was sane it was the boredom that got to me. Time stretched before me, behind me, around me. I almost wished for permanent insanity.

In the exercise yard I noticed that the green smear I had left on the wall had a line scratched through it, as if someone had taken their fingernail to it. Proof that there were others there! Real people. I was elated at the same time as I was appalled that there were others who were being treated the same as me. I rubbed my finger in the green slime and drew an L on the wall below my original mark. Maybe Faisal was there, and he would know that I was, too, when he saw it. The thought kept me going for a while, and back in my cell I hugged myself, thinking of making love with him, and before I knew it, I was allowing myself more than a hug. I didn't even care that the guards saw. To that extent, they had broken me. I had no dignity left, no privacy. But I still had my tattered soul.

Afterwards, I glanced over at the door. It was open but no one was yelling at me to show them my hands for the cuffs, or to stand back while they entered, tasers at the ready. What was going on? Was it a test of some sort? I noticed my heart speeding up, I was free to go, no one would stop me. I sat up slowly and swung my feet to the floor. Still no one shouted at me. Getting up onto my feet, I took some deep breaths. Running was the best option. Run fast and run hard. I clenched my fists as if round a relay baton, put my head down and charged.

Next thing I knew I was on the floor. I looked around me, dazed. The bastards had shut the door again. It had been a trick, a joke. They laughed at me, I was their toy. Wind her up and off she goes.

The marks on the yard wall disappeared, and worse, it was me that got rid of them. Spud shoved a bucket and cloth at me and told me to clean every last inch. When I'd finished, I threw the dirty water over him. I anticipated more hours hog-tied naked in the chair, but all they did was turn the heating off. I did star jumps and sit-ups to keep warm. It seemed like hours, but it was worth it. I hated them all. Small acts of rebellion were all I had.

I got to a point when I didn't like leaving my cell. I felt so exposed outside. By outside I obviously don't mean Outside. I mean away from No. 4. I couldn't think straight, I couldn't concentrate, I found it hard to remember things, and I felt raw, like the nerve endings were on the wrong side of my skin. And the noise. It was unbelievable. Straw's steel-capped boots on the floor as he walked, the opening and shutting of doors set my brain juddering. I couldn't cover my ears because my hands were shackled to my waist chain. And their voices were so loud.

Not only were they looking in my notebook, they gave themselves permission to write in it as well.

You should really be more helpful to Mr Smith you know. And by the way, my name isn't Spud, it's Jim.

Nothing was sacred. Nothing was mine except my thoughts. Sorry, Spud, I preferred the name I gave.

Mr Smith had a colleague with him one day. Mr Jones. He was shorter than Mr Smith, and had a huge nose that he kept blowing, except it looked like he was actually polishing it. I swear it got shinier and shinier as the interview went on.

'Your friend, Usman trained with an Al-Qaeda-related terrorist organisation in Pakistan.'

'I'm well thanks, how are you?'

'Don't get smart with me, Laila. Tell us what you know.' Mr Jones's voice was gruff.

'I don't know anything about Usman. I told all this to Mr Smith. He stayed at Faisal's sometimes, I don't know where he lived the rest of the time, or what he did.'

'What about friends? Who came to see him when he was there?'

'No one that I ever saw. He was very quiet, very private. I never saw him with anyone else.'

'Ever heard of Harkat-al-Mujahideen?'

I shook my head.

'What about Lakshar-e-Jafria?'

'No, never heard of him either.'

'They're not people, they're terrorist organisations. What about Faisal? Who did he associate with?'

I hated the way they called him by his first name, his usual name, as he called it. The one that his friends called him by. They should refer to him as Dr Choudhry. I felt my teeth clench.

'Well?'

'He had lots of friends.'

'What about these men?'

He threw mugshots of five men onto the table between us.

The failed bombers. Two weeks after the bombings, these men had thrown Britain into a state of anxiety even greater than that of the seventh of July. The original bombings, while horrifying, were a one-off, we were assured. Londoners were told not to give in to the fear, to go about their business as usual. And then, another terrorist attack. Helicopters filled the skies that day – how could you not be afraid? Everyone thought that this was the new world order after all, that our lives would be dominated by attacks such as these, and my friends and I were appalled, shell-shocked, terrorised.

Mr Smith pushed yet another photo towards me of a bearded man with green eyes and a haughty look about him.

'And him?' Mr Smith pulled out another photo, another man, younger, good-looking, with the same arrogant air. I'd never seen either of them before.

'No.'

'So you're trying to tell me that you've never seen your father or brother before? What do you take me for, eh? Some sort of fucking idiot?' He smashed a fist into the table.

My father? My brother?

'I didn't even know I had a brother – what's his name?'

No answer, the photos tucked away again so I didn't have another chance to see them.

'How about you? Who do you count amongst your friends, eh?'

'I have lots of friends, none of them terrorists. What is my brother's name?'

'Who's this?'

Another photo was put in front of me. I gasped. It was Kamila.

'Yes?'

I took a breath. Another. What should I say? I didn't want to land her in the shit too.

'I've met her a few times.'

'Oh, come on, Laila. You're not helping her, and you're not helping yourself.' Mr Smith sounded reasonable. Fatherly.

I relaxed a little.

All of a sudden, Mr Jones hurled himself across the table at me. His face was so close to mine I couldn't focus on it.

He yelled, 'Stop wasting our fucking time. We know you've been meeting with her regularly, and so has Faisal Choudhry. You seem to think we're idiots, but we have files on all of you including dates and times of meetings.'

I wiped his spit off my face as he continued in a calmer voice. 'So why not just co-operate, okay?'

'She's a friend. We see her because we like her. We have never plotted anything more than a surprise party for a mutual friend. Kamila throws great parties.'

Mr Smith and Mr Jones looked at each other and seemed to have some sort of telepathic exchange. Mr Smith turned back to me.

'We can tell you that Usman Wakim Khawaja was arrested in Pakistan and has been charged with conspiring to organise acts of terrorism.'

I couldn't get my breath. Usman, a real terrorist? I mean, they'd told me that they suspected it, but there was no way that gentle, quiet Usman was a terrorist. All he did was read. They must have got it wrong.

'And I expect we'll be charging your friend Faisal soon.'

Faisal? No way.

'You're wrong. He's a pacifist. He hates the religious zealots that explode themselves in shopping centres killing innocent people. He deplored the London bombings. He even wrote a letter to *The Times* saying so. And we went to the rally in Russell Square to stop the war and say no to more killings.' I felt sick. 'He hasn't got a violent bone in his body.'

'Yeah, yeah, yeah. And he knits fluffy bunnies to give to sick kids at Christmas.' Mr Jones laughed at his own joke. 'I don't know why you're trying to protect them. He's told us some interesting things about you. And the Pakistani police have sent us Usman's statement. You're mentioned several times.'

I stared at them. There was nothing interesting to know about me. What had they said? Had they incriminated me hoping to get themselves off the hook? No, they wouldn't do that, I felt guilty for even thinking it.

I laughed. A false laugh at first, just to do something, to show them how ridiculous they were, but it turned into the real thing. I laughed and I couldn't stop. Somewhere in there the interview ended, and I was taken back to No. 4.

I laughed until the tears started, and then they wouldn't stop.

They were lying. Usman knew nothing about me, and Faisal knew I wasn't a terrorist. He wouldn't make things up to get me into trouble.

I lay awake for hours. Did he, didn't he? Would he, wouldn't he? I hated Smith and Jones for planting the seeds of doubt, and I hated myself for watering them.

What did they know about my father and brother? I hated that they knew more than I did about my own flesh and blood, even though some of it was obviously lies and speculation.

I have a brother. That's weird.

Usman is a terrorist.

Faisal has been saying things about me. I don't believe it. I don't want to believe it. I won't believe it.

And Spud kept amusing himself by writing in my notebook.

Oh, Laila, you're in such trouble.

I loathed him. I hated that he reminded me that he was the one with the power, that he could do what he wanted. And why did he tell me his name? Was it meant to be a gift, a buttering up so that we could have a cosy chat sometime? Or did he hate the name I've given him so much that he didn't want me using it? SPUD SPUD SPUD.

~

There was a sprig of holly on my breakfast tray one morning. Was it Christmas? It had certainly been colder when I'd been in the yard lately, but I'd walkwalkwalkwalkwalk when I was in there and soon warm up. Christmas meant I'd been there five months. I'd been arrested just after school had broken up for the summer and Faisal and I were looking forward to a summer getaway. He'd taken three weeks off work in August and we'd booked a canal holiday in France for a week, and then two weeks in Italy because we were culture vultures. It was going to be my first time abroad; the pages of my new passport were virginal.

Five months. A whole term missed at school. I wondered what they'd been doing. Who would have directed the Christmas play? That had been my job for the last three years. I loved the excitement of the children in the lead-up to Christmas, even though it so often led to tears as Gretchen was chosen for the main part over Lily, or Shrinath given a song to sing but not Bogdan.

I pierced my skin with the holly. Was that what they meant me to do with it? Blood of Laila. I dug in the sharp ends of the leaves time and time again until my skin was dotted with red pinpricks. My arms, my legs, then off with the T-shirt and stab and scratch the belly, chest, neck.

I had been careful to turn away from the camera, but eventually even the sleepy guards came rushing, opened the door slot, yelled at me to stand back from the door, rushed in, tasers raised, and snatched the holly away. They were out again before I could say Merry Christmas.

There was no holly on the lunch tray, but there was a mince pie, and dinner was turkey with all the trimmings and Christmas pud with lumpy custard. As I picked at the food I wondered what Mum was doing, who she and Gran were having Christmas with. I sang all my favourite carols one after the other, quietly at first, but louder and louder until I was shouting 'Silent Night' at the top of my voice, and then a miracle – I heard someone join in. A real person, not a voice-in-my-head person. From far away, there was definitely another voice. A beautiful soprano. My Christmas present.

'Who are you? What is your name?' I yelled.

I couldn't hear the answer. I tried again. And then Spud came in and threatened me with a hose-down if I didn't stop. But there was someone there. Who was it? Had she been there as long as me, all this time and we'd never met? I was so excited to know that I wasn't alone, and so upset to know that someone was also in this hell.

The previous Christmas Faisal and I went to Thirsk. He was meeting Mum and Gran for the first time, and he was nervous which was sweet and humble of him, I thought. We drove up on Christmas Eve, the car full of food and gifts, and he asked questions all the way about Mum, Gran, the town, whether any of my friends would be there. That's when I knew I loved him. When he so obviously cared what my family thought of him and was anxious to make a good impression. Of course, they did like him, how could they not? He was kind, attentive without being obsequious, thoughtful, interested. And interesting. He had stories to tell about his childhood in Karachi, his travels in India, his work.

We walked on the moors in freezing fog and driving rain,

and he didn't complain once. We visited Gran's elderly friends, and he charmed them. We sat in pubs drinking real ale, and he didn't grimace once.

I thought about him. 'Faisal, wherever you are, Merry Christmas.'

He didn't make up things about me to get himself off, did he?

I couldn't stop thinking about the other person there. At least one, maybe more. A group of women who were never allowed to meet. I decided she was black. She sounded black. A gospel voice. A better singer than me. When would we have another excuse to sing? How could we communicate if not through song? My voice was still hoarse from the singing, so I couldn't shout.

I began to look forward to shower time, pathetic as that may sound. It was the only time that I was touched with anything approaching affection. At least, I pretended it was affection. In reality it was need, abuse of power, diminishing of dignity. Jabba reminded me again and again that she had all the control, yet I found myself feeling sorry for her. She may have had the power, but I had something she wanted. It must have been humiliating for her, and somewhere in her rotten, festering soul, she felt that. And degrading as it was, and even as I hated myself for it, I also knew that I needed that touch. It reminded me that I was a person with a body. A person in a body. It was easy to forget.

I tried closing my eyes and pretending she was Faisal, because he was so much more tender, eager to fulfil my desires, not just his own. It took a long time for us to get to making love. I think he had some inner conflict about it. He explained once that although his family was quite liberal in many ways, they still expected him to marry the woman they chose for him, and he said he didn't want to fall in love with me and have his heart always entwined with mine if he wasn't ready to stand up to his parents, break with tradition, and be with the person he wanted to be with. So when one day, he cupped my face in his hands and said that he very much wanted to make love with me, I felt overwhelmed. This was big. Monumental. I'd wanted him so badly, and here he was wanting me too, but I was suddenly aware of the full meaning of his desire. This wasn't just about making love, it was about futures and commitments. He'd thought about his struggle, and I hadn't even had one. Sex didn't have the same meaning for me, I'd slept with men and not loved them, although sometimes I'd convinced myself at the time that I did.

When we did finally make love, it was like an act of worship. A commitment to each other and all that lay beyond.

He would never betray me, would he?

I got to a point when I knew I couldn't go on any longer. My mind was going. The walls melted, gyrated, morphed into odd shapes. There were marks on them that moved. There was a bird flying around near the ceiling. I watched it for ages, wondering how on earth it had got in, convincing myself that maybe the guards had given it to me as a present. I thought about how maybe I had misjudged them. I would thank them. And then I realised that it was the camera. Not flying. Not even moving. The camera watching me and me watching it.

My eyes hurt all the time. I was constipated. My heart was all wrong, stopping for several beats and then thumping into gear again and pumping toohardandtoofast. I feel it in my throat. I asked to see a doctor. I waited.

. . .

Waited

waited

waited.

I thought I was going blind. I would kill myself.

I lay on my bed and hugged my knees to my chest. My hips dug into the thin mattress and the concrete beneath. My body ached.

I was alive. I would have been happy not to be.

I was disappearing.

I sat.

My head hurt. I had a red hand mark on my face. Jabba said I fainted and she slapped my face to bring me round. I remembered it differently. She had come into my cell and wanted me to go down on her. I'd refused and she'd hit me. Who was right? I didn't know. I didn't even care, except it gave me something to think about. Rightwrongrightwrongrightwrong.

I didn't know anything anymore. I was in the yard and started taking my clothes off, thinking I was going to have a shower. Straw handed them back to me and told me to put them back on and I cried.

I worried that I would not be given another notebook when I had filled the first one, even though I filled it with rubbish.

When I had to leave my cell it waited for me. When I walked back in, it breathed a sigh of relief and I did too. We belonged to each other. We needed each other. I inhabited it and it inhabited me.

I was not afraid of spiders anymore. There was one living on the ceiling. It descended when I slept, and grew. When I woke up it was covering me. It was almost as big as my cell. When I needed to get up it retreated to the ceiling and hid in its smaller form so that the guards didn't see it and take it away. Its job was to protect me.

After a shower, or was it exercise? Anyway, my books were gone. They had taken everything. There was nothing left.

I sat.

I did not move.

All day.

There was nothing.

I am nothing.

BOO!

Where was Faisal? I loved him.

I hated him.

Mr Smith showed me a statement Faisal had written.

He had betrayed me. I saw it then. I lost hope.

Hope was all I had.

There was no life in there. No hope. I sharpened a plastic knife against the concrete of my desk. I slashed and slashed and plunged it again and again into my body, my flesh. I welcomed the pain and then I felt it ebb away with my dying breath. I was so excited to be leaving.

I did not feel. My body had no substance. I looked down on myself as I floated near the light.

. . .

I was the bird.

There was blood, lots of blood.

PART II

5

March 2006
Yorkshire

I should have known.

I'd been in the hospital wing for some time after the stabbing incident, and then moved back to my cell on suicide watch. Every few minutes the camera would whir annoyingly on its bracket as it swept the room. The guards even looked in through the door slot at random intervals. I waited for them and imagined gouging their eyes out, smashing their smug faces with my bare fists. Even those who had treated me like a human were now making me angry. Why hadn't they let me die? The physical scars had healed.

I still wanted to be dead.

And then one day, who knows how long after I'd returned to my cell from the hospital wing, I had eaten my breakfast, washed my bowl and spoon and the door slot had opened. I'd been ordered out. Shackled, as usual. Taken to the shower. This time, shampoo, soap, hot water that kept running until I had scrubbed every inch of my body. Jabba had watched but not touched. All these taken together should have been clue enough to what was happening. But I was just enjoying the water on my skin, the smell of the soap, the lather of the shampoo, watching it drip down my body in white bubbly streaks. I turned away from Jabba and tasted it, acidy and chemical, disappearing on my tongue. It was these things that told me that I was real, that I existed. Taste and touch. Sight was no longer to be trusted.

Then my clothes. The jeans and T-shirt I'd so hastily put on when they came to Faisal's flat. The shoes that had hidden from me under the bed. Faisal's bed. It had been a warm evening last time I'd worn them.

My heart was thudding by then. This was not the way of things. Where was my blue jumpsuit, where were the chains? There were only hands holding me, kind ones, not Spud's bruising fingers.

I was led into a white room too big to feel safe. A woman stood in the middle, but I couldn't make out her features. My vision was fuzzy. I heard a familiar voice and the woman approached.

My mother.

She held out a hand to me, and I didn't know what to do. I wanted to laugh and cry, run to her. And yet, I was afraid. Was this really happening, or was it another of those tricks the guards played on me? I looked back towards the door to see if they were laughing, but there was no one there.

'Laila, pet, it's me, Mum.' Her arms enfolded me, our tears mingled as we pressed our cheeks to one another's, getting as close as possible. But too soon I became uncomfortable. I felt her disappointment as I pulled away, as repelled by loving touch as I had been desperate for it.

'Oh, pet, my darling girl. What have they done to you?' It was all she could say, as if I would be able to come up with an answer. I looked at her, and she'd changed. Her once lustrous skin was dull, her curly hair, styled for the occasion by the look of it, lacked vitality. Grey roots spread into the blonde-like tendrils claiming back the falsehood. What had happened to her? I tried to ask, but no words came. My mouth was too full of anger and hatred and fear to utter words of concern for my own mother.

She took my bag. It was small and light. A plastic shopping bag with my notebook, the books I'd read over and over until I could quote chunks of them. The only other possessions I'd been allowed in No. 4, the pencil, the comb and the toothbrush, had been taken away after all the blood. Mum had my laptop. I clutched my handbag, returned to me as I was released. It contained my phone with all my friends in it. My life on the outside.

Mum enfolded me in a big winter coat. I retreated into it as the last door whooshed open and I shielded my eyes from the sun. So bright, so unforgiving. I had to keep my head down. So cold. Frost clung to the ground, my breath turned to cloud on the air. No one was there to farewell me. There had been no explanations, no goodbyes, no apologies. For them, I had already ceased to exist.

My legs, unused to walking any distance, felt wobbly. I had gone into prison a twenty-seven-year-old, and come out an octogenarian. My mother had to help me to the car, all the way across an endless car park.

Colours. Too many to look at and some I couldn't even remember the names of. The grey of the road, the metallics of the cars. Grass. I had to look away. Tears hastened down my cheeks, and I had no idea why. I gulped the air. Adrenaline rushed through me, panic. I wanted my cell, the safe refuge of No. 4 which had been snatched away from me with no warning.

I hadn't been able to say goodbye, to thank Cedric the spider for helping me over my fear and for protecting me. I wanted to tell him to be wary of the guards, that they wouldn't understand him. I prayed that No. 4 wouldn't be fumigated before some other unfortunate was locked in there. In my cell.

My mother kept up a ceaseless stream of chatter, and yet I couldn't take in all that she was saying. The words congealed, like porridge left out too long, and didn't make it to my brain.

'...looking so thin... calendar every day... at home... couldn't work at... so worried... sleep...'

I concentrated on her voice, so familiar and yet it was like I was hearing it for the first time.

Eventually we reached her car. She opened the door for me, turned to put my bag in the back. I walked a few steps away, looked back towards the prison. I could hardly make it out. My vision, having only had objects within a few feet to focus on now couldn't adjust to the longer distance. I covered my eyes again, and all the anger that I'd been holding in welled in a great eruption of yelling, screaming, shrieking, bellowing. Nothing coherent – pent-up rage, fear, pain, horror. There were no words for all that.

I don't know how long I stayed there. I became aware of my mother standing beside me, a fragile smile on her face. I took her hand, looked at her, sucked in deep, shuddering breaths. I knew she wanted me to be normal. I wanted more than anything to be back in my cell, but I couldn't tell her that, it would hurt too much.

We left. She drove. I sat. I was reassured by the smallness of the car, but watching the blurry scenery overwhelmed me, so I closed my eyes to it, concentrated on the movement, the monotonous drone of the engine. Mum was quiet now but I could feel the questions burning her lips.

She wanted me to be happy. I didn't know how.

I stayed in the car when she stopped at a service station to get coffee and food. There were so many people. So much noise. I covered my ears, pulled my feet up onto the seat, let my head rest on my knees. When Mum came back and opened her door, I was startled and shrank away from her. I never want to see that look on her face again. Pain and sadness and anger all rolled into one, before she composed herself. She got in, stared out the front window. She didn't know what to say to me, and I still hadn't said a word to her. We, who had always enjoyed each other, who talked for hours about everything and nothing.

I felt my stomach lurch with anger. This was something else that had been taken away from me.

'What's the date?' I asked, finally. My voice sounded unfamiliar in my ears, bouncing off glass and plastic instead of concrete. We were still in the service station car park, the day dwindling towards evening. My teeth chattered with cold.

'13th March.' Mum swallowed hard and gripped the steering wheel, holding herself steady.

'March? 2006?'

'Yes, my darling. I'm so sorry.'

She apologised as if it was her fault that I'd been locked up for – how long was it? I couldn't work it out. My mind was foggy, slow.

'It was thirty-two weeks and four days. I crossed every day off on the calendar. When you didn't ring on the Sunday, I rang your house and the girls told me some men had come to talk to them about you and that they hadn't seen you and didn't know what had happened. I didn't know what to do. I was beside myself.'

I saw her begin to cry, wipe at the tears angrily, but I couldn't respond. I was disappearing again, like had happened so often lately. All I could do was wait and see if I came back.

All that time. I'd been in prison all that time.

I wrenched open the car door, ran to the edge of the car park and screamed. I hit a tree until my hand bled. I vomited. And then I collapsed to my knees shivering until Mum put her shawl around my shoulders and pulled me to my feet.

'It'll be all right, pet. Let's get you into the car and we'll get you home to your bed. Gran's waiting. She'll be wondering where we've got to.'

'Gran.' I was so relieved that she was alive. In the last few weeks I'd convinced myself that she'd died while I'd been away. I don't know why. Maybe with her dead, there was one less person to worry about, to wonder what they were doing.

My face felt strange, cracked. I was smiling. 'Gran.'

I lasted longer in Gran's embrace, but was still the first to pull away. Mum must have called her from the service station to warn her that I was – what? Strange? Damaged? Changed beyond recognition? Anyway, she didn't cringe when she saw me. She just got businesslike in the way she always did in a crisis, like when Granddad died – she'd made endless cups of tea and baked parkin, scones, biscuits, barmbrack. There weren't enough people in all of Thirsk to eat her cakes, but she wouldn't stop. I still can't eat parkin without thinking of Granddad. It was his favourite. He used to sit me on his knee when I was little and say, 'we'll share this piece, Laila,' and he'd wink at Gran then take a huge slice of cake and we'd take great bites, wedging the cake into our cheeks like hamsters before chewing, mouths stuffed. Gran would tut and put her hands on her hips, but she smiled too.

'We'll get some meat on those bones again in no time,' she said, handing me a plate stacked high with calories.

I took a bite of parkin and closed my eyes. It felt like home. Warm and safe and welcoming. Squashing the cake against the roof of my mouth to release the flavours, the same way I had as a child, I felt like I was drowning in sweet molasses and buttery sunshine. But after three or four mouthfuls I had to stop. I hadn't eaten food that rich and flavoursome in a long time, and it made me feel sick. I wanted to feel Granddad's strong arms wrapping around me, his mellow voice telling me that I'd get through this. But I was glad he wasn't alive to see me now. Laila unable to eat. Laila, skin and bone. Laila, unable to string two words together. Laila, full of rage and hatred.

'I need to go to bed,' I said.

Mum and Gran looked at each other. It was only just after six thirty. No doubt they had been expecting me to sit up with them, telling them about my arrest and incarceration over endless cups of tea. I couldn't do it. I needed to be alone. I felt as if there were beetles crawling all over me, my skin alive with anxiety. I didn't want to be in the cosy kitchen with its smells and memories. The headache that had started as a twinge behind my eyes was now a mallet pounding my brain. I wanted to talk to Cedric, to feel his reassuring weight on my body as I lay on my bed. His presence had made me feel real.

Next door in Mum's flat, my bedroom hadn't changed since I left home apart from several large boxes stacked in the corner. My things from London. Mum must have collected them for me at some point. Other than those, the room was as it had been the day I left home. Mum had left it as it was, waiting for me to come back or tell her I was gone for good. I looked at all my possessions. Who needed all those things? Posters on the walls, beads hung over the mirror, scarves spilling out of drawers, clothes in the wardrobe enough to dress a prison full of women. An assault on the senses, frippery and frivolity. I wasn't that person anymore. I had forgotten that I ever was. The only thing I wanted was the photo of Mum and Gran the first time they came to visit me in London. St Paul's in the background, Mum and Gran beaming at the camera, hair billowing round their faces in the strong November wind.

I lay on the bed, but the room, once my cocoon, now threatened me. Too big, too many memories, no lock on the door.

Ripping my duvet out of its glaring pink-and-purple cover, I tiptoed across to the bathroom. Smaller, safer, white. With the duvet in the bath, and all the towels from the airing cupboard on top of me for that reassuring weight, I dropped into a fitful sleep.

I dreamed about Granddad that night. He was standing in a river fly fishing. Slowly casting and recasting, so patient. His rod bent, he'd caught something. When he reeled it in, it was Cedric with me in a blue jumpsuit clutched in his eight long legs.

I sobbed. I wanted my Granddad, Cedric, the jumpsuit, my cell. In prison, imagining killing the guards slowly and painfully had often helped me get back to sleep. Now, with no guards to fantasise about, I ran my fingers over the scars on my body, each one a reminder of my time in No. 4. Each one a small triumph over the vigilance of the guards. They had taken away my freedom, possessions, privacy, dignity, my sense of justice and a future, but they couldn't take away my body. Sometimes, cutting with whatever I had to hand – cutlery, my pencil, paper torn from *National Geographic*, was all that reminded me I was real. When they were taken away as punishment, I used my fingernails, bitten to points. And there was always biting. My arms looked like a vampire had been at them.

In the morning I heard Mum on the phone.

'No, she's not all right. Of course she isn't. How could she be? But at least she's home.'

I imagined her playing with the cord like she always did as she listened.

'I don't know. Not today, anyway. We'll have to take each day as it comes.'

Peeking through the door, I watched as she picked some dead leaves off the plant by the phone.

'Absolutely effing furious. How dare they do this to her? I'm going to write to the Home Office again. Mmm... mmm... yes. Okay. Thanks.' She hung up and turned to see me standing in the doorway. Her cheeks were wet.

'Laila, pet, how long have you been there?' She smeared the tears across her face with the back of her hand.

'Not long,' I lied.

Mum put on her bright voice. The kind of voice I used in the classroom when I was introducing a piece of work I knew none of the children were going to want to do.

'Well, what would you like for breakfast then?'

'I don't know.' I'd fantasised about home cooking while I was in Solitary, but now that I was here there were too many choices.

'Porridge? You always used to like porridge.'

I shuddered, closed my eyes.

'Not porridge then. Toast? Eggs? Black pudding? Anything you like.'

I loved black pudding, but when I imagined thick slices of it on my plate, grease making a moat around it, I felt sick.

Same when I thought of eggs the way Mum made them, the yolks all runny.

'Toast.' Why were decisions so hard? Why did I want to escape to the bathroom again and get under the towels?

'I'll make tea,' she said as she put the bread in the toaster.

I sat at the table, remembering tea and talks there. Not only with Mum, but with friends, with Faisal when he was here.

I am a talker, usually.

Noticing Mum's shoulders heaving. I went to her, stood by her. I wanted to tell her that I was all right, or would be. But I couldn't, because I didn't know, and I wanted to be honest. Instead, I put a hand on her back and we stood like that, looking out the lace-curtained windows until the toast popped up and made us both jump.

'Do you want to talk about it, pet?'

'No.'

Mum hadn't said anything about not being able to get into the bathroom, but after that first night I stayed in my room. I heaved the mattress onto the floor, took extra sheets out of the airing cupboard and stretched them from the bed base to the chest of drawers to make a tent. Small, safe.

Some days later, as I entered the kitchen, Mum turned from the egg she was frying. Trying to sound casual, she asked if I'd heard from Faisal.

'I don't know what happened to him and I'm not sure I want to. He said things about me – to them – that... well, let's just say that whatever he said, it helped him more than it helped me.'

'Oh, pet. I'm so sorry. I didn't know.'

'I'm okay.'

I wasn't.

'Why did you ask?'

'What?'

My mother had never been good at acting. She flipped the egg and wouldn't look at me.

'Have you heard something?'

Slipping the egg onto a piece of buttered toast, she said, 'A letter arrived, pet. It was sent on from your address in London. I think it's from him.'

I clutched the table.

'Where is it? Give it to me. Please.'

'Are you sure? I don't want you getting upset.'

I laughed. The idea of not getting upset was preposterous. I lived upset. I embodied upset. Amongst worse things.

'Perhaps it's an attempt to explain what he did and why. It should make for interesting reading.'

'Well, if you're sure...'

I held out my hand.

Mum went to her bedroom and I heard the squeak of the bedside table drawer opening. All these months and she hadn't seen to it. All it needed was a bit of wax on the runners.

In my room, I examined the envelope. Jeanette had readdressed it in her scrawly handwriting.

Taking a deep breath, I pulled the letter out. Was this going to be his admission of guilt? An apology? Was I meant to forgive him for betraying me? He must think I was naïve as well as stupid.

I wasn't prepared for a love letter.

4th February
My darling Laila Farida,
I have been so worried about you, and this morning, as I was informed that my visa has been revoked and that I am to leave the country immediately, I was told that you have also been in prison all this time. I cannot express my outrage strongly enough. I had been so sure that you would have been released immediately, and I gained comfort from that.
I am so sorry that you were caught up in this diabolical miscarriage of justice, for that is what it is, I promise you. I have never, nor would ever, do anything to hurt you or anyone else, as I hope you know. As I know that this is also true of you.

My Love, I fear that I will never see you again. They are putting me on a flight to Karachi tonight and I doubt I will ever be allowed to return. It may be that after all you have endured in the last months, you never wish to see me anyway. I can only hope with every breath I take that that is not so, but that is a selfish wish, I know. Perhaps you are angry and have written me off; I could not blame you for that. I will not write again if I do not hear from you – your silence will tell me all I need to know.

I am a doctor, good at sewing together broken people. But I am broken without you, who are my soul, my heart, my Love, and I cannot repair myself.

When we were arrested, I had a book of Rumi poetry in my jacket pocket. It was, of course, taken away when we got to the prison, but after some weeks was returned to me. I suppose my captors had concluded that there was little threat in the devotional poems of a thirteenth-century Persian poet. So, while I was there I committed some of his poetry to memory. His poems were mainly written to the glory of God, but this one, I believe, was written for you. It has been on my lips a thousand times while we have been apart.

In the early dawn of happiness
you gave me three kisses
so that I would wake up
to this moment of love
I tried to remember in my heart
what I'd dreamt about
during the night
before I became aware
of this moving
of life
I found my dreams
but the moon took me away
It lifted me up to the firmament

and suspended me there
I saw how my heart had fallen
on your path
singing a song
Between my love and my heart
things were happening which
slowly slowly
made me recall everything
You amuse me with your touch
although I can't see your hands.
You have kissed me with tenderness
although I haven't seen your lips
You are hidden from me.
But it is you who keeps me alive
Perhaps the time will come
when you will tire of kisses.
I shall be happy
even for insults from you
I only ask that you
keep some attention on me.

You will always be in my heart.
Faisal.

There was something more, but it had been blacked out. I took the letter to the window, held it to the light, but the censor's pen was dark and would not yield up the information it hid. It must have been an address. His address. The address he would be expecting me to write to. Had been hoping for weeks already that I would write to.

From the words he had written it was hard to believe that he had betrayed me. How could I ever have thought that he did? That statement that Mr Smith showed me – now I realised what was wrong with it. I'd thought there was something at the time, but I wasn't thinking clearly. It wasn't signed. Mr Smith had written it to make me talk. My stomach clenched in rage.

Or was this part of some elaborate plot?

I slid to the floor, clutching the letter.

He betrayed me, don't be fooled by this.

He loves me, we are meant to be together.

He used me.

He loves me.

He is a traitor, a parasite.

He is the man I love.

In the end, all I knew was that I needed to try and contact him, that it couldn't end like this.

I traced my name lightly with a finger. Faisal loved my name. He would take my hands in his, gaze into my eyes and whisper it over and over again. 'My Laila Farida,' he'd say, 'your name is written in my heart.'

I sat, reading the letter again and again, and great sobs welled up making my chest heave, my heart ache. He was gone, but he loved me.

Gran came over later. 'I need some help with the curtains, Laila,' she said.

'What sort of help?'

'They've got to be washed. I need someone to get them down for me. I can't stand on a ladder these days. I'm getting old, you know.'

Gran had been getting old for as long as I could remember. Now she had obviously decided that I'd moped about as much as I needed to, or as much as she could stand and it was time to make me busy.

My body ached from lack of movement. I hadn't even paced since I'd been home, and that had been the sum total of my exercise for the last eight months. Perhaps it was time to get moving, to do something.

Next door, in her flat, she'd already got the ladder set up at the front window. She steadied it as I climbed. Unhooking the curtains, I glanced out the window to the street below. My distance vision was already restoring itself. I could see to the other side of the square with its red-brick-and-white-painted buildings, shop signs and the clock. A few cars were parked, others driving slowly along the road. The sky was heavy with clouds, snow would be falling on the high fells. People were hurrying about, heads down, going about their lives. All except one. A man was standing by the clock tower staring at me. I leaned closer to the glass, peered through to see who he was, but he'd gone.

Who was he? What did he want? Was he real? I couldn't trust my eyes, nor my perception any more.

'What's up, pet?' asked Gran.

'Nothing. Here – can you take some of the weight while I get the last of these hooks out?'

It took a fair while to get all the curtains down.

'And now to take them to the dry-cleaners,' said Gran looking at me expectantly.

'Oh, no – I don't think I can go out, I mean, there are so many people and it's started raining...'

'I'll be with you. You wouldn't want your old gran to have to carry all these on her own now, would you?'

I knew I was beaten. I squeezed her hand.

'I know what you're doing, Gran.'

She smiled, handed me a bag to put the curtains in, and grabbed her keys off the hall table.

'I'm getting you back to normal is what I'm doing, and the sooner the better.'

It was worse out on the street than I had thought it would be. Cars rushed past, spraying water over our legs, people under umbrellas or hoods knocked into us unseeing. I wanted to bolt back upstairs, into the safety of my tent, but Gran was holding on tight.

'All right pet, all right,' she said every time I flinched, as if she was soothing a scared animal.

The smell in the dry-cleaners made me gag. I'd never liked it, but had forgotten it was so overpowering. I had to leave, but that meant standing outside on my own while Gran waited for the receipt. I hugged myself, shifting from one foot to the other, keeping my head down. I thought I heard someone call my name. Shrinking back against the glass front of the shop, I quickly looked up to see who had called. And there he was again, the man standing still, watching me. He was by the letterbox. Tall, broad, ruddy-cheeked. I looked around to see if Gran was coming, I wanted to ask her if she knew him, but she was still busy. By the time she came out, he was gone.

I gripped Gran's arm as we walked back to the flat. I was being watched, I was certain of it. Had my release been some elaborate joke? Were they going to come and take me away again? Had Faisal's letter been part of the plot?

I shook my head. It was all crazy. I knew, even as I thought it, that it wasn't true. I'd been released because they had found nothing to incriminate me, and finally, grudgingly, believed that I was telling the truth. There was no one watching me. I was getting paranoid again. Deep breaths.

~

There was a knock at my door.

'Laila, Jeanette's on the phone for you. Do you want to take it?'

I leapt up. I didn't want Mum coming in and seeing the tent I'd set up. I slipped out and closed the door behind me.

My heart was thudding. The idea of speaking to a friend was terrifying, but I wanted to do it. I needed to do it.

I bolted back into my room.

I put my ear to the door and heard Mum say, 'Thank you for calling, and please thank the others and tell them all I'm grateful they've been phoning, it meant a lot.' There was a pause, perhaps she was listening to Jeanette talking, and then she said, 'She's not really feeling herself yet.'

It was true. I wasn't feeling myself. I didn't really know what 'myself' was anymore. Anxious. Angry. Fearful. Cut off. Paranoid. All those. But I had also been loving, caring, witty, patient and loyal. Where had all that gone? Were those traits still a part of me, hiding from me?

At dinner, by a huge effort of will, I managed to engage in the conversation. Gran was over, and she and Mum were talking about a neighbour, Mr Twedell, whose wife had just died.

'I remember him. He was Granddad's friend, the beekeeper.'

'Aye, that's right. Fancy you remembering that,' said Gran.

'I went with Granddad a few times, to get honey from him. He let me have some honeycomb. I thought it was the best thing I'd ever tasted.'

Mum smiled. 'Yes, and you came home and threw up on the kitchen floor!'

'I don't remember that bit.'

She laughed. 'Of course you don't, you ran off and left me to clean it up. You were fine!'

I saw her and Gran giving each other a look. They were

hoping this was my return to normal. They had no idea the effort it had taken to say those few words.

One night a car backfired out in the square and I wet the bed.

~

Mum had left for work. The phone rang just after she'd gone. It sat there, trilling innocently, and anger welled up in me. I wanted to throw it out of the window. Instead, hand trembling, I reached out and lifted the receiver.

'Hello? Hello? Is anyone there?' came a voice. A familiar voice.

'I'm here.'

'Laila? Laila is that really you?'

'I think so.'

Jeanette laughed. She thought I was joking.

'It's so good to hear your voice,' she said. 'How are you?'

I wasn't sure what to say.

'Are you still there?'

'Yes.'

'Look, your mother said you weren't very good right now, and God knows, why would you be after what you've been through, not that I know what that is, exactly, but it must have been awful. Oh, God, I'm ranting. What I wanted to say is, we'd love to see you. We've all missed you so much.'

'Thanks.' I knew it was an inadequate response, but I had no other.

'Look, I can't really talk right now – I'm just about to go into a meeting. I just wanted to say hi and see how you are.'

Jeanette. Dear diplomatic friend. I wanted to see her and all my other friends, but I couldn't imagine it. Having to talk, to tell them what had been going on in my life. I had no idea how much they knew, but Mum had been in touch with them. She can't have told them much because she didn't know anything. I couldn't stop thinking about it, but I wasn't ready to talk about it. I felt raw, exposed. A hermit crab between shells. I'd seen them once when we went on a school trip to the Blackpool aquarium. Vulnerable. Weak. Distorted.

I woke early after a nightmare. The street outside was quiet but for the council men emptying the bins, talking to each other, making jokes in the pooled light of the street lamps. They didn't know I was there. It felt strange, to see without being seen. But it also felt powerful to be the observer, and I couldn't pull my gaze away.

~

Gran cajoled me out of the flat again a few days later. She said she wanted a bit of help choosing the wool for a cardigan she was knitting for a friend. She was always doing something for someone.

I was getting more used to the noise and the general busyness of life on the outside, but the people still bothered me. There were so many of them, and some of them looked at me strangely like they knew where I'd been and why. I wanted to scream at them that although I may look a bit different, I was as English as they were – more so than the recent Eastern European immigrants that had settled in the area. No one made them feel like they didn't belong. Their skin colour didn't make them stand out. No one looked at them as would-be terrorists.

At least I didn't see that man again, the one that didn't move until suddenly he wasn't there. Maybe I'd imagined him. Stranger things had happened.

As Gran and I negotiated the crowded pavements I felt my heart speed up, beating harder. I couldn't get my breath. I pulled my jacket open, gasping for air, and clutching my chest. Gran said something from a long way away, but I couldn't see her, there was only grey where she should have been. I was panting, trying to draw air into my lungs, desperate to live now that it felt like I was dying.

Something stung my cheek. A hand held my wrist.

'Laila, Laila! Come on, pet, look at me.'

I lifted my heavy head and peered about. I was on the ground, Gran was kneeling at my side. Under her rouge she looked ashen.

'What happened?' I wanted to creep into my tent, close my eyes, sleep the headache away.

'You fainted,' said a male voice.

I looked around. A middle-aged man was kneeling on my other side. He was the one holding my wrist, taking my pulse.

'I'm a nurse,' he said. 'Has this ever happened before?'

I shook my head.

'Have you eaten anything today?'

I nodded.

'Well, I think you should go and see your doctor and get yourself checked out. Can you get up now do you think?'

I tried to draw my legs in and roll to one side, but nothing was working properly.

'Here, let me help,' said the man.

With his help and Gran's, I managed to get to my feet. I was shaking all over. A crowd had gathered to watch the spectacle. I wanted to tell them all to go, that I'd had enough of being watched, but the words wouldn't come.

I retreated into my tent the minute we got back to the house and stayed there for the rest of the day. Mum and Gran both came in at different times to see how I was, and neither commented on my arrangement, although they must have wondered about it. I heard Gran tell Mum I'd had a panic attack.

'How do you know what it was? She might be really ill.'

'My friend Betty has them sometimes. It was exactly the same as one of her turns. Exactly. Poor love.'

I was allowed to stay indoors for two days before Gran decided it was time to try going out again. She needed that wool and apparently couldn't buy it without my approval. This time, being a Saturday, Mum came too.

Going down the stairs to the front door, my heart started pounding again, but I took deep breaths and Mum reminded me that I could do this, that I was a fighter.

A few minutes later, out on the street, with the sun shining, Thirsk looked benevolent, welcoming, and in spite of the incident before, I felt better than I had in a long time. Being with Mum and Gran and in familiar places was working some kind of healing magic. Maybe I could consign all that had happened to a place where it didn't intrude on my daily life and claw my way back to some semblance of normality.

'This one, or the maroon?'

We'd got to the wool shop without me even being aware of it.

'The green, I think. I've always loved that deep evergreen.'

'You're right,' said Gran. 'Green it is.'

I watched her go off to pay and noticed a slight limp that hadn't been there before, a stoop of the shoulders that was new, and her coat looked a size too large. Gran really was getting old. The thought made my insides drop towards my feet. How old was she – seventy-six? Seventy-seven? With a jolt I realised that she must be eighty. She didn't seem so old, and yet suddenly I was aware that she wouldn't be around forever, and the thought terrified me.

She'd always been there. When I was young and Mum had

decided that she needed to make something of her life, Gran and Granddad had looked after me while she went to university in York each day. I used to sit in the shop while Gran served the customers. They all knew me. Everyone knew everyone in Thirsk in those days. There must have been talk about me, but apart from that one time with Mrs Rob, I never heard Gran talk about how come there was a little girl with dusky skin and dark hair in a family so blond. Perhaps if I hadn't been so well loved and protected I would have stood up better to those people who decided I was a terrorist because of the way I looked and the company I kept.

On the internet I'd found dozens of Choudhrys in Karachi. I considered sending a letter to every one of them in the hope that one reached Faisal. What sort of mischief could that have unleashed in unsuspecting Karachi households – a letter from an address overseas, written in English, professing undying love for a Faisal Choudhry. There may have been arguments, divorces, murders! Somehow, I had to find him.

The cardigan, it turned out, was for me, not a friend of Gran's. She gave it to me one morning when she popped in for a cup of tea. It was beautiful. The green we'd bought together made the trim, but the rest was in autumn russets, golds, reds and ochres. I put it on and watched the delight spread across Gran's face. She'd always preferred giving to receiving gifts. Granddad had given her a beautiful ring for their fiftieth wedding anniversary, and she'd been so embarrassed she'd seemed ungrateful. I smiled at the memory.

'Laila,' said Gran, drawing me out of my reverie, 'What do you think of the cardy – do you like it?'

I stroked the soft wool. 'It's beautiful, Gran. Perfect. Thanks.'

Her smile made her look young again, the sparkle in her eyes, the blush of her cheeks. I didn't need to worry about her – as long as she had people to do things for, she'd live until she was a hundred.

I'd been putting it off, but I couldn't procrastinate any longer. The new term was about to start and if I wanted to work at my old school, I had to call them. I had no idea what arrangements they'd put in place while I was away, nor how they felt about my disappearance. Mum had rung them when I'd disappeared, to tell them I was suddenly called away, but couldn't say where or for how long.

She'd been gently encouraging me to contact the school for days, but Gran would have been quite happy for me never to leave again, I think. She was still giving me jobs to do, happy to have me close by where she could keep an eye on me. No doubt Mum had told her about the nightmares I was still having, or maybe she'd heard me screaming from next door.

The dreams were always the same: Jabba and Spud and me in the shower, the tension building as Jabba undressed and Spud checked the video camera. As they approached me, I drew a knife from behind my back and stabbed them, blood spurting, looks of shock and pain on their faces until they sank to the floor. I always woke up before they died, their shrieks on my lips instead of theirs. If I'd had that same dream in Solitary, I would have felt a deep sense of satisfaction. I felt it was a measure of my humanity returning that it now horrified me.

On a Monday morning, I approached the phone in the hall as if it was a tarantula waiting to pounce. Dialling the number of the school, I tried to calm the churning in my stomach.

'Fulham Primary School.'

It was Mercy, I recognised her West Indian accent, the voice that always sounded a breath away from laughter. I pictured her there in the office in her bright clothes, her red nail polish, and the flower she always had behind her ear – real in summer, but at this time of year, probably silk.

My voice deserted me, the speech I'd prepared flew out the window and was carried by the wind to the moors and beyond.

'Wrong number,' I stammered, and slammed the phone down.

My heart thudded. Hearing Mercy's voice had made it all real – the school, the children, the job, leaving Thirsk to live in London again. I couldn't do it.

With Gran next to me I tried again.

'Fulham Primary School.'

'Mercy?'

'Yes. Who is this?'

'It's Laila. Laila Seaver.'

'Laila! My God, girl – we didn't know what had happened to you. Your Ma rang and said you went away, but she couldn't tell us where. Where in hell you been?'

'Where have I been... I... er... I'm here.'

'Well that's the best news I heard in a long while, I tell you, girl. Just you wait till I tell the others, they won't believe me. You been on holidays? You must tell me all about it. Oh, you just give me such a surprise. Such a good surprise.'

'Thanks, Mercy.' I didn't know how to continue. In the pause, I heard her telling the other women in the office that I was on the phone. Her voice was muffled as if she was holding her hand over the receiver, but she sounded excited.

'Er... Mercy, is Mrs Nair in?'

'Well, no, Laila, she left at Christmastime. Went to live in Bradford with her daughter. You want to speak to the new head, Mr Dietrich? He's in today getting ready for the new term.'

Mrs Nair gone? That was bad news. I didn't know what to do. I'd been preparing myself for days to speak to her. I couldn't talk to a stranger.

'No thanks, Mercy, it's okay.'

'Are you gonna come back and see us, Laila, tell us about your trip?'

Mercy had decided I'd been away, and maybe that was best. I hadn't lied, I just hadn't told the truth.

'Yes, yes, I'll do that. Soon.'

'You promise now?'

'Yes, I promise.'

I looked at Gran who nodded towards the phone.

'Actually, Mercy, I will speak to Mr Dietrich please.'

'It's all changed, Gran,' I said as I waited for the new principal to pick up. 'Mrs Nair's left. They've probably filled my position.'

She pulled me into a hug and stroked my hair.

'Now, now, pet. You don't know that for certain.'

'He's not answering his line,' said Mercy. 'I'll get him to call you, just give me your number.'

'Don't worry, thanks. I'll try again later.'

I turned to Gran. 'I'll write. It'll be easier.'

She smiled and I kissed her on the cheek and went to my room.

My laptop had been in the bottom of my wardrobe since I got home. I hadn't wanted to open it. Maybe I was being paranoid, but it was, after all, how 'they' had found out all about me and I didn't want them getting any more information. On the occasions I'd tried to find Faisal, I'd used Mum's computer.

Now my fingers hovered about the keys, but eventually I opened my email account. There was nothing there. Not a single message. No addresses even. They'd all been deleted. I went to my photos. All the pictures I had of Faisal, friends, holidays, silly snaps taken in drunken moments, gone. Search history, cleared. Lesson plans, notes for school, disappeared. My computer had been wiped of everything. My past had been eradicated. It wasn't enough that they'd stolen months of my life, now they'd deleted everything that connected me to my old life and my friends. I found my phone in the drawer where I'd thrown it the day I came home, plugged it in to charge, turned it on. Same thing – all my contacts deleted. I threw it onto my bed and grabbed my keys.

'I'm going for a walk, Gran,' I said as the door banged behind me.

I stomped through town glaring at anyone who so much as glanced at me, and set off across the fields. I hated Mr Smith and his crony, Mr Jones. I hated that no one in that nightmare place had told me their real names, so that I couldn't make a complaint against any of them. I hated the government that allowed them to get away with it. Or sanctioned it. Or ordered it. My hatred for the guards and Mr Smith and Mr Jones was a physical sensation in my gut. I almost wished I was a terrorist – I'd go and blow myself up and all of them with me.

I walked until I was exhausted and my throat parched. I gulped water from a spring, spitting out bits of leaf and twig and whatever else. I didn't care. If it made me sick, so what?

I yelled until I could yell no more. Fuuuuuccccckkkkk.

A flight of birds took off with panicked squawks, wings flapping wildly.

I sank to my knees, fell forward and let my head rest on the ground, clawing at the boggy mud until my hands were buried deep.

Faisal, where are you? What the hell is going on? I want you here, now.

When I got home, Mum and Gran were in the kitchen. Mum looked up guiltily as she stuffed something under her jumper.

'All right, pet? Had a nice day?' she asked.

Gran must have told her about the phone call and my hasty departure not long after.

'What's going on, Mum?'

'Nothing. Not a thing. Have a cup of tea.'

Gran cleared her throat. 'She's a right to know, Lynette.'

Mum's jaw clenched as she bit back the words that she no doubt wanted to hurl at her.

'Know what?' I asked.

'Your mother's had a letter. From the Home Office.' Gran looked at Mum, raised her eyebrows. 'Go on, show her.'

Mum's nostrils flared as she yanked the letter out and gave it to me.

I looked at it. Thick, heavy paper, formal letter heading. Mum and Gran were on the edges of their seats.

I took a deep breath, and read:

Dear Ms Seaver,
Having investigated the matter myself, and consulted with my colleagues in the Ministry of Justice, who hold responsibility for prisons, I am writing to inform you that there is no record of your daughter, Laila Farida Seaver ever having been arrested or incarcerated in any facility in the United Kingdom.

Yours Sincerely....

It was signed by the Home Secretary himself.

I stared at the letter, uncomprehending. Not arrested? No record of my imprisonment? The government was denying that it was picking people up and locking them away for months on end?

'I'm sorry,' said Mum. 'I...'

'It's not your fault. I just don't know how they can do this.'

'I only wrote because I thought you should be compensated, you know, financially, for not working and... and all that.'

She had no idea what 'all that' was.

'Thanks.'

'And I don't know what kind of flamin' fool they take me for – I collected you from prison didn't I? Someone told me where to go!'

'That's right, of course. Who was it, who told you?'

'I don't know. It was a phone call the day before. I'd been so worried I didn't even think to ask who was calling. I'm sorry.'

'It's okay. I'm going to my room now.'

I left Gran and Mum staring at each other over the kitchen table.

My chest was so tight I could hardly breathe. I paced my room as I had in my cell, to do something, to clear my head so that I could think, to calm myself. There were no records they said. Why?

Raised voices intruded on my thoughts. Mum and Gran were going at each other in the kitchen.

'I would have told her. I just wanted to wait until the right moment.'

'And when might that have been, eh? You always were one to avoid nastiness, Lynette, but sometimes these things have to be faced.'

'Oh, thank you very much. It always has to be your way,

doesn't it? You always know best. Well, Laila is my daughter, and you can take your interfering ways and get out. Now!'

Chairs scraped across the floor, footsteps approached. I got to the landing to see Gran, jaw clenched, opening the front door and Mum leaning against the wall, arms folded over her chest.

I'd never known them to fight before and was torn – who to go to?

Mum saw my indecision and shrugged, then turned back to the kitchen. She was slamming pots and pans around as I slipped out the door.

Gran let me in to her flat.

'You weren't supposed to hear that, pet.'

'Well I did. And I'm a big girl now, I can cope. But it wasn't worth the fight. Mum would've told me soon enough. Although I'm glad you forced her hand. It's as well to know.'

'You're a diplomat you are, if ever I met one,' said Gran. 'You just told me and your mother off and forgave us both in the same sentence.'

'What do you think it means, Gran? I mean, it's more than just not wanting to pay out compensation, isn't it?'

'Aye, pet, I 'spect it is, but I don't know what. Trouble is, they're bigger than us, and if they don't want us to know things, they just don't say. Your Granddad never trusted politicians. I used to stand up for them when he went on, but not anymore. Not now.'

The following Friday I got the train to London. Mr Dietrich had sent a neutral email back in response to my enquiry about my old job, and invited me in for a 'discussion'. I had spent hours trying to decide what to say. Should I tell the truth? Make up a lie? That would probably be the better option, but what would I say? I'd never been a good liar – my friends always saw straight through me when I tried to dissemble. So I'd focused on what to wear and what I would need to take for my one night in the city. I was staying with Jeanette and Bhindi at my old house, my room now taken by someone else. I wasn't looking forward to any of it. My heart was pounding as I said goodbye to Mum and found a seat on the train. I felt raw, the skin on my face tight.

A man came in, looked at me and moved to another carriage. Then a woman sat opposite me and got out a bag of food almost as soon as the train had started moving. Crisps, sandwiches, a pie of some sort, fruit. She placed them on the seat beside her and looked over at me.

'Help yourself, love,' she said. 'You look like you could do with it.'

Letting out a breath, I forced a smile, shook my head. Why did everyone think I needed feeding up, even complete strangers? I may have lost a bit of weight in prison, but I wasn't anorexic.

The woman took a sandwich and bit into it. With her mouth full of egg mayonnaise and lettuce, she started talking.

'Going to London are you?'

I nodded, got my book out of my bag.

'Work there, do you?'

The question made me feel anxious. I shifted in my seat, looked out the window. I knew I was being rude, that this perfectly pleasant woman was just trying to make conversation, but I couldn't answer. It was as if my throat had swelled, preventing any words from reaching my mouth. How was I going to explain my absence?

'I used to live there,' said the woman. 'Couldn't stand it. The noise, the crowds, the stand-offish people. Soon as I could I came back to Yorkshire. You know where you stand with folk here, not like them two-faced southerners.'

She was one of these people who asked questions merely as a conversational device to open a monologue. She didn't care at all that I played no part. In fact, it probably suited her quite well not to have to pretend interest in me. By the time we got to York, however, her ceaseless prattle was irritating me to the point of wanting to bang my head against the window. Or hers. Gathering my things, I said goodbye and bustled through to the next carriage.

What had happened to me? I used to be friendly enough, could talk to people. Now I wanted to be invisible, to move through the world without the need to engage with it.

The outskirts of London were drab and endless. Fields gave way to new estates of identical houses, which in turn gave way to factories, light industry, then dirty brick terraces with drab gardens backing onto the railway. At some stage, houses were replaced by shops, offices. Finally, we pulled into the station.

I sat until everyone else had gone and then took my bag off the rack and made my way slowly to the ticket barrier. There was building work going on all over the station as the glazed roofs above the platforms were being replaced, and a new concourse built. It was chaotic. A family with three children, several suitcases piled on a trolley and two more being pulled by a surly teenager, stopped right in front of me. I crashed into them, grabbed the trolley to stop myself from falling, and was treated to an earful of abuse. Ah, London. I hadn't missed it.

It was just after 12.30pm, I was hungry but had to get to school in Fulham by 1.30pm, and I was rooted to the spot. I couldn't decide whether to go by bus or Tube, eat first or not. Hot tears of frustration threatened and I brushed them away angrily. People swept round me tutting. They all knew where they were going. They weren't in a panic of indecision, sweat glistening in their hairlines.

In the end, there was no choice. There was no time to eat, and the bus would take too long. I plunged into the bowels of London and took the Piccadilly Line, trying to stifle the anxiety that had settled in my stomach. I was worried about my meeting with Mr Dietrich.

I was also feeling claustrophobic underground. I could almost feel myself being buried by tons of rock and debris and dying a slow death by asphyxiation. I tried to loosen my collar, I couldn't breathe, and was sweating like a pig. I had to get out. I ran up the escalator at Earl's Court, thankful to feel the drizzle when I emerged onto the street. It was a fifteen-minute walk from there, but I couldn't stand another minute in the Tube.

Without an umbrella my hair and coat were beaded with raindrops by the time I reached the school. I stopped on the other side of the street to look at it. It was a large Victorian brick building with a playground all around. It hadn't occurred to me that I would be arriving at lunchtime, that the pupils would be out in the playground. I wasn't ready for them.

Taking a deep breath, I went through the gate and headed towards the door. I hoped that if I didn't look at anyone, they wouldn't see me, but of course, that was naïve. An adult walking quickly through a playground always attracts attention. Soon I had a gaggle of excited children running along with me.

'Miss! Miss – where have you been?'

'Are you coming back?'

'Will you be teaching us again?'

'I did a project on frogs, Miss.'

'Jamil left the school, Miss – my mum says she's gone to Lebanon.'

'Can I be in your class when you come back? Mrs Banks is nice, but I like you better.'

'Miss, why are you crying?'

I made it to the door, tried to smile at the children who were now silent around me, wiped my face, and went inside.

Mercy was waiting for me at the office door. I'd never been more pleased to see anyone.

'Laila – my God, girl, but you've lost weight. What happened to you? You been ill?'

'Something like that. How are you?' She looked the same as ever, with the gap between her front teeth and her smile as wide as the sky. It was impossible, as always, not to smile in return. Her nails, lips and the silk hibiscus behind her ear matched perfectly.

She pulled me into a brief but tight hug, squashing me to her ample breasts. I could have stayed there, but she released me, looked into my eyes, and said, 'Mr Dietrich's a bit straight, but he's a good head. He had big boots to fill, but he's getting there. He's waiting for you now. You mind you come and say hello to everyone when you've seen him, okay?'

'Okay,' I said, and smoothed my skirt down as I turned towards his office, trying to breathe normally.

Mr Dietrich was a small brown man. Not as in brown-skinned – in fact, his skin was the only thing about him that wasn't brown. Suit, shirt, tie, shoes, hair, the frames of his large glasses and the eyes behind them. All shades of brown. It was disconcerting.

He shook my hand limply and invited me to sit. He went back behind his desk and sat in his higher chair, looking down on me. I sat up straighter. When standing, I was nearly a head taller than him and now, with my spine as erect as possible, our eyes were almost level. Before him on the desk was my personal file. He opened it and made a pretence of reading. I watched and noticed that he turned slightly pink under my gaze.

Eventually he looked up.

'Did you have a good trip down? I understand you're living in Yorkshire these days.'

'That's right. Thirsk.' I'd pulled my hankie out of my pocket and was twisting it between my fingers.

A smile flitted across his face and was gone. 'Good walking up there on the moors.'

'Yes.'

He looked again at my file as if he might find something new there.

'You have an exemplary record, I must say, Ms Seaver.'

I waited. There was a 'but' coming.

'Which makes it all the stranger that you suddenly upped and left. No resignation, no farewell to the children or the staff. Nothing.'

He looked at me expectantly.

Out the window I could see the children lining up to come in for afternoon classes. What I would have given to be out there with them.

'Am I to assume that you were sick?'

The temptation to agree to that lie was strong, but would only get me in trouble when I could neither describe the illness nor produce a sick note.

'I was... away.'

'Ah, I see. Away. As in overseas?'

That, too, would have been a lie that I couldn't have sustained. I'd never been abroad in my life.

'Away as in p–' I couldn't tell him the truth. 'Away as in... I had a sort of breakdown.' That was no lie.

'A breakdown? You mean you have a psychiatric illness?'

'Had. I had a few mental health issues. I'm fine now.'

'I see.' He ran a hand through his sparse hair. 'I'm sorry to hear that. And you had treatment for these "issues"?' I could hear the quotation marks around my words.

'Yes.'

'Where?'

'What?'

'Where did you receive treatment for these "issues"? In a hospital?'

'Er... yes. I mean no. No, not in a hospital.'

He looked at me as if I was shit on his shoe.

'Miss Seaver, forgive me, but I am having trouble here. Either you had treatment in a hospital or you didn't. Which is it?'

'Not in a hospital.' My lips were so dry they were sticking to my teeth so I could hardly get the words out.

'So you had mental health issues for which you didn't seek treatment in a hospital, but they were severe enough to keep you away from school, or from even contacting the school to let us know, for two whole terms. Is that right?'

There was a lump in my throat. He was a horrid little man with a total absence of compassion, and I didn't think I could work with him even if he did offer me my job back. I felt as powerless as I had been in prison, and unfortunately, these days that was a feeling that was always accompanied by the first stirrings of anger.

'All right, if you really want to know, I was in a detention centre.'

This clearly took him by surprise. I watched as he mouthed words, but no sound came out. He ran a hand through his hair again, and straightened my file on the desk.

'I was detained for several months under the anti-terrorism laws, never charged with any offence, and released. I expect it was because my father is Pakistani and that after the bombings last year the government and most of England allowed all their basest, most racist fears to come to the surface, causing them to lock up innocent people because of the way they looked.'

'And you can prove this?'

I laughed. 'Prove what? That the government is racist or that I was locked up? Why would I tell you something like that if it wasn't true?'

'I don't know... I don't know what to say. You must understand that we can't have you back at the school with that on your record. What if the parents found out?'

'There is nothing on my record. I wasn't charged with anything. You wouldn't have to record it anywhere. And the parents would only find out if someone told them.'

'No. Oh, no, no, no, no. That wouldn't do at all. I can't go doctoring records, it would cause–'

'Are you listening? There is no record to doctor.'

'It's not that. It's... well, procedures must be followed.'

I stood up and thumped the desk. 'You are a small man, Mr Dietrich, with small opinions, a small heart and a narrow outlook. I wouldn't work for you if you offered me double pay.'

He rose to his feet, placed his hands on the desk. 'And you, Miss Seaver, may rest assured that if I have my way, you won't get a job in any primary school in England, even on half pay, with your... your... record and your attitude. Good day.'

I resisted the urge to tell him to get fucked, picked up my bag, and left.

Once outside his office, I felt drained, shaky, had to lean against the wall and take a few deep breaths. I couldn't go and see Mercy and the other office ladies. I slipped out the door and across the playground hoping they didn't notice me skulking away.

What a nasty little man. Obviously I'd have to construct a lie and be able to maintain it if I were to get a teaching job, and felt exhausted at the prospect.

It was still only just past two in the afternoon, and neither Jeanette nor Bhindi would be home before six.

The rain had stopped, thankfully, so I got myself a

sandwich and a Coke and went and sat in Brompton Cemetery. The grey of the gravestones and the weather matched my mood.

The cemetery was quiet with its trees and shrubs growing amongst the old, lichen-covered gravestones. There were a few larger mausoleums, family tombs, but most graves were modest. I read a few headstones, but started feeling bleak and teary, so stopped. It was just beginning to hit me that I would never see 'my' children again, that deep down, I had expected to get my job back and pick up where I'd left off. I stomped through the graveyard, and came across Emmeline Pankhurst's grave next to a gnarly tree with weeds around it. A tall, red sandstone Celtic cross marked her resting place. We had something in common, both having been incarcerated. She'd described her experience as feeling like she was being turned from a human being into a wild beast. I could relate to that.

Rain started falling again and I made a dash for the station. With hours to go still before I could go to my old house, I decided to go to West Hampstead.

Standing in the street outside Faisal's house forty minutes later, I knew it had been a mistake to come. I hunkered down into my coat as the rain fell hard and constant. The once beautifully tended, albeit tiny front garden was overgrown by weeds. Free newspapers and rubbish were strewn over the path to the front door. The curtains were shut, or I might have risked peeking through the window. It looked as if no one lived there. What had I been hoping? That it would be as we left it, that I would be able to go in and have a look around, touch things that Faisal had touched, lie on the bed where we had lain? I laughed at myself. How pathetic was I? I was just about to leave, when the front door opened. A young girl wrapped her scarf around her neck and pulled her hood up as she trotted off down the road without looking in my direction. So that was it. There would be no trace of Faisal left. The house had been relet. Rain and tears mingled on my face.

~

Almost as soon as I got there I knew that it had also been a mistake to come to my old house. I'd been hoping for a chance to sit quietly with Jeanette and Bhindi and catch up. We'd spoken on the phone a couple of times, but I was looking forward to talking properly. Unfortunately, Bhindi's young cousin, Preety, had moved into my old room and her friend Scarlett was visiting her. They didn't have an ounce of tact between them.

'So, I hear you were in prison. Cool!' said Scarlett when we were introduced. I shot Jeanette a scowl, and she had the decency to look abashed.

'What was it like?' asked Preety, her mouth full of hummus and cracker.

'I don't really want to talk about it,' I said through tight lips.

'No, of course, but was it really gruesome? Did you get hit on by the other inmates and stuff like that?'

'Shut up, Preety, I told you not to say anything.' Bhindi turned to me. 'I'm so sorry, Laila.'

'Let's go out, shall we?' I suggested.

Bhindi and Jeanette led me into the lounge and looked at each other. 'Well... we've asked a few people over – they wanted to see you.'

I groaned and sank into a chair.

'Sorry – we thought you'd want to catch up with the gang, you know...'

'Yes. Thanks. It's a lovely idea. It's just that I'm exhausted and I haven't had much practice at socialising recently. I'm pretty shit at it these days.'

'They won't stay long, I'm sure.'

Jeanette and Bhindi went to their rooms to change out of their work clothes, and I sat wishing I'd gone straight home. I could hear Scarlett and Preety talking in the kitchen.

'Do you think she really is a terrorist?'

'Well, you know what they say, there's no smoke without fire, and Bhindi said she was locked up for months. People don't get put away for nothing, do they?'

'She doesn't look like a terrorist, though, does she?'

'That's the clever thing, though, isn't it – anyway, what does a terrorist look like?'

I covered my ears, squeezed my eyes shut, brought my knees up to my chest and screamed at them in my head. How dare they say those things? And if they thought them, who else did? Were all my friends wondering about me, talking about me behind my back? I had to leave. Jumping up and grabbing my bag, I'd reached the hall when Jeanette came down the stairs.

'Laila – what's the matter – where are you going?'

'I can't stay. I'm sorry, it was a mistake, I'm not ready for this.' I tugged the door open.

She was by my side before I could get out.

'Don't go, please. I know it's not easy, but hiding away isn't the answer.'

I looked at her and saw the concern on her face.

Fists clenched by my sides, I said, 'Answer me one question. How many of you think I did something to get locked up for? You've obviously talked about it, so tell me, what do you think I did?'

Jeanette reacted like I'd hit her, putting her hands up in self-defence.

'What are you talking about? None of us thought you'd done anything. None of us could believe what had happened.'

'So how come Bhindi's cousin and her friend think I'm a terrorist?'

'What?'

'They're in the kitchen talking about me. "No smoke without fire", "Looks like a terrorist". Is that what you all think?'

Jeanette tried to take my arm but I pulled away.

'Laila, I promise you, I never thought you were guilty, and to the best of my knowledge, no one did. If those two morons...' – she nodded towards the kitchen – 'are talking about it, it's because they don't know you, and they're about as mature as kindergarten children and think that everything in the world is black or white.'

We stood facing each other, while I thought about what she'd said. Was she being truthful? I wanted to believe her. I needed to trust her. I wanted my life to be normal again.

Taking a deep breath I let my bag drop from my hand.

She led me back into the sitting room, sat me down and poured me a glass of wine, which I knocked back quickly and held out my glass for another. Preety and Scarlett went out, and by the time Bhindi joined us I was feeling quite tipsy.

Through my alcohol-haze I decided it was actually nice seeing Jemma, Pete, Dimitri, Col, Soula and Jools. It's just that they stayed and stayed, chatting, wanting to know when I was coming back for good. The wine flowed, pizzas arrived, and I had less and less to say. I felt like I was disappearing into the fabric of the chair, a bright, floral design, and I was the greenery in the background. I didn't want to be there anymore. Much as I loved my friends, I felt overwhelmed and after a while, couldn't even make myself join in the conversation. I saw Jeanette giving them her meaningful look, as if to say, 'I think she's had enough,' for which I was very grateful, and they started making leaving noises.

'Where's Kamila?' I asked from the depths of my chair.

Everyone stopped talking and looked at each other, then at me and quickly away again.

I saw the blood drain from their faces. Jeanette's eyes were watering. Jools suddenly found a mark on her jeans fascinating.

'What's happened to her?' I struggled to sit upright.

Still no one said anything, and no one would look at me. Finally, Pete cleared his throat.

'She disappeared about the same time as you, Laila. We didn't hear from her for months, and then she was back. She'd been arrested, same as you. It hit her really hard. She... she...' He couldn't finish the sentence.

'She what?'

Silence met my question. My heart started beating faster.

Finally, Pete almost whispered, 'She killed herself, Laila.'

6

'No,' I said quietly. And then louder, and suddenly I was screaming and yelling, crying, tearing at my clothes. I didn't want it to be true, but how often had I wanted to kill myself while I was in Solitary, and since? Only the thought of what it would do to Mum and Gran had stopped me.

I felt hands on me, stroking my back, my hair. I shoved them away and leapt out of the chair, tore out of the room, out of the house.

It was Pete who found me, huddled between two cars, hiding.

'Hey, Laila,' he said, sitting beside me on the kerb, pulling me towards him, enveloping me in his coat.

'It was before Christmas. I guess they didn't keep her in prison for as long as they kept you.'

I sniffed.

'She wasn't the same when she got out. She wouldn't talk to us about it. And she was angry, really angry. She wrote letters to the newspapers, stood outside Parliament and shouted at any MP she saw. She looked for you. We'd all looked for both of you when you disappeared. None of us knew what had happened.

When she came out she told us which prison she'd been in and we started writing, asking about you. We never received a response. The rest of us were pissed off and frustrated, but she got angrier and angrier. Then she went quiet. We all thought maybe she was getting over it. God knows, we didn't know how to help her. And then we got the call. Her mother rang Jools to tell her and give her the details of the funeral. It was awful. Fuck. She left a note, blaming the government, but we all feel guilty, we all let her down.' He shook his head, pinching the bridge of his nose.

'Then your mum rang Jeanette to say you were getting out, and we were all really happy, but freaked out too. What happened if you did the same? We took turns ringing your mum every day when you first got out, to make sure you were okay.'

'I know, thank you,' I said, resting my head on his shoulder. 'Why didn't anyone tell me – about Kamila I mean?'

'We didn't know how you'd react. We didn't want you to do the same.'

I couldn't respond for the lump in my throat. We sat, quietly for a while until I started shivering.

'Pete – did you ever think…?'

'Not for a second. I know you. You're not a terrorist.'

'Thank you. I just had to know.'

'I know.' He smiled. 'Want to go back?'

'Not really, but I suppose we'd better.'

'Look, Laila, I know you don't want to talk about it now, but if ever you do, well, I'm here.'

'Thanks, Pete.' Big, kind, quiet Pete. He'd always been a good friend. We'd had a brief fling when we first met. Not even that brief. I do him a disservice calling it a fling too. We went out together for several months, but I always felt that he was too good for me. Too kind, too even-tempered, too patient. I'd ended up being quite the bitch, just to get a reaction from him, but all I ever got was his confusion, the hurt in his eyes when I said something cruel. I was ashamed of myself even at the time, and yet I couldn't seem to stop it. I wanted him to get angry and tell me that I was horrible, that I didn't deserve him, that he was going to leave me if I didn't treat him better, but he put up with it all, and I kept going. My friends noticed what was going on and suggested I see a counsellor, that I obviously had some problems. I told them to fuck off and mind their own business. But I did go and see a psychologist eventually, and together we explored the idea that I was taking out my anger towards my absent father on him, but maybe that's just a pathetic excuse. Months after I'd ended it – by text, no less – I apologised to Pete, tried to explain it all, and he forgave me, just like that. And yet he isn't a doormat, he's just one of the best people I've ever met. He's an exceptional person. I often thought, after that, that it was a shame that he was the one who copped all my anger. My subsequent relationships were quite different.

Kamila had been one of the first people I'd met in London. I gravitated to her immediately. She was so bubbly, everyone wanted to be around her. She was also one of the first Pakistanis I'd ever spoken to properly. I don't count the people who ran shops in Blackpool and Whitby where we occasionally went to "see the sea" as Granddad put it. She was bright and funny and so obviously comfortable with who she was, a third generation British Pakistani, brought up in Southall in a community of Asians. Her experience had been so different to mine. I was the only Asian in Thirsk when I was growing up. By 2001 I was living in London, one of thousands of Asians, and I'd deprived Thirsk of a large chunk of its multiculturalism.

She'd taken me under her wing, introduced me to her big, boisterous family who all made me welcome and took it upon themselves to educate me in their ways. They were loosely Muslim, in that none of them prayed daily, let alone five times a day, but they kept the main festivals, and fasted during Ramadan. Her father worked in customs at Heathrow, her mother was a librarian, although I wondered how she kept quiet at work – she was loud and always had a joke to tell or an opinion to share. They'd had an arranged marriage, but had been allowed to meet beforehand, and get to know each other. Their neighbours on one side were Indian, on the other, Bangladeshi. In their street there were also a few Afro-Caribbean, white and mixed-race families. There was more racial diversity in that one street than in the whole of North Yorkshire. I loved it. I was the same as them. And although it hadn't really registered before, I realised that in Thirsk, people must view me as different. Not white, not like them. In Southall particularly, but in London generally, no one looked at me as if I was some sort of outsider. Not then.

Her death wormed its way into my consciousness. I lay awake all night trying to understand what had been going through her mind right before she did it, the despair and desolation that prompted her to act. Was I stronger than her? Had my experience been less traumatising somehow? Was it weakness that made her kill herself? I had no answers. I only knew that I would never see her again and that I would miss her. I was sad. And so angry.

In the morning I rang Mum to tell her I'd be getting a later train home, and set off to Southall. I had no idea what I was going to say, or if my visit would be welcome, but I had to go. It was Saturday, so her mother at least would be home, even if her father was working a weekend shift.

Walking from the bus stop I remembered the first time I'd been there, the way I'd gaped at the Asian shops selling saris, other Asian clothing I didn't even know the names of, spices, sweets, vegetables I'd never seen before. This was a whole new experience. Kamila laughed at my questions but patiently answered them:

'What was that building?'

'A gurdwara.'

'A what?'

'A Sikh temple.'

'Why are some women wearing saris and others those suits with the long tops and baggy trousers?'

She answered that one with another question – 'How come you're wearing a skirt and I'm in jeans?' Point taken, Laila put in her place. I felt stupid, and didn't like it. She'd put her arm through mine then, and promised me that one day it would all feel familiar.

Now, walking up the path to her parents' front door, I took some deep breaths. I wasn't sure I could face their grief while my own was so raw. I wanted to run away.

Her mother opened the door. Or rather, the ghost of her mother. She'd lost so much weight I hardly recognised her. She peered at me.

'Mrs Malik, it's Laila, Kamila's friend. I just heard–'

'Laila! Of course it is, I see now. Allah be praised, you're safe. Come, come.' She ushered me into the sitting room, sat me on a chair, and called for her youngest daughter, Zerena, to make tea and bring snacks.

She sat opposite me, on the edge of the sofa, her hands playing with each other in her lap, never still.

'I'm so sorry about Kamila. I only just heard what happened.' I was trying desperately not to cry.

'Thank you.' She looked down at her hands.

'I don't know what to say. I'm just so sorry.'

'There are no words, Laila, no words that can tell what happened, or describe the desolation. She is gone, that is all.'

Zerena came in with a tray of tea and biscuits, put them

down on the coffee table, and escaped without making eye contact. Mrs Malik didn't make a move to pour the tea, so I did, and used it as an excuse to move over, sit by her and take her hand. Eventually, she looked at me, giving a trace of a smile.

'It is good of you to come, Laila. Kamila was very fond of you. We all were. You are always welcome here.'

She put her hand on her heart, took a deep breath with eyes closed, anguish etched on her face. 'I have felt unable to go on, but I know I must. I have a husband, other children who need me. Tell me, Laila, you were also in prison, was it so awful that she had to take her own life?'

How to answer that one? I thought carefully before I answered.

'I can understand why she took her own life, yes. In prison you are made to feel like nothing, a nobody. It was like I was invisible, yet watched all the time – I can't really explain it.'

'But you didn't take your own life, Laila. You are still alive.'

It felt like an accusation, although I knew it wasn't intended as one.

'I tried, but yes, I am alive.' I hadn't even told Mum about my suicide attempt. I bit down hard on the inside of my cheek to stop myself from crying.

She clasped my hand then, held it so tight that it hurt, but I didn't move. She had asked me why her daughter killed herself, and I was still alive and talking to her. What made us different? I wished there was some comfort I could offer, some explanation. I know that if my mother had been in her position she would have asked the same, trying to find answers for the questions she would have been asking herself – should I have done more? Could I have done something to stop this? I shuddered.

When her son, Taban came in, he nodded a greeting to me, put an arm round his mother, and put his other hand over ours. She loosened her grip, rested against Taban and wiped her eyes.

It was time to go. I couldn't bear the weight of her grief any longer. It was cowardly of me, but I couldn't stay.

'Come again, Laila, any time. Please.'

I promised I would, leant down to kiss her sunken cheek, and fled.

I had to go and see her. Kamila had been such an important part of my life in London. I knew where she'd be. The cemetery wasn't far.

Her grave was in a new section and was very simple; a white stone was all that marked it. I'd had to find it on a map and then count out the newly turned graves until I found hers. I sat next to her, saying her name over and over again, feeling the shape of it in my mouth. There was a lump in my throat that constricted my breathing, and my ribs felt too tight around my heart. I spoke to her, asking all the questions I knew I'd never get answers to.

'So, Kam, here I am. Sorry I haven't been to see you before now, but you know the reason for that. It was shit, wasn't it? We might have been in the same place. We could even have been next door to each other for months and not known. What was it they thought they had on you? Did you know Straw and Spud, Jabba and Ireland? Maybe you had your own names for them. Did they do the same to you as they did to me, or worse? Was that what broke you? How come I'm still here and you're not? How could you leave us all? Were your friends and family not enough to help you through? You don't have to answer that. I know. I was there, and I almost didn't make it either. I'm just so sorry that I wasn't there for you, and I'm so sad that you're not here for me. You and Faisal were two people in the whole world who might have known what it was like for me, and neither of you are here to talk about it. I don't know how to live my life now.'

I wiped the tears away with the back of my hand.

'I don't know what to do anymore, Kam. I can't forget, or pretend it didn't happen. I can't look forward. The world makes no sense anymore. Is that why you did this?' My throat was so constricted I hardly recognised my own voice.

I became aware of other people, a family visiting a grave close by. They cleared weeds, wiped the stone marker and sat on the ground, heads bowed. A little boy climbed onto his mother's lap and tucked himself into the contours of her body.

I sat quietly, letting my grief mingle with theirs until they left.

'So, Kam, all I can do is carry on where you left off. I won't let your death be the end. If people don't know your name and what happened to you, they soon will. I'm not sure how, but I'll work it out, I promise. Wish me luck, and if you have any words of wisdom, now would be a good time to share them.' I looked at the simple stone at her head. All was silent except the cooing of a pigeon.

As the train pulled out of King's Cross, I watched London recede until it was a smudge in the distance, confident that I wouldn't be there again for quite a while.

It was a dry, crisp evening when I arrived in Thirsk, the street lights shining on the buildings, warming the stone, making the red-brick houses look brighter. As I walked home I thought yet again about my time in London, the dreadful interview at school and finding out about Kamila.

Back home, I opened my laptop and typed Faisal's name, hoping for some miracle, but knowing that as always, there would be nothing to lead me to him. Then, tapping in the letters of my father's name, only to find the same old Afridis. Over the years, I returned to my search, time and time again, broadened it to include Islam, the politics of Pakistan, the geography, demography, trade, the Taliban, visa requirements and travel to Pakistan. I became an expert on my father's country – Mr Smith must have been so excited to find all that in my laptop. The only thing I never found out was where my father lived and how to get in touch with him. I began to think he didn't want to be found.

Thinking of Mr Smith made me angry. I was still confused as to why the Home Office was denying that I'd ever been in prison. I presumed it was the case for other people who were rounded up in the government's cruel knee-jerk response to the bombings. I wanted to do something, make contact with these others. I needed to talk to them about our shared experience, but I had no idea where to start. What did Kamila do? She wrote to newspapers Pete had said. So I emailed him to see if he knew which papers had printed her letters.

His response came quickly.

Hi, Laila. It was so good to see you. I hope you're managing okay with the news of Kamila's death. Shit – how could you be? What I mean is, I meant it when I said you could talk to me, anytime.
As to her letters, not a single newspaper published them. It was like there was some blanket ban on the whole thing. That's one of the things she got so angry about. I think she'd made contact, or tried to at least, with a guy called Jake she knew from uni –

```
apparently he is a bit of an agitator. I don't
think it came to anything.
I wonder now whether if she'd been able to
talk about her experience to someone who'd
been through the same thing, she would still
be alive. But it doesn't really help to think
like that, does it? It's just that we all feel
so guilty that we didn't notice how desperate
she was feeling. Please, if you don't want to
talk to me about it, talk to someone – I
couldn't bear it if – well, you know.
Sorry to be so maudlin. I'll call soon.
Pete xxx
```

Jake. I knew Jake. I shuddered at the thought of him. She must have been desperate to contact him. A creepy guy with no friends who hung around on the edges of groups in the bar, trying to be part of something. On the occasions when he had been included, because someone felt sorry for him, he quickly became offensive and got himself excluded again. His social skills and personal hygiene left a lot to be desired but he was very smart. A total geek.

A blanket ban on information getting out, Pete had said. Denial right from the top that people were being kept in solitary confinement for months on end. An experience itself which was a form of torture, and then to have it denied. I couldn't let it go. For Kamila's sake as well as for my own, I had to let the world know how a civilised country like England was treating its own citizens. And if the newspapers wouldn't print anything, the internet was the place to start.

Facebook, MySpace, a blog, letters to charity organisations that work in prisons, posts on forums about the criminal justice system... I'd think of more as I went along.

When Mum came in, hours later, I was lying in a foetal position on my bed. I had been thinking what to write and had had flashbacks of the abuse in the shower, Jabba's hands all over me. I spent most of my time trying not to think of my imprisonment, it was still only too vivid in my memory and in my dreams. Now, in bringing it to the fore again, I wasn't sure how I'd cope. I still felt dirty, ashamed, humiliated. And angry.

'What's happened, Laila?' she asked, rushing over and curling herself round me. 'Whatever it is, you can tell me.'

So I did. I started with the recent past – Faisal's house let, the awful Mr Dietrich, Kamila's suicide. That was all I meant to say, but once I'd started talking, I couldn't stop. I told her about my time in prison – the fear, the loneliness, how I wanted to kill myself or the guards, how much I missed her and Gran, how even now I didn't think I'd ever be normal again. The only thing I didn't tell her about was the incidents in the shower. I was too ashamed. She stroked my hair, whispered soothing words, but as I went on and on, I felt her body shuddering and heard her sobs.

'Oh, my poor, poor girl, I had no idea. We'll get you right, pet, we'll get you right. You've been through the seven levels of hell, but you're home now, and we'll look after you.'

I felt suddenly exhausted. I wanted to be looked after, to let my guard down finally. I wanted to do nothing.

Later, still lying on my bed, I heard Mum and Gran talking in the sitting room.

'I'm glad she's talking about it finally, but I could hardly stand to hear what she told me. It's an outrage that anyone should go through that. We've got to do something.'

'For now, all we can do is make her feel safe and loved, pet. Then we'll work out what to do when she's stronger. For now, though; love, love and more love.'

'You're right, Ma. Love, love and love. I can do that.'

'I know, pet, I know.'

I smiled to myself, shifted to a more comfortable position, and drifted off again.

~

Over the next couple of weeks Mum and Gran were true to their word. They cossetted me. One of them was always around, if not in the same room, at least in the flat. When I went out they offered to come, and if I said no, had tea and food waiting for me when I returned. They tried to anticipate my every need, and became completely overbearing in the process. Much as I got annoyed at times, though, I loved them for it. I felt protected. It's what I'd wanted, and it's what I got.

And while they were making endless cups of tea and all my favourite things to eat, I was writing blog posts, Facebook and MySpace messages, letters to prison charities, posting on online forums relating to criminal justice, chatting with people online who were appalled at my story and wanted to help get the message out. My posts and messages were reposted, and I was getting words of support from strangers all over the world. I saved them all to an external hard drive that I hid every night and every time I went out. If anyone got hold of my computer, I wasn't going to have them getting rid of all this.

Even though not one person who'd written had been through the same ordeal, I felt comforted to know that I was believed, that people were outraged that something like that could happen. And as a side effect of what I was doing, I was beginning to feel myself again, with something I felt so strongly about to focus on. And the more messages of support I got, the more strongly I felt about what I was doing, the more I knew I was doing something worthwhile not just for me and Kamila, but for Faisal and all the others who had no voice.

I was shocked and angered, too, to find that I also got my fair share of hate mail, people who said, as Preety had done, that there was no smoke without fire, that with a name like mine I was bound to be a terrorist, that all us stinking Muslims should go home. Those messages I deleted, but their hatred burned into my soul.

There were messages of sympathy about Kamila too, and I sent them all on to her family. It wouldn't bring her back, but I hoped they were some small comfort. Taban emailed me to say he was glad I was getting the word out about what had happened, and thanked me, belatedly, for coming to see his mother.

```
She continues much the same, but I know she
appreciated your visit. She does not work
anymore, but she is following your blog and
your news with some interest, which is
something. If you felt able to come again, I
know she would value it, as would we all.
Taban.
```

He offered the invitation lightly, almost as an afterthought, but I knew it was a plea from a son desperate to help his mother, and even so, I didn't think I could do it, not then.

It wasn't long after Taban's email that things started hotting up.

I received an invitation to attend the Home Office. Declining was not an option. A car would pick me up.

Three days later, on a mild day in late April, I was sitting in a steel-and-glass office in Marsham Street with someone I presumed to be a very junior secretary. He was young and pimply, with acne pits and thin, wiry hair, cut short. His Adam's apple was too prominent.

'Percy Worthington,' he said, extending a hand on a wrist so narrow it looked breakable. 'Thank you for coming.'

'I didn't think I had a choice.' I looked straight at him, demanding eye contact. He reddened and looked away.

'Please, sit. Tea? Coffee?'

'Neither. I know I wasn't invited here to drink tea. Perhaps you could tell me what I am here for?'

He ran his hand down the length of his tie then patted it smooth against his crisp white shirt. His fingernails were bitten.

'Yes.' He cleared his throat, his Adam's apple bobbing alarmingly. 'Miss Seaver, it has come to our attention that you are spreading rumours about certain... shall we say, events.'

Rumours? Spreading rumours? Not only was that insulting, it meant that my internet activity was being monitored. I should have known.

'I beg your pardon?' I said with as much ice as I could muster, even though I could feel the heat rising and was barely able to contain my fury.

'You've been writing posts about terror suspects being subjected to lengthy spells in solitary confinement and abuse at the hands of guards. You have even alleged that a' – he consulted some notes – 'A Kamila Malik committed suicide as a result of such an incarceration.'

'It is no allegation. If the government that you work for had had the decency to acknowledge her experience and apologise, or maybe if they had the moral fibre to admit that they'd fucked up, she would still be alive. Better still, don't put innocent people in solitary in the first place. Do you have any idea what it's like? The isolation, the fear, the fact that you know you're losing your mind and can do nothing to stop it?'

Percy cleared his throat again. 'Now, now, Miss Seaver, no

need to get upset.'

I saw every shade of red.

'Oh, I'm not upset, I can assure you, Percy.' I was on my feet, jabbing at the air between us with my index finger. 'I am furious. You call me in here to patronise me, to slap me over the wrists for telling the truth. You're trying to tell me that I didn't actually go through all this, that I'm mad, perhaps? That would be convenient for you, wouldn't it?

'And are you telling me that I'm making up the fact that my best friend is dead because of your fucking government and its secret policies? Do you even know what they're doing, or do they lie to you too? Have you been to the prisons where terror suspects are held? Do you know what it's like to be held without charge for weeks or months on end, abused sexually and physically by the guards who are supposed to be there to look after you? To have no privacy, no contact with the outside world? No, you have no fucking idea.'

My breath was coming in short gasps. Percy was backed into his chair and looked like he needed a stiff drink.

He held his hands up in surrender.

'Miss Seaver, I can see that this is very upsetting for you, please, sit down. I'll order us some tea.' He picked up the phone.

'I've told you, I am not upset, and I don't want your fucking tea.' I had both hands on the desk, leaning towards him.

He swallowed hard and stood up. 'All right. I must tell you, as a representative of the government – your government – that we are doing all we can to keep this country safe from outside threats. You will be aware that security has been tightened in public places following the bombings, and we are very serious in our endeavours to keep Britons safe from harm in whatever form it may appear. Your activities are not helping in this regard. In fact, they could be said to be breeding fear, and although I'm sure you mean well, I believe that if you think seriously about what you're doing, you'll agree with me. I have therefore been charged with requesting, in the national interest, that you cease all such activity immediately.'

'I beg your pardon? You honestly think that I'm "breeding fear"? I'm doing no such thing. I'm just telling the truth. If you can't cope, that's your problem.' My heart was beating so hard I thought he might see it through my clothing.

'Well, in that case, I have to inform you that if you do not cease this activity, steps will have to be taken.' Again, the bobbing Adam's apple.

I laughed. 'Government mind games. What activity, exactly, are you so scared of, and what steps will you take?'

'I'm afraid I can't say. That is all, Miss Seaver. You have been warned. The car will take you home. Good day.'

'I don't want your bloody car. I'd rather walk.'

'As you wish,' he said, picking up the phone again as I stormed out.

I stood outside taking deep breaths. I pulled my phone out to call Mum and tell her what had happened, but put it away again. They were probably monitoring my calls too.

Still furious, heart beating wildly, I went to a park by the river and paced.

What could they actually do? What were these "steps" that could be taken? Could they put me away again? I didn't know, but what I did realise as I calmed down a little was that I was getting to them because people were beginning to ask questions. My blog posts and emails were being taken seriously by enough people that the Home Office was getting worried. That was a good thing. And, afraid as I was, I couldn't stop now, when they'd all but admitted that they were concerned that their secret was out. As well as feeling intimidated, which had no doubt been the intention, I felt excited, exhilarated even. I felt so good that I decided to go to Southall.

~

'Laila! You have come.'

'Hello, Mrs Malik. How are you?' She still looked dreadful.

'As you see me is how I am.' She swept her hand up and down to indicate her clothes that fell in folds over her shrunken frame, the hair that escaped its clasp. 'But it is good to see you. I was hoping you'd come to see us again. I have something for you.'

She limped from the room, only to return again a minute later.

'Open it,' she said as she handed me a package wrapped in brown paper.

'I was going to send it if you didn't come,' she said.

I sat with the parcel on my lap and carefully inched my finger under the sticky tape. Mrs Malik held her breath as I lifted the clothing out of the paper.

'It's beautiful,' I said, holding the shirt to me. It was turquoise with cream trimming and embroidery.

'It was Kamila's. She would have wanted you to have something of hers. And I want that also. It is called shalwar kameez. Shirt and trousers. Also there is dupatta, the scarf. Here, put it on.'

She placed the scarf over my head, throwing one end over my shoulder.

'Thank you. I'll treasure it.'

She smiled. 'Wear it well,' she said.

Taban and his brother, Zafran, came in, sitting across from us on the sofa.

'It's good to see you, Laila. We've all been reading your blog.'

I looked at Mrs Malik, who nodded. 'It is true, we read every word you write.'

She looked at her sons, then back at me.

I smiled. 'I know that nothing can bring Kamila back, but I want people to know the truth.'

'Yes, I know. I am glad that you are doing it.'

'Well, I think the right people are getting to hear what I've been saying.'

Taban sat forward.

'Laila,' he said, 'has something happened?' His forehead was creased into a frown.

I told them about my encounter with Percy Worthington, leaving out the swearing and finger jabbing.

'Laila, you must not get into trouble,' said Mrs Malik, her hands clasped as if in prayer.

Zafran looked impressed, Taban was still frowning.

'Perhaps you have done enough,' he said. 'We don't want you to get into trouble.'

'Well, not too much, anyway,' said Zafran, smiling. Taban shot him a filthy look.

'It's okay, Taban, leave him.' I said. 'Because in a way he's right. The amount of trouble I get into is an indicator of the number of people who are hearing about it and the questions that are being asked. It's how it goes. And we're supposed to have freedom of speech here, so what can they do to me? I'm just telling the truth.'

'What you're doing is telling a truth that the government doesn't want people to hear. Please, Laila, for my sake, for Kamila's sake, be careful,' said Mrs Malik.

'I will, Mrs Malik, I will. But I can't stop altogether, not now.'

I stayed another few minutes and when I left, Taban saw me to the door.

There was a question that I had to ask.

'Taban, why do you think Kamila was arrested and not anyone else in the family?'

He looked away, studying the plant on the hall table. I

thought he wasn't going to answer, but after a few moments, he spoke in a low voice, full of pain.

'I have wondered that myself so many times. I know that she wasn't what they said she was, a terrorist. The only answer I can come up with is that she was in contact with our brother, Asim and that he is in some kind of trouble.'

'Asim? What kind of trouble?'

'He went back to Pakistan. My father forbade him to go, but he went anyway. None of us were allowed to have any contact with him. My father cut him off completely. But Kamila has always done what she wants, and she and Asim had a special bond, even from childhood. They always had secrets, were always standing up for each other.' He smiled sadly. 'She was writing to him. We were all questioned, and our computers taken away for a while, but ours were returned. Kamila's wasn't, and then she was arrested.'

'So you think Asim is involved in...?'

'I don't know. My sister is dead. I don't want to believe that my brother is a bad man, and I have no proof, but if I am right, then he must be doing something that made her a suspect.'

I didn't know what to say. Could he be right? I'd met Asim a couple of times and hadn't warmed to him, and he'd made it pretty clear that he thought I was a complete waste of space, but was he a terrorist?

'Shit,' was all I managed to say in the end.

'Shit indeed,' Taban agreed. 'Laila, we're – I'm – grateful for what you're doing. I think it's because of you that my mother feels that life is worth living again, but it is dangerous. Please be careful, and let me know if I can help in any way. We have, of course, written to the Home Office demanding answers, but my father won't let us do more. He's defeated by what has happened, and turns to the Prophet for answers now. He says what's happened is the will of Allah and we must accept it. My mother and the rest of us can't do that, but neither are we prepared to go against my father's orders. That's why we follow your work so closely and support you in what you are doing.'

I hadn't known how to ask, but now that he'd offered, there was something I wanted. And yet, it seemed far too much. I bit the inside of my cheek.

'What?'

'No, it's okay. Don't worry.'

'What, Laila? I can tell it's important, but if you don't ask, I can't help.'

I drew a deep breath and avoided his gaze.

'I was wondering if you might write a short piece on how you've tried to cope with losing Kamila, the effects on the family and...'

He had gone very still, but I heard his gasp and glanced up to see the tear that tracked down his cheek.

'I'm so sorry. Please, forget I asked, I shouldn't have.' I put my hand on his forearm, wishing I could take the words back, cursing myself for being so insensitive.

'It's all right, Laila. No need to apologise. I just – well, you took me by surprise, that's all.' He wiped his face.

'Forget it. I don't need it.' I wanted to get out of there.

He looked down at the carpet as if he'd find an answer there. 'I don't think I can.'

'No, that's fine. See you soon then,' I said, turning and practically running down the garden path.

Asim, a terrorist? Was he the reason Faisal and I had been arrested too, because we were friends with his sister? I couldn't believe it. It was too spurious a connection. I thought of quiet Usman again. Was he really a terrorist or had Mr Smith made that up too?

7

A week later, a letter arrived from Taban.

Dear Laila,
I gave a lot of thought to your request. I don't want to do anything that will jeopardise your safety, nor can I sit here any longer doing nothing. As you are unwilling to stop writing your blog in spite of your trip to the Home Office, it seemed to make sense to try and do what you asked. It hasn't been easy. In fact, it's been one of the hardest things I've ever done, but in a way I'm glad you asked me to do it. It helped to tell you about my suspicions the other day, and it has helped even more to write my feelings down rather than live with them constantly revolving around in my head. Also, you will see when you read it why I am worried for you. I don't think Kamila told anyone else what she told me, and I hadn't told my family until writing this letter because I didn't think it would help them to know.
You will see why I say again, be careful.
If I can do anything more, let me know.
Taban

I looked out the window, steadying my breath, nervous about reading it now that it was in front of me. It's one thing to ask someone to write about their sister's death, and quite another to read it. I had to, though, for Kamila and her family, for the others that had begun to contact me recently who had been through the prison experience.

To whom it may concern,
My sister, Kamila Malik, was arrested and held in solitary confinement for several months under the government's anti-terror laws. She had done nothing. She was charged with nothing.
Before she went into prison, she was an intelligent, gregarious, fun-loving woman who would have done anything for anyone, and who always had a kind word for everyone.
When she came out she was broken, always retreating to her room, hardly able to speak a word, unable to bear the company of people, even her family. She spent most of her time writing away furiously. She wanted people to know what had happened to her, what was happening to others. Not one newspaper published her story.
We, her family, and those friends who came to see her, had no idea how desperate she was becoming, how much pain she was in, how forcing the government to acknowledge what they were doing had become her obsession. In the last few days of her short life she started saying that they were coming for her again, that she was being watched. I thought that she was just scared and that her fear bred this suspicion. I do not know the truth of the matter. I only know that she felt unable to go on, and that she took her own life.
In the note she left, she said that she couldn't stand the pain of what had happened to her, and the betrayal she felt by her own government in continuing to deny her experience. She also said she felt ashamed that she was letting her family down, leaving us behind to grieve. I think it is the people who locked her away who should feel shame.
And now there is a hole in our lives, but it is bigger than Kamila ever

was. It is vast and deep and wide. And it is filled with guilt and anger and immeasurable sorrow. Any one of us would gladly take her place, just so that she could live. My mother cannot leave the house, my father drags himself through the days. Me and my brothers and sister keep to the shadows for fear of unearthing memories too painful to keep, too glorious to forget.
Even though it is some months since Kamila took her life, I don't know how we will ever get through this and live our lives as we did before. I think we will not.
Taban Malik.

I lay on my bed and sobbed. To have written that, to be the ones living it – I couldn't imagine the pain, the despair. I would not let it be for nothing.

Later, I wrote a short blog piece, scanned and added the letter. Then I rang Taban to thank him and let him know it was posted.

'Thank you, Laila,' he said. 'It has eased my mind a little to write it down. I hope it helps others.'

'It will,' I said. 'It's very powerful.'

Taban brushed my comments off with an 'mmm', and went on, 'But Laila, what I said in the letter, that Kamila believed she was being watched, please take it seriously. The more I think about it, the more worried I am about you.'

I tried to ignore the fear his words evoked.

I couldn't settle to anything for the rest of the day. The letter and Taban's warning had jangled my nerves, but I was determined not to let myself be cowed. I went out walking, but the moors didn't have their usual calming effect on me. The birds didn't hold my attention and I couldn't even enjoy the wild flowers.

Every few steps I looked about, half expecting to see men in black suits following me. Only a small part of me thought I was being ridiculous.

When I got back, I tried reading a book to take my mind off everything, but I couldn't concentrate. Eventually, I went next door to see Gran.

'What is it, pet?'

I wanted to ask if she'd seen strange men hanging around, but I knew it would freak her out.

'I just came for a cup of tea.'

Gran smiled, boiled the kettle, filled the teapot, stirred it three times clockwise before putting the lid on and then the tea cosy.

'Gran?'

'Yes.' She took my hand, turned it over, stroked the palm.

'I miss Granddad. He used to sing to me. No one else does.'

She nodded. 'He had a lovely voice.'

'Do you miss him as much as I do?'

Gran sighed. 'Probably more, pet, probably more.'

I hugged her, we shed a few tears, and then Gran got all businesslike again. Tea and getting businesslike was how she got through everything.

'No good crying. It won't bring him back.'

She was right – tears didn't bring people back, or my grandfather and Faisal would both have been there with us.

A few days later, another letter arrived, postmarked Rome. I didn't recognise the handwriting. I ripped it open. A single piece of paper fell out, torn from an exercise book by the look of it.

FAC is in Peshawar. I thought you should know.

I read it again, hardly breathing. FAC had to be Faisal. He was in Peshawar. I had a city, if nothing else. But who had sent it? I turned the paper over but there was nothing else. I checked the envelope for a return address, but there was none. Was it true, was Faisal in Peshawar? I turned my computer on to google hospitals in Peshawar but I couldn't get the internet up. I turned it off and on again, and still no internet. I rang Mum at work to see if she'd done anything to the router. She hadn't. It had been fine the day before – I'd been monitoring the response to Taban's letter on my website, which had been huge.

I rang the internet provider. After talking to a computer-generated voice who couldn't understand what I was saying, I was eventually passed to a real person who couldn't help me, and put me on hold while he tried to find out who could. After talking to three more people, I finally spoke to the manager. My contract had been "interrupted".

'What? By whom?'

'I'm afraid I can't divulge that information,' she repeated slowly, as if I was an imbecile or hard of hearing.

'And "they" can just do that?'

'Yes,' she said.

I could feel my blood pressure rising, like my head might explode.

'And did they give a reason?'

'They don't have to. There's nothing we can do.'

She was curt, she sounded like she was talking to a criminal or a terrorist.

'So you ask for no evidence, no information. You just do as you're told, is that it?'

'Yes, that's how it goes. I can't help you. Goodbye.'

She hung up. I stared at the phone in my hand and then very carefully replaced it in the base station so that I didn't throw it across the room.

I rang another provider. I was on a blacklist. It was the same for every single one I tried. I had been hog-tied as surely as if I was on that chair in my cell fully shackled.

Or had I? My internet may have been cut, but there were other ways to get into my account. I grabbed a jacket and headed out.

At the library, I tapped my foot and sighed a lot until a spotty boy with braces finally finished what he was doing. Sitting at the computer, I logged on and typed in my blog address. Nothing. Facebook, same. Email, gone. Everything had been hijacked, just like my computer had been wiped of all my history before I was given it back, now there was no trace of me at all on the internet.

How dare they – how fucking dare they? If they wanted to silence me, this wasn't the way to go about it – first the warning at the Home Office, now this. Well, it wasn't going to be the end. I'd just have to get creative. I ran home to get my external hard drive, then back at the library, set up a new account in a false name. I was back in business, for a while at least, until whoever was stalking me found me again.

Then I googled hospitals in Peshawar but Faisal's name didn't appear in any of their staff lists. Another blank.

I was still angry when Mum got home that evening. I'd gone walking after leaving the library, and once again hadn't been able to calm down. I'd felt so much closer to finding Faisal only to find that I was no further forward after all. And I was being victimised for telling the truth. I felt as powerless as when I was in solitary.

I wouldn't be stopped. I already had another idea.

'I'm scared for you, Laila,' Mum said when I told her what

had happened. 'I don't want you to get thrown in prison again. You've done enough, surely.'

I'd never known Mum to back down so easily. We were as stubborn as each other. It had caused fights and then days of not talking to each other when I was younger.

'I'm scared, too, Mum, but I've got to keep going, you know that.'

She flopped into a chair and swept a hand through her curls.

'I don't know what to say, pet. You've taken on a fight you can't win with this one. They've arrested you once, they can do it again.'

My heart battered my ribs. I swallowed the bile that rose in my throat. I was frightened, but I had to keep going, it was the only thing that gave my life purpose. I answered Mum hoping that I sounded more confident than I felt.

'Then it's all the more important for me to keep going, isn't it? They wouldn't dare arrest me again, too many people would know about it this time.' I wasn't convincing myself. 'If they did, there'd be people on the outside fighting for me.'

'Your gran and me fought for you last time – do you think we just sat back and did nothing? We went to the police, called the Home Office repeatedly, got our local MP involved. Useless bugger that he was. We were frantic.'

'I'm sorry, I didn't know,' I said, sitting next to her and taking her hand. But it made sense. Mum wouldn't have sat quietly and waited. 'Is that why you lost so much weight?' I smiled.

'Yes, pet, better than any other diet I've ever tried, but I've lost enough now, so don't go getting arrested again, okay?'

I shuddered. 'I certainly don't want to.' My stomach churned at the idea. 'But you know I can't stop, don't you?'

She sighed, squeezed my hands in hers. 'Yes, I know.'

'I think I'll have to go to London for a few days, talk to some people there.'

'Do you want–'

'No, Mum, I don't want you to come. You stay here and look after Gran, I'll be careful.'

'Your gran needs about as much looking after as Attila the Hun.'

I smiled. 'Must run in the family then.'

~

The next day, I went to do some errands for Gran. At the greengrocer I stood choosing fruit. It took a while. One of the pleasures I'd discovered since getting out of solitary was food, particularly the smells and textures of fresh fruit. I could stand for hours, literally, sniffing and prodding. With a pineapple at my nose, I became aware of a man standing in the doorway.

'Can I help you, duck?' asked Ivy, the shopkeeper.

I looked over. He was tall and clean-shaven, his hair cut short. And he was looking at me. Our eyes met and he quickly looked away.

Ivy looked at me and shrugged her shoulders.

I was rooted to the spot. Who was he? I'd never seen him before, was sure he wasn't a local.

He picked up a cabbage, pulled out his wallet, threw a five pound note on the counter, and walked out.

'Wait – there's change!'

He didn't even look back as he strode across the road. At the first rubbish bin he passed he tossed the cabbage away and kept walking.

'Well, that was odd, wasn't it? Must have more money than sense I reckon,' said Ivy, hands on her hips.

I couldn't reply for the constriction of my chest.

'Are you all right, flower?'

'Fine. Yes, fine, thanks Ivy.' I paid for the pineapple that was still in my hand, stuffed it in my bag and ran home, checking over my shoulder all the way.

Was I being paranoid?

~

I decided it was time to go back to London. I couldn't live my life hiding away in Yorkshire. I'd be careful, but I had to go. There were things I needed to do in London that couldn't be done from home.

Mum tried in vain to talk me out of going. We fought, she cried, she begged. In the end, Gran wouldn't even talk to me she was so angry at my decision, but I was adamant. I hated leaving on such a sour note, I couldn't remember a time when they'd been so pissed off with me, but I had to go. I hoped that when I got back they'd forgive me.

I decided to leave my mobile at home and buy a cheap phone and a prepaid SIM card.

I was scared, but it was also energising. I had been doing too little for too long.

CCTV cameras were another hurdle. I didn't want to be recognised if I was being followed, but nor did I want to cut my hair, so I'd had to work out another way to change my appearance. I bought a pair of the weakest glasses I could find from a chemist, and wrapped a scarf round my hair – not a Muslim-looking scarf, a brightly coloured African print one, hippie-style. I wore eye make-up and lipstick, which I didn't normally. I hardly recognised myself. It was perfect.

In London, I booked into a cheap hotel near King's Cross station, giving my name as Mary Morgan and paying in cash even though this wasn't the type of place that would ask questions. In fact, the woman at the desk seemed so stoned that I doubted she'd even remember taking my money and handing me the key. The whole place smelled of dirty carpet and cigarettes and I didn't want to think what might be happening behind all the closed doors I passed.

When I saw my room I determined not to spend any more time there than was absolutely necessary – the bed sagged and the sheets were grey and thin from washing. The pillowcase was stained from other peoples' heads. I hardly cared. The important thing was not to be found, and here, I was a nameless, faceless nobody.

I took a deep breath and got ready for my meeting with Jake. I'd contacted him after Taban mentioned him. I hadn't seen him since he dropped out of university midway through second year, or maybe he was asked to leave. He'd been involved with the uni radio station, and had got into a lot of trouble for airing his subversive views and for interviewing known drug dealers and other lowlife. We hadn't been friends, but he had had a bit of a thing for me, which I'd found uncomfortable at the time, but which I was now hoping to use to my advantage. Taban had sent me his number from Kamila's address book and I'd rung him from a phone box in Thirsk the day before, and arranged to meet.

He hadn't changed a bit in the last eight years. He still looked a bit like a rat with his sharp features, deep-set eyes and wispy brown hair tied back in a thin ponytail. He was sitting at a table in the back corner of the pub, nursing a pint and staring at a girl at the next table. She seemed completely unaware of him.

I got myself a drink and sat down opposite him.

'Hi,' I said, already wondering if this was a mistake as he looked me slowly up and down and raised an eyebrow.

'Wouldn't have recognised you,' he said.

I laughed nervously and pulled at my scarf.

'Good thing I recognised you then,' I said. I hadn't told him much about why I wanted to meet. I'd asked him when I rang if he had any contacts in radio these days, and he had said he still dabbled. He hadn't asked much, and I wondered if he'd thought that it was just an excuse to see him again as he edged his chair closer to mine and smiled.

'So, how've you been, Laila? Long time no see.'

I moved my chair away slightly.

'I'm not so bad. What are you up to these days?'

'Oh, you know me, a bit of this, a bit of that.' He grinned, showing yellowing teeth.

I sucked in my lips. He'd never been one for small talk, and he was no different now, so glancing around the pub to make sure we wouldn't be overheard, I launched into my spiel.

'Did Kamila get in touch with you?'

He frowned and shook his head. 'Why would she?'

I took a deep breath and caught a whiff of his cheap aftershave. It was better than the BO he had smelled of at uni.

'It's a long story. The thing is, I need your help. I have news that I need to get aired.'

He leant away from me and crossed his arms. 'Oh yeah?'

'Kamila and I were detained under the anti-terror laws and now the government is denying that anyone was locked up. Kam has since killed herself.' I stopped for a moment, closed my eyes, tried to compose myself. 'I've been in contact with other people who were arrested and spent time in prison, and we want to pressure the government into owning up to what's happening.'

He sat very still, his expression a mixture of interest and perhaps disappointment that I wasn't looking for anything else.

'Go on,' he said eventually. He didn't seem shocked or upset about Kamila.

I told him the bare bones about my time in solitary, the lingering consequences in my life that meant I found social situations stressful, had no work, that I thought I was being watched.

'Hence the cloak-and-dagger stuff?'

'What?'

'You look like you're wearing a disguise – badly applied make-up, a stupid-looking scarf, glasses that really don't suit you, if you don't mind me saying.'

'Thanks. But you're right.'

'Thought so. Go on.'

When I finished telling him everything, he raised his eyebrows.

'That's some story. Is it all true?'

I bristled. 'Of course it is. Why would I make it up?'

'I dunno – people do crazy things for a few minutes of fame.'

'Not me,' I said, getting up. It had been a waste of time seeing him. He was still the creep he'd been at uni.

'Hey, hey, hey, not so fast. I've got a reputation to uphold, you know. I can't just tell my listeners any old thing and expect them to keep tuning in. Can you prove any of it?'

I rolled my eyes. 'No, which is what the government wants. They've taken down my blog and I can't get an internet provider to connect me which is precisely why I need to get my story out to as many people as possible, so that they start asking questions. The more people who ask, the more difficult it'll be for the bastards to deny it.'

He thought for a minute, chewing on a fingernail. 'Okay. I'm in. Come to this address tomorrow at eleven and we'll do an interview.' He pulled a business card out of his top pocket and threw it across the table.

I felt a rush of gratitude towards him.

'Thanks, Jake.'

'And now, let's get drunk and reminisce.'

'Oh – I'd love to, but I'm really sorry, I'm meeting a friend.' I looked at my watch. 'In fact, I'd better get going or I'll be late. See you tomorrow. And thanks again.'

I picked up my bag and rushed out the door.

I felt bad. I was using him, but I couldn't bear to be with him a moment longer.

~

I spent the evening with Pete in a shabby pub in Willesden, far enough from our usual haunts that none of our other friends would be there. Once he'd got over my appearance, I gave him the briefest outline of why I thought it was necessary.

'Laila – don't do anything stupid, will you?' he said.

'Define "stupid".'

'Oh, you know, anything that could get you into real trouble. You're doing a great thing, but sometimes the cost can be too high.' He turned his pint glass on the stained wooden tabletop. 'Don't get arrested again, okay?' He looked up, frowning.

'I won't. I wouldn't survive another stint in solitary. I'm being as careful as I can, and I have a plan. Please, don't worry about me. Anyway, I didn't come here tonight to talk about me, let's talk about you.'

Pete sighed but got the message. After making me promise that I'd call him if ever I needed anything, he settled into his usual steady self, talking about his work, our friends, the state of the world. It was like old times, and I was calmed and reassured by his presence, as I'd hoped I would be. I pretended that life was back to normal and that this was just another night out with a friend, and for minutes at a time, I did forget all that had happened. Pete made me laugh, he distracted me from what my life had become. We sat close, drank too much, and when his hand touched mine, I didn't move away. He offered his couch, and although I was tempted to stay with him, to prolong the sense of companionship, I made my way back to the hotel and crept up to my room to spend the night trying to shut out the sounds of people having sex in the room next door, drunken shouting down in the street, and the loud banging of doors.

Approaching the address on Jake's card the next day I experienced a growing apprehension. It was in a part of London that had been forgotten in the rush towards gentrification, and people loitered in the streets watching each other and anyone else who trespassed into their area. I imagined drug deals, knifings, child abductions, muggings. I held tightly onto my bag, and walked with purpose, trying to look confident and not make eye contact with anyone, through a council estate of tall tower blocks surrounded by car parks and an asphalted playground where several teenage boys were spraying graffiti on the swings and lopsided roundabout.

Jake's house was just down the street, in the shadow of the towers. The doorbell hung on exposed wires and when I rang it I heard the sound ricochet around an empty-sounding hallway. I tried to smile and stop my feet from bolting.

'Who is it?' asked a robotic voice through the entryphone speaker.

'Laila. I'm here to see Jake.'

'Jake who?'

My insides dropped. Was this all an elaborate hoax? I bit my lip.

'Jake Garner.' There was a query in my voice.

'Come in,' said the voice, and the door opened immediately. Jake was standing in the hall hanging up the entryphone.

I wanted to hit him. He'd known who it was all along. I couldn't afford to put him offside though, so I swallowed the words I wanted to say, and instead fixed the smile back on my face and said hello.

'Sorry about that. Can't be too careful, you know. Not in my line of business.'

'What exactly is your line of business?' I asked, following him along the dingy hall. The wallpaper was adorned by large damp patches, which accounted for the unpleasant smell. The lino on the floor was mostly grey and worn, although a few patches of yellow at the edges revealed its original colour.

'I told you, this and that.'

I remembered his penchant for mystery. At uni he was all smoke and mirrors and sleight of hand. We'd all thought he was like that because there was nothing underneath and he didn't want anyone to find out. Was he still the same, full of piss and wind, or was he really into something dodgy?

He reached a door and paused, his hand on the doorknob, and then with a flourish, opened it and said, 'Welcome to my Pleasure Dome.'

To say I was shocked would be a huge understatement. He invited me into a room that was light and airy and furnished with what to my untrained eye looked like expensive designer pieces. It was such a contrast to the exterior of the house and the hallway that I couldn't quite take it all in.

'Yeah, I get that reaction a lot,' said Jake, grinning.

'Why?' was all I could say.

'Let's just say that it's good for me to give a certain appearance, keeps me under the radar, which is handy, but I don't actually want to live like that. Anyway, want a coffee, or something stronger?' He gestured towards a glass-fronted cabinet full of booze.

'I'm fine,' I said, looking around. There was something creepy about this whole set-up. 'What do you actually do? And don't fob me off with "this and that", please.'

'This and that sums it up, and is about as much as you need to know. Now, do you want my help or not?'

I needed his help, and he knew it. I knew no one else who had access to a radio show. He had all the power, and once again I was in the position of having to go along. I closed my eyes and took a deep breath.

He was right by my side when I opened them again. I jumped.

'Does anyone else live here?' I asked, hoping that we weren't alone.

'Nah, just me.'

'Big house for one.' Did he hear the anxiety in my voice?

'We're very private here, the house is completely soundproofed.'

'Oh.' I wanted to run.

'We'll go through shall we?' He nodded towards another door.

'Through?' I asked.

'Yeah, to the studio.'

'Oh, the recording, yes, that'd be great.' I giggled in relief.

He smiled, seeming to take pleasure in my discomfort. I just wanted to do the interview and get away.

Jake pulled a picture aside and punched numbers into a keypad on the wall. A lock clunked. The door opened onto a professional-looking studio with mixing desk and mics, but also several computers and extra hard drives.

'Is this all for recording?' I asked.

'Nah, I do other stuff in here too.'

'Like what?'

'Oh, you know...'

'No.'

'I play around a bit, cause a bit of trouble here and there.'

I looked at the computers, all of which were on and had rows of numbers scrolling down the screens.

'You mean you're a hacker?'

Jake pursed his lips and looked up at the ceiling as if expecting to see his answer there. 'Am I a hacker? Yes, I suppose I am.'

He looked proud of himself.

'So, who do you hack?'

'Anyone and everyone. Last big project was a bank in Bahrain.'

'What? You hack into banks and steal money?' That would explain all the expensive furniture.

'Nah, nothing like that. We just hack in and say hello, we're here. It puts the wind up those arrogant pricks who think they're impenetrable.'

'We? There's a group of you?'

'Yeah, it wouldn't be so much fun on your own. Gotta celebrate your victories with someone. Anyway, it takes a few heads to get around some of the systems.'

'So where are the others?'

'Around and about. Sweden, South Africa, Germany, New Zealand, Watford, places like that.'

'And you really want me to believe that you don't make any money from it? How do you afford all this?' I swept my arm around, indicating all the equipment.

'I build internet security systems so people like me can't hack into those big businesses.'

I looked at him and laughed. 'You create havoc and then sell the companies the means of keeping you out?'

'Yeah. Clever, eh?'

'You could get caught.'

'It'll never happen. It's not that hard to hide in cyberspace if you know how.'

'I wish I'd known. Being visible got me in a whole lot of trouble.'

'Yeah, well, tell me your story, and then we'll work out the angle for the interview. What we'll do is record it today but hype it for a couple of weeks. Put it up on MySpace, a Facebook page, some well-timed snippets on my radio show, and then we'll air it when people are already hooked. That way it'll get replayed and hopefully go viral. That's what you want, isn't it?'

I was impressed. Jake seemed to know how to go about these things. And delaying the airing for a few weeks was perfect.

Several hours later, we'd recorded a half-hour interview and a few shorter pieces as teasers. It sounded great. He was a surprisingly good interviewer, asking the right questions to help the story unfold.

'It's a wrap, as they say in the movies.' Jake leant back in his chair, hands behind his head.

'Thanks, Jake. Are you sure it's not going to get traced back to you – I don't want you to get into any trouble on my account.'

'Not a chance. My security is tighter than a weasel's anus.'

I thought how attractive it would be to be invisible like that.

'Can you set one up for me?' I asked. 'A new internet identity that no one would be able to trace is very appealing.'

He got up and came round to my side of the desk, getting too close. I wanted to leave, to get away from his advances, but if he was as good at internet security as he said he was, it was too good a chance to miss. I let him put his arm around me for a moment.

'Okay. Let's do it,' he said, and grinned, and went back to his computer.

Sooner than I would have thought possible, I was back online with an identity that wove through Tunisia, Mozambique, Denmark and Gibraltar. Jake assured me that even his team of hackers would have trouble getting into my account. He explained that government agencies tracked tag words, like terrorist, Islamist, rogue state, training camp, and the names or makes of a number of weapons and terrorist organisations. With my new security I could stand outside the Home Office with my laptop and type all of the tag words in without anyone being able to trace them to me.

'Well, that's the theory anyway. I wouldn't put it to the test if I were you, you know...'

'Wasn't planning to, Jake, but this is great, thanks.'

There was one more thing I needed, and I asked if he could help with that too. Turned out Jake was very well connected.

'Not a problem. Leave it with me,' he said. 'Now, how about a drink?'

I owed him, but the way he was leering at me made me uncomfortable. 'Just a quick one then,' I said, and threw down the gin and tonic he mixed me as fast as I could, edging away from him along the sofa. Maybe I should have mentioned being raped in prison when he interviewed me – surely he wouldn't behave like this if he knew?

Putting the glass down on the coffee table, I got up, thanked him again and headed for the front door.

'Wait!' he said.

I thought he was going to pressure me to stay, and was ready with more excuses, but instead, he peered through the spyhole in the door, then went into the front room and looked out the window.

'Here, have a look. Recognise the geezer in the denim jacket?'

I took a peep from behind the curtain.

'No, never seen him before. Who is he?'

'No idea. And that's a worry, coz I know everyone round here. Any chance you were followed?'

I thought quickly. Could I have been? Had my disguise not been as successful as I thought? Heart thudding, I said, 'I don't know. I don't think so, but...'

'Fuck.'

'I'm so sorry. What can we do?'

'Double fuck,' he said as he bit on a knuckle. He led the way to the kitchen at the back of the house, all shining steel and granite.

'What do we do?'

'Nothing, for now. Let me think.'

He paced the kitchen while I chewed my nails.

A few minutes later he checked to see if the man was still there.

'Gone,' he said as he came back into the kitchen. 'Probably just here for some smack after all. You'd better go, and keep your head down until you're right away from here.'

I did as I was told, not even glancing up from the pavement until I was going into a station to make my way back to the hotel. No one was behind me, but I'd had enough – the clandestine meetings, the fear of being followed, and worse, thrown back in jail. There was no doubt that the shit would hit the proverbial fan once the interview was aired.

I was ready to leave and I had a plan.

PART III

8

July 2006
Pakistan

I didn't tell anyone I was leaving except Mum, who begged me not to go, and then threatened never to talk to me again if I did. After sticking to her guns and ignoring me for almost a week, during which time I was making my preparations, she came into my room.

'What about money for this trip?'

'I'd been saving for going away with Faisal, so now I'm using that money to go and find him. Got my passport too, thank God. I doubt they'd give me one now, but they haven't taken it away either.' I didn't tell her about the passport in the name of Asma Iyer that Jake had managed to get me through his dodgy contacts.

Mum looked disappointed, as if she'd been hoping that if she couldn't talk me out of it, there might be another way to stop me. She closed her eyes momentarily, and sighed.

'Sorry, Mum.'

'Will you try and find your father?'

'Do you mind?'

'No, if you're going, I'd rather you found him, perhaps he can keep an eye on you. If he's really sensible, he'll tell you to come home.'

'I have to go, Mum, please try and understand.'

'I understand you wanting to find Faisal, of course I do. And I understand you wanting to meet your dad, but why now?'

'Because I need to find Faisal and see if we have a future together. I can't just leave it like it is.'

'But it's not safe.'

'I don't feel safe here either though. I'll be careful. I'm not going to do anything stupid. If I haven't found my father or Faisal in two weeks, I'll leave, I promise, okay? I'll go somewhere else. You could meet me in Paris for a holiday or something.'

Mum looked at me, biting the inside of her cheek.

She left the room and came back a minute later.

'Here, take this. If you find your dad and he doesn't believe who you are, give it to him. He'll recognise it, and know where you got it.'

She put a necklace into my palm. It was a silver filigree hand on a black silk ribbon.

'It's a Hand of Fatima. He gave it to me as a promise of his return when he had to leave. He'll remember.' There was a tear in her eye.

'You still love him, don't you?'

'Can't help it, pet. He was the love of my life, plain and simple.'

I squeezed her arm. 'I'll find him and bring you an up-to-date photo.'

'You'll have to nail his feet to the floor to get one.' She smiled. 'He hates having his picture taken.'

I remembered the photo of him that my mother had shown me all those years ago. A stiff, young man staring straight into the camera. My father.

~

At Heathrow I could almost feel the CCTV cameras pivoting on their stands, tracking my every move, and was convinced I was being watched by people in uniforms, fellow passengers, cleaners, duty-free salespeople, all of whom knew who I was and where I was going. In passport control, I took my time choosing which line to stand in, and finally chose the one where the official smiled most. As she looked at my picture and then up at me, I tried not to shake.

'Holidaying in India, Miss Iyer?' she asked.

I nodded, a tight smiled fixed to my lips.

'Have a good time.'

At security, I was asked to stand aside, take my shoes off and was patted down. I wondered if they would feel my heart racing, but again, I was allowed to pass.

I almost skipped to the departure lounge and sat waiting for my flight to be called. I was flying to Delhi. From there I would pay cash for a flight to Peshawar.

On the plane I read the safety card from start to finish, flicked through the *Inflight* magazine, watched closely as the flight attendant showed us how to inflate our life vests and noted where the emergency exits were. I ate my meal, went to the toilet and used all the lotions and creams on offer, and then sat looking out the window at the clouds, trying to imagine how high we were above the ground. But mostly I sat feeling relieved that my fake passport had passed scrutiny.

The novelty of flying wore off pretty quickly, stuck in a seat with little leg room next to a large man who belched loudly as he drank his way across Europe, and then fell asleep and snored in my ear. After a while, I started trying to read the guidebook I'd bought, so that at least I had an idea of where to stay and some places to eat. It was a long seven hours.

I'd left London in jeans and a T-shirt but in Delhi I rushed into the toilets and changed into the shalwar kameez Mrs Malik had given me. I thought I might as well look the part, even though I didn't know how to play it. I splashed water on my face to freshen up, and took a look at myself in the full-length mirror. I felt self-conscious, pretending to be someone I wasn't, trying too hard to fit in. Taking a deep breath, I went to the ticket counter and bought a flight to Peshawar. Another few hours and I was arriving in Pakistan.

Looking out the window as we came in to land, I was struck by the size of the mountains. I knew they were high, but nothing prepares you for them stretching away to the horizon when seen from above. Big and brown, a few white peaks, some green in the valleys. And then we were down, roaring along the runway. I pulled my scarf over my head when I saw other women doing the same, and thought of Kamila. Having grown up in a Muslim family, she would have known what to do here. I was wearing her clothes, but they gave no clue as to how to behave.

In the terminal, I was struck first by how small and dingy it was. The ceiling was low and everything looked a little shabby, even though there were men with brooms sweeping the floors and one with a duster flicking lazily at the glass as if hoping the dirt would fly off of its own accord. The signs were all written in Urdu, the official language of Pakistan, but comfortingly, added the information underneath in English, still widely spoken, all these years after Partition and us Brits leaving that particular catastrophe to be dealt with.

The second thing I noticed was that there were very few women, and no others that seemed to be on their own. I tried to make eye contact with one of them, but she averted her gaze.

Then I became aware that as the only unaccompanied female, I was attracting a lot of attention. Men stared openly, and they, unlike the women, didn't look away when I stared back. In fact, I was the one who broke eye contact, feeling uncomfortable under their scrutiny. What was the form here? Was I allowed to stare back? Were they allowed to look at me like that in the first place? I wished I knew more about the culture, and wondered if I should have confided in Mrs Malik and asked her for some tips, but the fewer people who knew about me leaving England, the better.

The queue for passport control was large and rowdy. People were shouting across the large hall at each other, gesticulating, wafting spicy breath and acrid body odour over me. The air conditioning wasn't working and sweat trickled down my spine.

At the immigration desk, a man dressed in a beige kurta pyjama, the men's version of the shalwar kameez, rattled off what might have been a series of questions.

I looked at him blankly.

Obviously thinking I was a simpleton, he repeated himself more slowly.

'Sorry, I only speak English,' I mumbled, feeling embarrassed.

'Oh. English – coming here for first time? Where are you staying, please?'

'At the Welcome Hotel, I think.'

'Ah, many people used to stay there. Journalists and the like. You will like it but the Pearl Continental is better. More comfortable, bigger rooms, a generator for when the city electricity is not working.'

Electricity not working? Of course. I'd read about that in my guidebook. The capital of the North-West Frontier Province, and they couldn't even keep the electricity running. I began to feel the familiar churning of my stomach that was the prelude to panic. I took some deep breaths, smiled at the immigration official and said, 'Oh, I see. Well, I'll try the Welcome first and see what happens, I suppose. Thanks.'

'Have a good time. Go to the museum. We have a very fine museum.'

I collected my suitcase from the carousel and dragging it behind me, walked on slightly shaky legs into the arrivals hall of Peshawar International Airport. I'd been unable to track Faisal down but I scanned the hall anyway, heart quickening, in the hope that somehow, by some miracle of telepathy he knew I was coming. I had imagined him there, waiting patiently, greeting me with a wide smile and his loving gaze.

Of course he wasn't there. With mounting apprehension, I made my way to the doors that would eject me into Pakistan.

Nothing in any guidebook could have prepared me for those first few minutes.

The colours were all wrong. The sky was too blue, the buildings too reddish-brown. There was a breeze blowing dust and litter around, swirling it up into the air in energetic gusts before losing the will and letting it fall. My feet in their sandals, and the cuffs of my trousers were soon the same reddish brown as the street.

The women I'd seen in the safety of the airport had disappeared and I felt conspicuous and vulnerable. Not that the men leered, it didn't feel sexual. Their stares were more curious and slightly affronted that I would be there, in their world. But they certainly knew how to stare. I pulled my scarf well down over my forehead and avoided eye contact. With so little knowledge of the culture I didn't want to invite any more attention than I already had. The crowd thickened and then dispersed quite quickly as cars pulled up and luggage, parcels, boxes and people were loaded and driven away. Soon there were only a few of us left.

I looked around for a taxi rank. The guidebook had promised one, but I couldn't see it anywhere.

'May I be of assistance, madam?'

I whirled around, scarf fluttering from my head, to see an elderly man with a crocheted skullcap peering at me through thick, black-framed glasses.

'I am sorry to disturb you, but I was behind you at passport control and heard you saying that you speak only English. Can I offer you my services?'

Half of me was so grateful that I wanted to hug him, and the other half was wary of being taken advantage of. The guidebook, my Pakistan bible, had warned of people who seem friendly but only want to get you to spend all your money in their relatives' shops and restaurants. Or worse.

'I beg your pardon. I have not introduced myself. I am Nasruddin Ali Khan.' He bowed.

'Pleased to meet you, Mr Khan. I'm Asma.' I shucked my daypack and let it slip to the ground at my feet. 'I don't suppose you'd know how I can get to the Welcome Hotel would you?'

'Indeed I would, Miss Asma, it is not far from here. I will hail you a taxi. Please, stay here and I shall return.'

He scurried away, and I wiped the sweat from my face with the end of my scarf before draping it over my head again. The sun was beating down fiercely, and there was no shade. Within minutes, a taxi drew to a stop and Mr Khan got out and held the door open for me. Gesturing for me to get in, he spoke to the driver.

'I wish you well, Miss Asma. Enjoy your stay.' And with that, he closed the door, waved and walked away. Winding the window down as fast as I could, I called my thanks after him, feeling ashamed that I'd ever thought he might be anything other than a gentleman. He didn't even look round, just lifted a hand in acknowledgement and kept walking.

The taxi driver, a youngish man with an ugly scar under his right eye, made no attempt at conversation, leaving me free to take in the sights. We drove along a wide main road, hugging the centre to the annoyance of the cars, buses and trucks that tooted and tried to get past. The driver seemed completely unaware of the frustration he was causing behind him. Possibly because he had no rear-view mirror, and the wing mirrors were hanging at odd angles. Static buzzed on the radio and occasionally burst into speech, foreign and tinny.

The buildings we passed were an odd assortment – old pinkish sandstone, once grand, but now in need of a loving hand, interspersed with new brick or breeze-block monstrosities with garish business signs held aloft on metal scaffolding. A huge old colonial building was set back from the road with manicured lawns in front of it.

Turning off one road, we slowed down to merge with the traffic on another main road, narrowly missing a truck with the most amazing decorations: a mountain scene, complete with pheasant and sparkling stream, and adorned with tinsel and streamers, fairy lights and a bank of horns across the top of the cab which were constantly blaring to make everything else get out of its way. There were no lines in the road to separate the lanes, and it seemed that the biggest and loudest vehicle got right of way. I clutched the sides of my seat and prayed that the seat belt would hold in the event of a crash. I wasn't hopeful, since when I'd done it up the driver had laughed and shaken his head.

Apart from the chaos, my main impression remained the dust. It looked like it hadn't rained for months, and all the soil from every field for miles around had blown into town to compete with plastic bags and bits of paper swirling in the air. The smells through the open window were of exhaust fumes and hot metal, an undertone of melting bitumen.

The next turn took us into a narrower road, with cars, donkey-carts, motorbikes and pedestrians weaving their way along with no care for one another. The taxi driver leant on his horn, but it didn't make any difference. In the same way that he'd been oblivious to other drivers on the road, now they ignored him. Still he hooted, but there was a smile on his face and he looked quite relaxed. It was all a game.

The buildings were smaller, a hotchpotch of styles and degrees of decay. This was not a wealthy part of town. It was like nowhere I'd ever been before, and although I was curious, I was also horrified. It was like I imagined Dickensian London, full of pickpockets and dens of vice, not a place for the unknowing to venture. And yet it was here that the taxi stopped. I almost changed my mind and asked the driver to take me to the Pearl Continental after all, but clenched my teeth and said nothing. I would not be beaten by fear.

The driver helped me out with my case. I got my wallet out, but he shook his head, gestured with his thumb back the way we'd come, and said, 'Man pay.'

Even more ashamed that I'd suspected Mr Khan of being a scammer, I thanked the driver, and he drove away, still smiling.

I turned to look at the hotel. It was four storeys high with air-conditioning units stuck on the outside like barnacles. It needed a coat of paint and the windows could have done with a clean, but I didn't care. I just wanted to be off the street, have a shower, something to eat and bed.

There was a man behind the front desk, removing his lunch

from between his teeth with a toothpick, inspecting the shreds intently before popping them into his mouth again.

'Hi, I was wondering if you have a room?'

He snapped to attention, put the toothpick in his pocket and opened a large ledger.

'Single, madam?' he asked, looking at me for the first time. His eyes were a remarkable green.

'Yes. With an en suite if possible.'

'Anything is possible at the Welcome Hotel, madam. You will find that I am right.'

I smiled, a laugh in my throat, but he was serious and it would have seemed rude to respond in anything but the same tone, so I bit my lip and stifled my giggle.

'That's great,' I said as he picked up a pen and wrote something in the book. There was a computer beside him on the desk, the screen blank.

'Name?' he asked.

I gave him my name, passport number, address in England, reason for visit, and handed over a wad of rupees for a week's stay. I calculated that it came to less than forty quid. And that included breakfast.

'My name is Khalid. Anything you need, you have only to ask me.' He gave a little bow, his right hand on his heart.

'Thank you, Khalid, that's good to know.'

My room was on the second floor overlooking a courtyard with cane furniture and rather limp-looking potted plants. It smelled faintly of disinfectant and strawberry air freshener, which was comforting somehow. The bathroom was damp, however, with the dank odour of an underground cave. It had paint peeling from the walls and ceiling, but at least it had a bath with shower over it, and a toilet, if somewhat stained. Water dripped from the sink taps along moss-green trails to the plughole.

I tried the light switch. Nothing happened. The fan didn't work either. I lay on the bed, glad to be alone at last.

The enormity of what I'd done was beginning to sink in now that I had actually arrived. And then I sat bolt upright. I'd given my real name and passport number to Khalid. Did it matter? I took some deep breaths and calmed myself down. Asma Iyer had left England. As far as the government knew, I was still in Yorkshire being a good girl and minding my own business. No one would look for me here.

Sitting in my room, I let out a deep breath. 'I'm here. Where are you, Faisal?'

In spite of the heat in my room I must have slept, because I dreamed I was in a museum full of crumbling statues looking for Faisal, until the electricity started working again and the fan heaving itself into action woke me up. I was disorientated. There was a mosquito bite on my arm that I'd scratched in my sleep. I looked out the window and saw a couple having a meal in the courtyard below, but the idea of leaving my room was too much. It felt like I'd used up all my courage just getting here, so I searched through my bag and found a snack bar from the plane and had that for dinner with the last of my bottled water.

Having slept all afternoon, I stayed awake all night, wondering what the hell I was doing. I tossed and turned in my single bed with its scratchy sheets, breathing deeply to quell the anxiety that made my heart beat too fast. As the sun rose, I got up, took my sweaty nightdress off and stood under the shower. Tepid water trickled over me and then stopped. I cursed and pulled on some clean clothes.

Khalid was at reception, looking at the computer screen, which was full of strange squiggles. Urdu writing, of course. I craned my neck to try and see better, but he angled it away from me.

'Can I help you, madam?' he asked.

'Oh, yes, I was wondering where I get breakfast?'

'In the courtyard, madam.' He gestured towards a wide door. 'English or local?'

'Er... English,' I said.

'As you wish. It will be brought to you out there.' He turned back to the computer. I was dismissed.

The couple I'd seen from my room the day before was at one of the tables, and three men were at another. That was it. Not wanting to talk to anyone, I took a table in the far corner and sat with my back to them all. It was already warm, and the air smelled of fried eggs and something sweet that I couldn't quite place. When a waiter in a startlingly white kurta pyjama arrived a few moments later, I discovered what it was – along with the eggs and toast was a small vase of frangipani, which he put on the table before bowing and backing away.

I was hungry, and grateful to have something to eat that I recognised, but I did wonder what a local breakfast was. The waiter reappeared with a teapot, cup and saucer, and sugar bowl.

'Kahwa,' he said as he held the pot under my nose. 'Peshawari speciality. You like?'

It smelled all right, more like green tea than the PG Tips we drank at home.

'Yes, I like,' I said, and smiled at him. He looked away.

'Good. You put sugar, that is best.' Then he ran back to the kitchen.

I had a notebook with me, as I always did these days. I'd written every day since prison. This new journal would be a record of all my faux pas, if nothing else. A record of cultural do's and don'ts. I imagined the first entries:

Don't assume the worst of everyone, especially older men with glasses.

Don't make eye contact with young men.

Try local.

I wondered how many more points I would have written by the end of the day and began, for the first time since my arrival, to feel excited at the prospect of exploring this new world. Would it ever feel familiar, a place where I could find my way, feel at home?

I couldn't concentrate on anything else until I found Faisal. Exploring the town would have to wait.

'Can you tell me how to get to the nearest hospital?' I asked at reception.

'Are you unwell, madam?' asked Khalid.

'No, not at all. I am looking for a friend who works there.'

He looked relieved. It was probably inconvenient to have sick guests.

'That is good. It is not far. Khyber Teaching Hospital, world class. I can order a taxi for you.'

'How far – could I walk?'

'You must walk for about twenty minutes and you will be there.' He pointed in the direction I had to go. 'But it is on GT Road which is not a nice place to walk. The road is busy with many trucks.'

'It's okay, I'll give it a go. Thanks.'

It wasn't okay. As soon as I stepped out of the hotel I was in a heaving mass of humanity and a nightmare of traffic. Cars, trucks, buses, ox-carts, mopeds carrying whole families and all their possessions swept within inches of me. Pedestrians crowded the narrow pavement, men walking two or three abreast and not moving aside or separating for people coming in the other direction. There were few women about, and they were all hiding under black scarves pulled down low over their foreheads and pinned across their faces so that only their downturned eyes showed. As I'd noted the day before, however, I was an object of interest because my face was showing, and I quickly decided to cover it with the end of my dupatta. The difference was instantaneous. I may as well have disappeared. Nobody looked at me. Men looked over or through me, their gaze sliding off the scarf as if their eyes couldn't catch hold of it. The anonymity, however, was almost outweighed by the discomfort it caused. Even breathing through my light scarf made my breath hot and within a minute or two I was sweating and having to wipe my face every few seconds. How did they do it, those women who wore the veil all the time?

I gave up and hailed a taxi, settled myself in the relative calm of the back seat, and closed my eyes. I was going to find Faisal. It's strange how anxiety and excitement can feel the same.

The hospital was busy. People scurried, ambled, loitered. Some were pushed in wheelchairs, others sat looking patient, or perplexed, or bored. There were signs to different departments: Oncology, Pathology, Neurology, Paediatrics, Physiotherapy, Endocrinology. And Orthopaedics. They were written in Urdu with English underneath. An arrow pointed along a wide corridor.

Taking a deep breath, I stepped round an old man who was buffing the tiled floor and started towards orthopaedics. And, hopefully, Faisal. The first sign was for the outpatient clinic. It was worth a try. Opening the door, I entered the waiting room. There was a desk just inside the door, three doors labelled Consulting Room, and dozens of chairs in neat rows, all filled.

'Good morning,' I said, approaching the receptionist who sat behind a pile of medical notes. 'Do you speak English?'

'Of course,' she said, looking up and smiling.

'Great. I was wondering if Dr Faisal Choudhry works here?' I held my breath.

'No, we have no Dr Choudhry here. Perhaps you have the wrong name?'

Stifling my disappointment, I assured her that the name was right, but perhaps the hospital was wrong.

'Is there another hospital with an orthopaedics department?'

She nodded. 'It is very near to here, in fact. You can get there in five minutes only by taxi. The Nasir Teaching Hospital. Maybe that is why you got confused – both are teaching hospitals, you see.'

'Yes, that's probably it,' I said, and thanked her.

Outside, I hailed another taxi and we swung into the mayhem of GT Road once again and then onto another main road before screeching to a halt at the kerb.

Nasir Teaching Hospital was a grey concrete boxy building, more run-down than the bright, shiny Khyber. Outside, at a window marked Pharmacy, dozens of people sat on plastic seats on a patch of dusty concrete waiting for their medications. Inside, the walls needed painting and there were holes in the lino flooring. There was a strong smell of bleach that caught in the back of my throat. I couldn't see any signs for the orthopaedics department, so I asked at the main reception desk.

'Excuse me, is there a Dr Faisal Choudhry working here in orthopaedics?' I crossed my fingers and held my breath.

'I'll check,' said the man at the desk, and tapped the name into his computer. 'Yes.'

I let the breath out and my heart started tap dancing against my ribs. I wanted to laugh and jump and punch the air. All the tension I'd been feeling dissipated, only to return moments later. I was going to see Faisal – would he still want to see me? Did he still love me? I took another deep breath.

'Where would I find him?'

The receptionist consulted his computer again. 'He's in surgery today.'

Damn. 'Until what time?'

'Orthopaedics has operating time until lunchtime today then clinics in the afternoon.' He waved a hand in the direction of a corridor. 'You must go along there and ask.'

I rushed away, barely aware of the people around me, and found a door marked Clinics.

I entered a huge hall with at least a hundred strangely silent people sitting on wooden benches or the floor, leaning against the walls, or standing around looking bored. Against the far wall was a small reception desk with a lone woman sitting behind it.

I picked my way through the crowd trying not to bump into anyone, and approached the desk.

'Good morning. Do you speak English?' My usual opener.

'Yes.' She was bent over some notes, rubbing something out angrily.

'I was wondering if Dr Faisal Choudhry would be in later?'

'Yes. Clinic from 2pm. Do you have an appointment?' Finally, she looked up.

'Er... no. I'm a–'

'Well, he is very busy, fully booked. So many people are waiting.' She nodded towards the waiting area.

'All these people?' Surely he couldn't be expected to see them all?

'Not all. Other clinics and other doctors are here also, but he is fully booked.'

I wasn't about to be put off.

'Well, could he fit me in at the end if I waited?'

'Do you have a referral letter?' She held her hand out expectantly.

'No, not as such.' I decided to appeal to her emotional self. So far there was no evidence that she had one, but I had to try.

'Look, I'm actually a friend of Dr Choudhry's from England. We... er... worked together in London. I'm only in Peshawar for a day or two and I'd like to surprise him. I don't mind waiting.' I smiled and raised my eyebrows hopefully.

The receptionist ran an appraising eye over me and pursed her lips. 'Come back at five thirty.'

'That's fantastic. Yes, I will, thanks. Oh, and could you keep it a secret? I really would like to surprise him.'

She nodded curtly and turned back to her work.

I looked round at all the people waiting and silently wished them all well, hoping they lived long, happy and prosperous lives. The doors to the consulting rooms were all still shut, and I wondered which one Faisal would be behind. We were no more than seven hours from seeing each other and he had no idea I was there. I had to force my feet to turn towards the exit. Five thirty was a lifetime away.

I spent what seemed like hours at the museum wandering through the dusty halls, reading about the exhibits on labels that were peeling off the walls and looked like they'd been written in the 1950s. The glass of some of the cases was so dirty it was almost impossible to see what lay inside. After a while I couldn't concentrate on trying to see the relics. Instead, I watched the people. A group of schoolgirls solemnly listened and took notes as their teacher explained something to them, pointing energetically at the case behind him which held several small statues of Buddha. An old man peered into a cabinet full of old coins. Others drifted in and out. A museum official approached and said something. In the end he asked in English if I'd like a guided tour.

'No, thank you,' I replied, looking at my watch. Twelve forty. This was going to be a long day.

I took a seat and pulled my guidebook out. Lots of things to see and do that would fill the time, but none that I could get excited about. I decided to go back to the hotel.

The taxi driver was young. He hardly looked old enough to drive, but once we'd been through the usual, 'I don't speak Urdu, Pashto, Dari or any of the other languages spoken locally', he decided to practise his English on me.

'How do you like Peshawar, madam?'

'I haven't seen much of it yet, I only arrived yesterday.'

'Then you must allow me to be your guide. I will show you the best places to eat and shop, the sights to see, the offices to book tours and so on and everything.'

'It's okay. I just want to go back to my hotel,' I said through tight lips. So here he was, the scammer. He was going to take me to his uncle's clothing store, his cousin's restaurant, his father's tour company, his grandfather's spice emporium and God knows what else.

'It is nothing, madam. Just a quick tour.'

'No. Thank you. I'll get out here.' I reached for the door handle.

'No, madam! It is not safe – it is main road. And I think you do not know your way back to the hotel.'

'Well please just take me there. I don't want a tour today. Maybe another time.'

He was quiet a moment. I wondered if I'd offended him, but I didn't care if I had. He'd been pushy, and I'd pushed back, that was all.

'Madam, I understand what is happening. I, too, have read the papers that tell visitors to beware, but I am not one of those men who try to take advantage of others. I am Pashtun and an Afghan.' He said it with pride, sitting straighter in his seat.

'Oh,' I said. I'd been rumbled and felt embarrassed. But this could also be part of the scam, a double bluff. *I'm not who you think I am, you can trust me, I'll look after you.*

'Do you know what it is meaning to be Pashtun?' he asked.

'No, not really.' Not at all.

He manouevred around a cyclist with an enormous load of car tyres tied to his bike, and continued.

'We live by the laws of Pashtunwali. The first rule it is called melmastya, meaning hospitality. It is our honour and our duty to respect all visitors. You are visitor. So it is my honour to show you round. Please.' He turned briefly to smile at me.

I glanced at my watch. Still only one fifteen.

'Well, in that case, a quick tour would be okay, and if you know where I can buy a SIM card for my phone, that would be great.'

'Oh, my uncle owns a phone shop.'

I groaned.

'I am joking only, madam.' He laughed, swerved to avoid a truck that was driving towards us on our side of the road, and said, 'My name is Saleem. I will look after you.'

'I'm Laila,' I said and then realised I'd done it again, given my real name. But what could it matter, he was only a taxi driver. I thought I'd never see him again. 'Your English is great, how come you speak it so well?'

'My family has been living between Afghanistan and Pakistan since just after the Russians invaded my country. We are refugees. I was born in the Kochi Gahi Camp.'

'A refugee camp?'

'Indeed, yes. There are some English aid workers. They run a school that is a real school, not one run by Imams who teach only how to recite the holy Qur'an. I reached the final class by the time I was sixteen and was about to take my exams for university entrance but then I had to work instead of pursuing my dream of continuing my education, because my father, may he rest in peace, died, and so I look after my family.'

'That's such a pity – I suppose there was no other way?'

'It is my duty, and I am proud to be able to support them.'

'Do a lot of the children in the camp go to school?'

'Most go to the madrassas. My family are Muslims, of course, but my father, may he rest in peace, knew that they are the training ground for fighters, and he did not want us to fight. He wanted us to live, that is why he left Afghanistan. When it is safe to do so, we go back to our village, but usually we have to leave again very soon.'

He said it all so matter-of-factly, but I couldn't imagine a life like that, moving from one place to another, having to flee for my safety. And yet, hadn't I just done that very thing?

'I'm sorry–'

'There is nothing to be sorry about, Madam Laila. Life is what it is, that is all.'

'Laila,' I said. 'Just Laila. And instead of a tour of Peshawar, could we go to your camp?'

He flicked a glance at me and then looked back to the road.

'I'd really like to see it,' I said.

'We can go there because you are my guest. Many people say it is not safe for foreigners, but that is not true.'

'Okay.'

'We are passing the Bala Hissar now.' He pointed to a huge pink brick fortress. 'It is ancient fort that is now home of the Frontier Corps. Now I am being tour guide.' He laughed.

At the base of the high walls, people were sitting on blankets trying to sell dusty piles of fruit and vegetables.

'And now we drive towards my country, towards Afghanistan,' said Saleem proudly.

'How far is it?'

'Less than one hour.'

I hadn't realised we were so close. The idea both thrilled and terrified me.

A flash of blue in my peripheral vision caused me to turn. It was a person walking along the side of the road covered from head to foot in what looked like a sheet.

Saleem obviously noticed me looking.

'She is wearing burqa. Many women cover themselves when they go out. It is their custom from religion. They feel safer also.'

I could understand wanting to feel safe, but the burqa looked unwieldy. The woman was having to hold it up to step over the rubble at the side of the road, and the only opening was a square of mesh in front of her eyes.

'We are nearly there,' said Saleem.

We were driving uphill, the engine straining. Low buildings started crowding the sides of the road. The signs were brightly coloured and written in several scripts. The fronts of the shops were open, the owners sitting outside on upturned oil drums or stools. Most of them seemed to sell electrical goods. Not just hairdryers and mixers, but huge air-conditioning units and industrial size fans and everything in between. And guns. Lots of guns, big and small. Mostly big. Crates stacked outside one stall had AK-47 stamped on them and an example of what was inside displayed on top.

Saleem drew to a stop, switched the engine off and turned to me.

'Please cover your head and stay with me. We will get SIM card.'

I did as he asked, and as an added precaution, pulled my dupatta across my face again. There were no other women about. I felt unsettled as I got out of the car. Where were they all? It was as if life here was only lived by half the population. And that half of the population was now staring at me. Keeping my eyes on the ground even as they longed to roam over the goods on offer, I followed Saleem's feet in their plastic sandals into a shop.

'Assalamu alaikum,' said Saleem.

'Wa alaikum assalam,' a voice replied.

I couldn't help it. I looked up to find myself being stared at by a middle-aged man in a dirty brown kurta pyjama which strained over his huge belly.

Saleem and he spoke in low voices, and I wondered if I was the subject of their conversation. They went on and on, casting occasional glances in my direction, and I wondered if I'd been conned after all. What was Saleem saying to him? I turned to leave, suddenly afraid. I felt so powerless, not understanding the language, being the only woman for miles around.

'Madam Laila – do not go outside on your own!' Saleem's voice had a hard edge to it.

I turned mid-step and looked at him, heart thudding.

'Please.' His voice was soft again. 'This man is from village on the other side of valley from where I live in Afghanistan. It was rude of us to talk with you here, but he was telling me news from home. He has just come back. And also, even now, some members of the Taliban are here, in very next shop, buying guns and rocket launchers. My friend suspects there is big offensive coming soon. So you must stay close to me so that I can keep you safe, isn't it. We will buy your SIM card now and then we will leave.'

My stomach dropped. My interest in seeing where he had grown up went out the window, I just wanted to get away. I wanted to trust Saleem but I couldn't quite convince myself to.

Outside, a crowd had gathered round the taxi. My heart skipped a beat and then started pounding. Saleem seemed angry. He said something to the men, pushed his way through them to the car, then turned and gestured for me to follow. I half ran, head down, not wanting to come eye to eye with a member of the Taliban. Saleem held the door for me and I scrambled into the back and scooted into the middle, where I sat with my thighs burning on the plastic seat through the thin cotton of my shalwar.

'What was all that about?' I asked when we were safely on our way.

'What?'

'All those men, what did they want?'

'They wanted to hire my taxi or for me to take something for them into town and deliver it, that is all.'

That wasn't all, and I knew it by the way Saleem flicked me a look in the rear-view mirror but wouldn't hold my gaze. He said no more until we arrived back at the hotel.

'How much?' I asked, businesslike.

'SIM card was one thousand rupees, madam.'

Gone was the friendly chat, the informal use of names.

'And the taxi fare?'

'Was my privilege and my honour, as I said.'

I didn't know what to say. I counted out the rupees, the sums so big they seemed like Monopoly money, and added another two hundred. I had no idea how much I really owed him.

'That is too much,' he said.

'In my country we tip people who have helped us.'

He bowed his head in acquiescence and gave me the SIM card. I noticed he'd written his name and phone number on the packaging.

'That is my number if you need taxi, or anything else, any time.'

I looked at him and he looked away. How could you tell what people really meant if they wouldn't look you in the eye?

'Thanks again, Saleem,' I said as I got out of the car. He tooted once and drove off.

It was nearly three thirty, and feeling safe back in the hotel, I thought no more about Saleem and our trip, as thoughts of Faisal and our imminent meeting filled my head.

In the tepid shower I gave myself over to fantasies of a romantic dinner in a quiet restaurant, catching up with each other's lives, and then making love on silk sheets that smelled of frangipani.

As I dried myself, however, a much more prosaic issue pressed on me – my stomach rumbled, and I remembered that I hadn't eaten since breakfast. I didn't feel ready to brave the street food, so I changed SIM cards, put Saleem's number in my phone and left for the hospital figuring I'd find something to eat there.

When I got back to the orthopaedic clinic there were still a few people waiting. The receptionist recognised me from earlier and actually smiled and beckoned me over.

'So, friend of Dr Choudhry, you are back.'

'Yes,' I said.

'You have had a nice day?'

'Yes, thanks. It was fine.'

'That is good. So, now you can tell me everything.' She leant across her desk conspiratorially.

'I'm sorry?' I was thrown by the change in character.

'I am not busy now, so we can talk. I would like to get a job in England, perhaps you can help me. You said you worked with Dr Choudhry. You are a lady doctor?'

'Um, no, not as such,' I said.

The receptionist looked disappointed. 'A nurse then?'

'No, not a nurse either.'

'Then what?'

'Actually, we didn't work together, that was a bit of a lie. We're friends. Good friends.' I found myself sweating slightly.

Her eyes narrowed. 'I see.' The friendly confidante had disappeared leaving the ice maiden in charge again. 'Take a seat.' She nodded towards the chairs, most of which were now empty, and turned back to her computer.

The door to one of the consulting rooms opened and a patient limped out. I felt a jolt of excitement, only to be let down when the receptionist sent someone else in. The minutes ticked by, each one longer than the last, until finally the last patient shuffled out.

The receptionist looked up long enough to tell me to go in.

Heart thumping and legs shaking, I pulled my dupatta over my head and across my face and went through the door.

Faisal was sitting behind a desk writing in a patient file. He looked worn out, fine lines radiating from his eyes, his forehead deeply furrowed. He leaned his head on one hand as he wrote. I was just about to rush over and promise to make him feel better, when I noticed a nurse standing in the corner watching me approach. I hadn't envisaged that we'd have a witness to our meeting. A small sinking feeling started in my stomach.

'I'm the last,' I said.

He looked up, surprised. 'English?' he asked.

I nodded.

'And what is your name? I thought we'd seen the last patient.'

'Laila Farida Seaver.' I was so nervous that my voice didn't sound like my own.

He gasped, half stood, sat down again and gulped. 'Laila?' He looked over at the nurse who was watching his every move.

I dropped the end of my scarf, uncovering my face. 'Yes, it's me!' I laughed, wanting him to jump up, rush round his desk, take me in his arms and tell me how much he'd missed me. Instead, he stayed where he was as if pinned there by the gaze of the nurse.

'Laila,' he said again, shaking his head. He started stacking the patient files that were on his desk. 'It is good to see you, if rather a shock. Are you in Peshawar for long?' He glanced up at me and away again.

'What? Is that it? It's good to see me? Faisal, what's going on?'

He looked at the nurse again as if she was his puppet master or his guard, and then back to me. 'It would be good to catch up, to talk about old times. Please leave your phone number at reception and I will call you.'

I wanted to scream. This was the man who had written me love letters, who said that he wanted to spend eternity with me.

Was he now intimating by his glances at the nurse that they were in some sort of relationship? Surely that must be it. She still hadn't said anything, but when I looked at her, she raised a knowing eyebrow and gave me a smug smile. My heart sank.

'Don't bother, I can see I made a mistake,' I said. I turned and ran out the door, wiping the tears from my eyes as I pulled the scarf back over my head so that the receptionist didn't see my tears.

~

I walked. With no idea of where I was going, I kept on, my scarf across my face to hide my grief and confusion. What had happened? I couldn't make any sense of it. Faisal had been so distant, there was no way I could reconcile that beautiful letter and poem he'd sent me only a few weeks ago with the reception I'd just received. He'd treated me like an old acquaintance, and an unwelcome one at that. Could he have transferred his affections so quickly? Did he think that because I hadn't written, I wanted nothing more to do with him?

I found myself in narrow backstreets, open-fronted shops on both sides, men sitting outside them chatting to one another. The only other woman was wearing a burqa, and she was attracting no attention whatsoever, while I was being stared at, appraised, even with my dupatta over my face. Clearly in some areas that wasn't enough. I hated this country and everyone in it. I wanted to be anonymous, to have no identity. To be a faceless, nameless nobody.

I approached the woman.

'Excuse me, where do you get these?' I asked, tugging gently at her burqa.

She pulled away, grasping it more tightly around her, turning away from me.

'Please, where can I get a burqa? I need one.'

She turned her whole body to see me, the mesh allowing no peripheral vision. I could barely make out her eyes behind it.

'Street, street,' she said, lifting her chin once, twice.

'Two streets from here?'

'Yes. Two.' She turned and walked away.

'Thank you,' I called after her.

The streets were too crowded to run, even though I wanted to get to the shop as fast as possible. I could feel the gazes of all the men following me, piercing me like needles in the back. Walking as fast as I could, dodging barrows and people, men cooking delicious-smelling meat over open flames, I reached a row of shops with burqas hanging outside and crowding the walls inside. I stopped at the first one and pointed.

'How much?'

'One thousand rupees, from China, but not good cloth.' He rubbed the fabric between his fingers and frowned. 'Better inside, come.'

'No, this one will do.' It was black, tent-like.

'Nicer ones inside,' he repeated.

'Please, just let me have the burqa. Here.' I shoved the money into his hand and dragged the garment off its hanger. Stuffing it into my bag to try on later, I left the shop. I just wanted to be invisible.

I found a main road and tried to orientate myself, but I hadn't taken the time to note any landmarks and everywhere looked the same. I tried to stop a man to ask for directions, but the very time I wanted to be noticed, I was ignored, again and again.

By the time I found the hotel, and climbed the stairs to my refuge I was angry. Not just at Faisal, although he certainly bore the brunt of it, but at the whole world. I was even angry with my father for not knowing I was there and coming to find me. I kicked the wall when the fan didn't work.

Mostly, though, I was angry and hurt and confused about Faisal. How dare he treat me that way? He would have been more polite to a stranger. And the nurse – he hadn't had one in clinics in London, so why did he need one now?

I chewed on a fingernail, seeing her unmoving form before me, her gaze never leaving me. There was a smugness about her, and then there was Faisal's stiffness and formality with me. Had I been replaced? The thought filled me with despair.

I pulled out his letter again. I knew it off by heart, but still carried it everywhere. I loved knowing that his hand had formed those beautiful words, that his heart had felt them, that his mouth had probably spoken them as he wrote:

I am broken without you, who are my soul, my heart, my Love, and I cannot repair myself.

Howling in pain, I scrunched it up, threw it in the bin and sobbed.

Later, I started writing in my journal, trying to make sense of what was going on. I found the physical act of writing soothing, and committing my thoughts and feelings to paper made them more manageable somehow. As I wrote, I knew I had to talk to Faisal. He owed me an explanation for his behaviour. All I could think was how much I loved and wanted him. If he'd moved on, I'd have to find a way to accept it.

To talk to him, I needed to find him on his own without that bloody nurse hanging around. I pulled the burqa out of my bag. Time to go native.

Sitting on my bed, the material draping over my knees to the floor, part of me was horrified at the idea of putting it on, and another part was fascinated – who would I become in that thing? Unseen, I could do anything, go anywhere. I was both thrilled and appalled at the thought. Would a monster be unleashed, or a mouse? Slowly I stood up and tried to work out which way it went. I placed it over my head. How did people wear these things? The mesh cut my limited view into two-millimetre squares. Breathing was the next issue. It had been bad enough just with a scarf over my face that at least let in a little air. The burqa, being heavier cloth, was suffocating. I was soon overheating, my breath hot and moist, making it hard to breathe at all, but when I put the fan on, the fabric billowed all around me without cooling me down. I pulled it off, gasping, and let it drop to the floor where it looked like a deflated parachute.

I ordered some food – lamb with some salad and flat bread. I ate with appreciation, having not had anything since a dry and tasteless samosa at the hospital. The meat was hot and glistened with fat but it was delicious, just the right amount of spice. The bread was light and the greenery fresh. As I ate, my plan crystallised. I fell asleep thinking of Faisal, a smile on my face.

I was up early but I couldn't manage breakfast. I had some kahwa tea then went back to my room to put on my covering.

Out on the street every gust of wind blew it around me.

Grabbing it tighter under my chin, I started out. It was hot and claustrophobic. Finally, I waved down a taxi and gave the name of the hospital. Ten minutes later I was standing outside watching people entering and leaving through the main door. I'd thought about hiding behind a tree, but then realised that I had no need. I wished I'd had a burqa in England when I was being watched, and then thought that there it would have had the opposite effect – I would have stuck out like an eskimo in the Sahara.

There was little shade and it felt like the sun was beating down especially on me, roasting me in my personal tent.

And then Faisal appeared, in a crisp white shirt and slacks, carrying a briefcase, marching towards the door. I stepped into his path.

He looked at me without recognition. My heart stopped, but then, of course, he couldn't possibly have any idea who I was.

He said something in some incomprehensible language.

'It's me, Faisal.' I had meant to say more, to demand an explanation, but my throat had closed up and my mouth was dry.

'Laila?' He took a step back, and then leant forward again, peering at me through the latticework and then looked around the busy hospital entrance. 'What on earth are you wearing that thing for?'

I started to explain but he interrupted. 'We can't speak here, but I will come and see you. Where are you staying?'

'At the Welcome Hotel.'

'I know it. I will come later. Now I have to be in surgery.'

'When?' I asked.

He started walking away, only to turn and say something in Urdu as his nurse caught up with him and they walked into the hospital together.

I didn't know what to think. He had seemed less distant, but

I still had no idea what was going on. I would have to wait to find out, and I didn't know how I'd manage.

Outside the gates I took the burqa off and called Saleem. I still didn't know if I could trust him, but I had no one else to ask and I needed to know more about the place, the customs, what was permissible and what wasn't. He arrived after a few minutes, screeching to a halt beside me, a smile on his face.

'Madam Laila! Here is your chariot. Come, come, I will show you the sights today.'

He leapt out of the car and opened my door for me.

'Thanks, Saleem.'

'A friend, isn't it? I am your good friend.'

'Yes.'

'I hope you are,' I added under my breath.

'So, where would you like to go?'

'I have no idea. Actually, let's get something to drink and find a place to sit. Is it okay for a man and a woman to be out together?'

'Sure, of course. What you like? KFC?'

'God no! Something local.'

His face fell, and then he smiled. 'Okay. We have Peshawari speciality. Let's go.'

We sat at a table on the street next to the man who cooked the lamb kebabs Saleem ordered for us. He started telling me about the sights he wanted to take me to, but I had other things on my mind. I'd invited him out for a reason, and I wouldn't let the opportunity go by – I had questions.

'Before I came, I read that in Pakistan, women don't have to cover themselves, but it seems that they all do. Why?'

He looked into the middle distance as if reading the answer from a poster on a building across the road. 'Holy Qur'an says that women must be modest.'

'I know, but it said that about all people, not just women. It never said that they had to cover completely, did it? I read that even Muhammad's wives didn't cover their faces, so why do women have to now?'

'For some it is the way they want to be modest, to show that they are good Muslims, and so that no man who is not a relative can see them. For others it is custom, for some political, some are told to by their husbands or fathers. And you must understand that here in Peshawar we have religious government at the moment, the Muttahida Majlis-e-Amal. They are not as bad as the Taliban who terrorise my country but they are strict. Have you noticed that there are no posters of people anywhere, not even outside cinemas?'

I had to admit that I hadn't even noticed there were any cinemas.

'Aha! That is because holy Qur'an says that images of people and animals are not allowed, so film posters are only so much writing-writing now. And no music is allowed in the streets, and if you play it too loud in your own home even, police can come and stop you. They demand that women should be modest, and that means covering completely unless they are at home. But women can go out on their own, unlike when Taliban were ruling my country, and they can work and study. All these things are good, no?'

It wasn't fair. But there was no point in getting angry with Saleem. It wasn't his fault.

'What about foreigners, what are we allowed to do?'

'You can do anything, of course. But you may have the problem because you don't look foreign.' He held his forearm next to mine, not quite touching. 'See? We are same.'

He was right. We had exactly the same skin tone. The colour that in North Yorkshire had made me stand out now offered me anonymity.

'My father's Pakistani and my mother's English,' I said.

'And we Pashtuns have lighter skin because we are not really Pakistani at all. We are descended from Alexander the Great!'

Clearly I needed to do my history homework. I had no idea Alexander the Great had been anywhere near here.

'But Madam Laila, I think you will find that your father is Pashtun. Our tribal lands extend all over this region and have no care for borders.' He gestured to the hills and surrounding land with a sweep of his arm. 'You are Pashtun. I know it. It is the green eyes.'

I put my arm next to his again, accidentally touching his forearm. Saleem pulled it away as if my touch had burnt him.

'Sorry, Saleem. No touch, right?'

'That is right, Madam Laila – even married people do not touch in public. It is haram.'

'Forbidden?'

'Yes. Not allowed.'

'So what else is haram?'

Again he thought for a moment before answering. 'Same like your bible I think, but also no alcohol and no pig.'

I tried to remember the Ten Commandments – no murder, adultery, cheating, taking the name of the Lord in vain – I got stuck there. But there were cultural customs to take into account too, layers of subtle rules that I had no idea about. It dawned on me that perhaps I had unwittingly done something haram the day before and that had prompted Saleem's strange reaction. I bit my lip. Maybe it wasn't that he was untrustworthy, but that he'd thought I was.

'Saleem, did I do something to offend you when we went to the bazaar?'

He looked surprised and shook his head a little too vehemently. 'No, madam, of course not.'

'What was it?' I asked, not believing him. 'If you don't tell me, I can't learn the right way to behave.'

He looked embarrassed.

'Saleem?'

'No, Madam Laila, you did nothing wrong. It was I who wronged you. I should never have taken you to the bazaar, it was unsafe. That man in the shop, he... he thought I was... that is to say, he wanted relations with you and thought I was–'

'What? He thought you were my pimp, is that it?' I laughed, glad that it was nothing more than that. And then I shuddered. If I had gone on my own, what would have happened? 'Why didn't you tell me at the time?'

'Because I was ashamed. I had taken you there, and it was my duty to protect you, not allow people to have incorrect thoughts.'

'That wasn't your fault, it was his.'

Saleem didn't look convinced, and I suspected that nothing I said would make him change his view. Now that the misunderstanding was cleared up, I had a favour to ask. I'd made contact with Faisal, now was the time to try and find my father.

'Saleem, I have never met my father, but I think he might still live here. Could you help me find him?'

His face lit up. 'But of course. I can try. What is his name?'

'Afridi. Janan Farudin Afridi.'

'Ha! You see? I said you were Pashtun. Afridi is Pashtun name. Clan name. One of the big clans. We will find him.'

'Really?' He sounded so confident. Surely it couldn't be that easy. 'When I looked there were so many Afridis.'

'Yes, many, but they all know each other or someone who knows someone. I will talk to my friend Mahmoud and he will help. He knows everyone.'

'That's great.' I was beginning to get excited. 'But Saleem, if you or your friend find him, could you not tell him about me? Could you just give me his address? He doesn't even know I exist

– he left England before I was born. I don't want to scare him or make him angry.'

Saleem nodded. 'Pashtun man is very honourable. He would not leave his wife if he knew she was having baby. I will do as you ask.'

I felt excited now that finding my father seemed possible.

'Do you have brothers and sisters, Saleem?'

'Yes, I have one brother who is younger than me, and three sisters. Two are older and married and the youngest one is still at school.'

'Do they wear a burqa when they go out?'

'Yes, all of them.'

'Because it is expected?' I tried to keep the negativity out of my voice.

'Partly. You must remember that they all had to wear it when we went back to Afghanistan during the time the Taliban were in charge. But it has always been more common for women in the country to cover themselves. It is tradition. Now my eldest sister wears it because her husband says she must and my youngest sister wears it because she is very beautiful and does not want the attention of men. She wants to finish school before she marries.'

'And the middle sister?'

'She wears it because she is very ugly.'

Saleem tried to look serious, but there was a twitch at the corner of his mouth that gave him away.

'Oh, so she would make people ill if they had to look at her?' I smiled.

He laughed. 'You are very clever, Madam Laila. You knew I was saying a joke.'

I nodded. 'And you're very wicked,' I said. 'Your poor sister would be hurt if she knew you said things like that.'

'No she wouldn't. She is the most beautiful of all, and she knows it!'

Saleem drove me round the city pointing out places of interest, but I became anxious and couldn't concentrate. Faisal hadn't said what time he would come, and I wanted to get back so I didn't miss him.

'Goodbye, Madam Laila,' said Saleem as I got out of the taxi and handed him some money. 'I will find your father for you!'

There was a note for me at reception. Khalid, on duty as always, gave it to me as he told me what it said.

'You must meet Dr Choudhry at seven pm in the evening here. He will take you for dinner.'

'Thanks, Khalid.' I hoped he hadn't heard the thumping of my heart. 'Do you read everyone's mail?'

'Yes, madam. It is my duty. Letter can get lost. Memory cannot.' He tapped the side of his head.

Based on my own recent experience I doubted that very much, but said nothing. I was just glad that the note hadn't said anything more personal.

I had three hours to get ready. Or rather, fidget, pace, wring my hands, sit, stand again almost immediately and pace some more. In the end, I had a shower, tried to decide whether to wear Kamila's shalwar kameez or a dress. I didn't want to stand out, but I still felt like a kid in fancy dress when I went local. In the end I opted for a long skirt, a modest top and a shawl I could draw over my head if necessary. And then I sat on the edge of my bed and waited for the minutes to tick by. At two minutes to seven, I went downstairs.

Faisal walked in as I reached reception, looking perfect in jeans and open-necked shirt. I was glad I'd chosen the skirt.

He gave a stiff little bow.

'Laila, you look lovely. Shall we go?' He smiled but didn't wait for an answer. Turning, he led the way to his car, glancing along the road in both directions. Opening the door for me, he brushed his hand against my back to guide me. A shiver of anticipation ran up my spine and I almost gasped.

The sun was setting in glorious pinks, purples and oranges. I was about to comment, but when I looked at Faisal, he was concentrating hard on the road and checking the rear-view mirror frequently. He sat very straight, passed the steering wheel from hand to hand to turn the corners. I guessed he didn't drive very often. He hadn't had a car in London. I sat silent, not wanting to break his concentration, but also not knowing where to begin. I wanted answers, but now I was with him, I'd forgotten the questions.

We left the city behind and drove through farmland. The car headlights lit up low drystone walls, and I felt suddenly homesick for Yorkshire. As if reading my mind, Faisal asked how my mother and gran were.

'They're fine,' I said. 'Just the same, really.'

'I am glad.'

'Where are we going?' The city was far behind us, the mountains looming ever closer, great bulky masses against the evening sky.

Faisal seemed unaware of my concern. 'To the house of a friend of mine. Dinner has been prepared.'

My insides fell. Were we going to have dinner with other people and make polite conversation all evening as if we really had only been acquaintances in England? If that was the case, I couldn't bear it.

'Faisal, I...'

'Don't worry, we will be alone. There is a lot we need to talk about.' He looked at me briefly and smiled.

In that moment, I relaxed. His smile was the same as ever, inviting trust and confidence.

'We will be there soon. For now, it is enough to have you here in this car with me.'

The house was up a narrow, dusty lane off the main road and surrounded by orchards. It was a large, two-storey brick building with a stone barn to one side.

'Here we are.'

The front door opened and an elderly man hobbled out.

Faisal got out and said 'Assalamu alaikum,' to the man, who bowed.

He opened my door and said, 'This is Sajjad. He is from Afghanistan and he's a very good cook. Come.'

We went into the house and up the stairs, out onto the roof. A table had been set for two, with candles in jars offering the only light apart from the stars overhead. Faisal pulled out my chair and I sat down. Sajjad appeared with a jug of apricot juice and a bowl of almonds.

'Thank you,' I said. 'This is lovely.' He bowed again and left.

As soon as he was gone, Faisal took my hand.

'I can't believe you're here.'

I smiled. 'Are you glad?'

'Glad? I am beyond delighted. When you didn't write I thought you hated me for all that had happened. I couldn't blame you, but my soul sickened. Every day I wanted to speak to you, to beg you to come, but I knew it was unfair to ask. When I wrote to you before I left England, I said I would understand if you hated me and never wanted to see me again. And when I got back here, there were other reasons for not wanting you to come.'

'Other reasons? Have you changed your mind about us?'

The smile slipped from his face.

'Not at all, but I am being observed. Even here in Peshawar, where I am well known and regarded for my work, there is suspicion. I expected a visit from the police when I arrived back, but having been cleared of any wrongdoing in England, I thought a friendly chat and a warning not to consort with the wrong people would be it, and then all of a sudden, that nurse is helping at all my clinics and in surgery.'

'But why?'

'Why her, or why am I followed?'

'Both, I suppose.'

'As a male doctor, I have to have a female nurse for the women who do not want to be examined by a man. And she is a policeman's wife, so she can report back daily. And I have to say that she is good at her job – both her jobs. The patients are comfortable with her, and she lets nothing I do escape her eagle eye.'

'I still don't understand why you're under surveillance though.'

He looked down at our hands, still entwined. 'Do you remember Usman, my cousin?'

I nodded.

'Well, it turns out that he is a member of a terrorist organisation.'

'I know. They told me.'

He shook his head and took a deep breath. 'You must believe me when I tell you that I never knew. You must know that I wouldn't have let him stay with me in England if I did. He was in prison here, but managed to bribe his way out. I think he is in Afghanistan now, but I can't be sure. I suspect they think he'll contact me at some stage. I don't want to get you involved again, but now you are here, I can't stay away. I was very careful to make sure I wasn't followed this evening – it's not even my car.'

'So that's why we're having dinner here in the back of beyond?'

He smiled. 'That is why. It is to keep you safe. And so that we can be alone.'

He withdrew his hand when Sajjad arrived again carrying a tray of steaming rice and mutton stew.

'Can you imagine what it did to me to see you yesterday and not be able to take you in my arms? I thought I would die. And then I couldn't explain and you ran out – I thought I might never see you again. I sent boys out to all the hotels in the city to find you. I felt like the Artful Dodger with his little gang. In fact, one of my young spies told me at lunchtime today where I could find you, but by then, of course, I already knew. Thank you for coming back.'

Sajjad had disappeared again and Faisal got up and came round the table. I stood and walked into his arms.

'Laila Farida, how I have longed for you.'

'And I you,' I said, tilting my head up for his kiss.

'Oh, my Laila.' He sighed. I pulled him closer.

'Let's eat and talk. We have the whole night ahead of us, but I must know what happened to you and how you have been since...'

How could I tell him all that had happened? And yet, how could I not? He would see the scars on my body, faded, but still there.

'Were you in solitary confinement?' I asked. He nodded. 'Then you know what it was like. The boredom, the desperate need to talk to someone, anyone, the yearning for contact and the revulsion when you got it.'

Faisal gasped. 'No, no – please don't tell me that you were... I can't bear to think of it.'

'There was a female guard who... but none of the men touched me.' A small lie, to protect him from the truth. Surely that was okay? I felt like I was talking about someone else so well had I buried my feelings about it all.

A tear teetered on his lower lashes. 'I am so, so sorry. I

cannot tell you how terrible I feel to have subjected you to that. It is all my fault.'

He kissed my fingers one by one.

'It wasn't your fault. How could it be? But what about you?'

'Anger, despair, emptiness. That was the worst, I think, when I thought there was nothing. I went a little mad.'

'You too?'

He smiled. 'Yes, me too. And then I started reading Rumi and thinking of you, and I knew I had to stay strong in order to see you again. When I was released and they told me that you were still being held, I was so shocked. There was no reason to lock you up. And I was told you would be released only after I was safely back here in Pakistan. I was so angry with your government, but I could do nothing. I felt so weak and pathetic.'

'Which is what they wanted, and why I was watched after my release too. They wanted to intimidate us.' I could feel prickles of rage.

'So you came here, to get away?'

'I came here to find you, and because I no longer felt safe in England.'

'And you thought you'd feel safer here?'

I didn't like the way he laughed as he said that.

'I came because I love you. Perhaps I was being naïve, but I thought that together we would be okay. Maybe I was wrong.' I withdrew my hand from his, but he caught it again and held on tight.

'And maybe you are right.'

Sajjad returned to clear the last of the food away, and Faisal told him that he could go home to his hut on the other side of the barn. Sajjad nodded.

'He's mute,' said Faisal. 'The Taliban cut out his tongue for telling lies, or at least, that's the charge they trumped up.'

'That's awful.'

'Yes, but he manages.' He took my hand again. 'I don't want to talk about him, though, not now.'

I agreed and we sat next to each other, looking at the stars but I felt unsettled. Faisal seemed to want me there, but there was something else, something I couldn't quite put a finger on. Was he being cautious because Sajjad had seen us together? Was he worried that somehow we would be found out? Or was he wondering how a relationship like ours could work in a country like Pakistan?

'I thought that your parents might have found you a wife,' I said, leaning against his shoulder.

'They have.'

My heart skittered. I looked up at him.

'Three so far.' He smiled.

'Three?' I gulped. 'And?'

'I have met none of them. How could I when my heart is full of you?'

'Don't you dare do that to me again,' I said, swatting him on the arm.

'Never again, Laila Farida, never. I'm sorry. I will take you to meet my parents and tell them that I have found my wife and they need look no more.'

'Are you sure? Will they approve of me?'

'They will love you. They are traditional in some ways, but I believe they will accept that I have made my own choice. For now, though, you're all mine.'

He took my hand and led me down the stairs.

In bed, Faisal ran his fingers over the scars on my body, wanting to know how I'd got each one. He winced when I told him that they were all self-inflicted and then kissed them with feather-light lips.

'I wasn't as strong as you. Hurting myself was a way of

getting through it all, but I don't think I would have lasted another week in there,' I said, sighing under his touch.

'I also tortured myself, but it was with thoughts of you, of never seeing you again. I would spend hours imagining my life without you. Then I'd tell myself that if I didn't eat for a week, everything would be all right. And after a week, another week, just to make sure. In the end a tube was pushed down my throat and I was force fed.'

I shuddered. 'That's awful. We should have believed in each other, but I have to tell you–' I raised myself up on one elbow and looked into his eyes. 'I was told you'd implicated me in something. I didn't want to believe it, but they were so forceful. They even showed me a statement you'd written. I obsessed over it. In the end, I did believe it, they were very convincing. I'm so sorry. I know you didn't really write it, but then–'

'It's okay, Laila.' He pulled me closer, kissed my eyelids, my cheeks, my mouth. 'We are together now. That is all that matters.'

I rolled on top of him. 'No more talk now.'

'As you wish...'

The light was breaking over the city and the muezzins were calling the faithful to prayer when finally, we fell asleep.

9

'It is best if we are not seen together, my love, I will drive you to the city, but–'

'It's okay. I'll get Saleem to come and pick me up.'

Faisal raised his eyebrows. 'Saleem?'

'My personal taxi driver.'

'You have a personal taxi driver and you call him by his first name?'

'Yes, he's really sweet and feels it's his duty to show me the sights and look after me. Some Pashtun code of honour or something.'

'Pashtunwali. I know it. Where have you been so far?'

'Well, to be honest, not that many places, but he did take me to where he lives – Kochi Gahi. Lots of little...'

'That place is not safe. I cannot believe he took you there. It's more common name is the Smugglers' Bazaar. I do not trust this man.'

'Faisal, it's fine.' I laid my hand on his arm. 'Honestly, it was okay, and I asked him to take me there. I wanted to see where he lived and I needed a SIM card. It's all good, really.'

He didn't look convinced. 'Just promise me you won't go there again.'

'All right, I promise.'

He smiled and pulled me closer, hugged me tight. 'I don't want anything to happen to you.'

'I know. It's fine, just let me call Saleem and you can tell him how to get here, and then off you go.'

I handed him my phone and listened as he talked. I couldn't understand a word he said. I watched his mouth form the incomprehensible words and remembered his lips on my body.

'Laila? Are you all right?' Faisal looked concerned.

'Oh, yes, of course. Just daydreaming. He speaks English, you know.' I nodded towards the phone.

'Yes, I thought he must since he's managed to tell you so much about life here, but I need to practise my Pashto. Anyway, he said he'd be here in half an hour, but I'm afraid I have to go.'

'That's okay. I'll sit on the roof and wait.'

'I'll see you soon, my love.'

He looked into my eyes, cupped my face in his hands, and kissed me. 'Laila Farida, I love you.'

'I love you more,' I said.

'Impossible.'

I watched his car raise dust as he drove down the dirt track and turned onto the main road. Stretching and yawning, I felt satisfied in a way that I hadn't since before that night in July last year. The man I loved was back in my life. I hummed to myself as I climbed the stairs to the roof.

Beyond the orchards, a flock of goats wandered in the field, a young boy following them trailing a stick on the ground. In the distance, the mountains loomed.

Saleem arrived a few minutes later. I met him at the front door.

'What are you doing in this place?' His eyes swept over the house and barn.

'I had dinner with a friend. Let's go.'

'So, Madam Laila, I will take you back to the city?'

'Yes. But tell me, what's that way?' I pointed away from the city.

'That way is the mountains and a few farms. It is the way many smugglers take to get in and out of my country. This is not a good place.'

I went out later and found a bazaar that sold just about everything, and so cheap. I bought some silk for Gran to make herself something, and a brass vase for Mum. I wished I could afford to buy a carpet. Khalid, the receptionist, had told me that Peshawar was famous for its carpets because of its position at the crossroads of so many trade routes. I spent a couple of hours in a shop, being shown one after another whilst being plied with green tea and almonds.

'So. What you like?' the shopkeeper had asked, switching to English seamlessly when I told him I didn't speak anything else. He seemed to have no problem at all with the fact that I'd thrown the front of my burqa back so that I could see the carpets and drink the tea. He didn't, however, make eye contact with me at any time, instead letting his eyes roam over his carpets like a lover admiring his beloved.

'I have no idea. I know nothing about rugs.' I was feeling overwhelmed by the colours and styles in his small shop. Carpets piled on top of each other in tall stacks, tottering towards the ceiling.

'We have Baluchi, Bokhara, Afshar, Kazak, Afghan, Chobi, Gabbeh – you name it, we have it.' As he spoke he pulled various rugs out of the piles as examples of each.

'You like this one?' asked the portly Mr Khan, sweating slightly from tugging at his carpets.

'It's very beautiful, but I can't afford it, I'm sorry.'

'What you can pay?'

I was too embarrassed to say how little I could give him for it.

'Come now, madam, you like? You have!'

'I've only got a hundred pounds sterling,' I said apologetically.

You'd have thought I'd told him that I wanted to eat his mother for dinner the way he went off.

'This is beautiful rug, silk rug, hand dyed, hand woven. Must pay a thousand pounds!' He waved his hands as he spoke, and I thought at one time he might even take a swipe at me for insulting his carpet, his shop, his person.

'I'm very sorry.'

I pulled my burqa back on and beat a hasty retreat, feeling embarrassed but also annoyed until I realised that with so few tourists in the north these days, times must be tough for him.

I was exhausted by the time I got back to the hotel. Wiping the sweat from my forehead, I looked for Khalid. Sure enough, he unfolded himself from behind the counter and told me there was a message for me.

'Okay,' I said. 'What does it say?'

He smiled a proud smile as he would at a young child who had learned the rules, and recited the message as he handed it to me.

'I hope you got home safe and sound. Can I pick you up at the same time tonight? The Artful Dodger. Please, who is this Artful Dodger. It is a strange name, is it not?'

I smiled. 'Yes, it is. It's actually a character from a book by Charles Dickens, and my friend is making a joke.'

'Ah, a joke, like a pet name, isn't it?'

'Yes, something like that.'

'Shall you make a reply?'

'Oh, I don't know – how would I get it to my friend?'

'The boy over there, he is waiting.' Khalid pointed to a child in a dirty T-shirt and shorts, who was passing the time by smiling and winking at himself in the mirror on the wall.

'In that case, yes.'

Khalid passed me a pen and some paper. I slid it to the end of the counter and wrote, *Home safe and sound. Same time is fine. See you then...* I wondered how to sign it. I didn't want his nurse to know my name, although she'd probably already found it out somehow. But Faisal had used a pseudonym, and so would I. I signed it *Oliver*, folded it, and gave it to Khalid.

Khalid opened it and read it, while I watched open-mouthed. Privacy had a different meaning in Pakistan, obviously.

'That is another joke, isn't it? Because your name is not Oliver, I think so.'

I smiled. 'Yes, a joke. How much should I give the boy?'

'Five rupees only,' he said, and called the boy over, gave him the note and the money. The boy winked goodbye to himself in the mirror and ran off.

At seven, I was waiting in the foyer wearing Kamila's shalwar kameez, hoping Faisal wouldn't think I was trying too hard to fit in.

He rushed in a few minutes late, gave me a small bow, and went over to Khalid. They talked in urgent whispers and Faisal passed him some money, then he went to the door and peered out before turning back to me. 'The car is outside. Please, shall we go?' He sounded stressed.

'What was all that about?' I asked as we drove off.

'I'm not sure, but I think I was followed. As I got here, another car stopped over the road and two men just sat there. It was too late to go again without looking suspicious so I sat in the car for a few minutes pretending to be on my phone, and they left, but I wanted to be sure that the receptionist could be trusted not to say anything in case they came back.'

I swallowed hard. Could it be me they were keeping an eye on, not Faisal?

'Followed by whom?' I asked.

'One of my nurse's husband's cronies no doubt. Laila, this is a complex place. There are those who cross the borders regularly to fight or train in Afghanistan, and they are heroes. There are others who speak out against the bloodshed, and they are villains.'

'That doesn't make sense.'

'I know but that's how it is. I am a pacifist and therefore not to be trusted. But let's not talk about it again.'

'Okay. Where are we going this evening?' I asked.

'To Charsadda, a town about twenty minutes from here. I do not know anyone there, nor they me. We will be left in peace. By the way, you look beautiful tonight. Did you get the suit here?'

'No, it was one of Kamila's.'

He looked over at me, smiling.

'She gave it to you for coming here?'

It hadn't occurred to me that Fasial didn't know about Kamila, but how could he? I took a deep breath.

'No. Her mother gave it to me. Look, there's no easy way to tell you this, but Kamila's dead.'

'What?' The car swerved as Faisal turned to me, stricken. 'It can't be true – what happened?'

'She was also arrested. When she was let out she discovered that the government was denying that anyone had been detained. She tried to let people know what was happening, and kept meeting with lies and deceit. After what she'd been through it was too much to live with.' I wiped my eyes and blew my nose. 'I'm so sorry, Faisal. I should have told you sooner. I know how fond you were of her. We all loved Kam, didn't we?'

He pulled in to the kerb and sat staring at the headlights coming towards us.

'I can't believe it. You're saying she took her own life?'

I nodded, unable to speak the words.

'Inna lillahi wa inna ilaihi raji'un,' he said under his breath. 'I don't know what to say. Why was she arrested? What had she ever done? Was it because she knew me? Am I to blame for her as well as for you? I cannot bear it.' He covered his face with his hands and rocked gently backwards and forwards. I didn't know what to say or do. We had spent time together, the three of us; we'd been away for weekends together, too, her and her boyfriend, Waleed, Faisal and me. Silence seemed the only response. I took his hand and let my breath settle into the same rhythm as his. Deep inhalations, long sighs.

After some time, he lifted his head and looked at me. 'If I had known, please believe me, I would never have let Usman stay. How can I live with what has happened?'

There were tears in his eyelashes and he looked crushed, his shoulders sagged and his body slumped in the seat.

'Faisal, Kamila wasn't arrested because of you. My theory is that it was because of her brother, Asim. He's out here, in Pakistan somewhere, and all he tells the family is that he "travels".'

He looked up and stared past me out into the night. After a

lengthy pause, he said, 'You think he has joined a group, that he's fighting?'

'It's possible. I never trusted him. There was something about him, he was always so cold and distant. You must have met him at Kam's some time. What did you think of him?'

Faisal's brow creased into a frown. 'I think I met him once.' He put his arms around me, holding me close. He let out a long breath and seemed to relax a little.

'He and Kam had some sort of special closeness.' I spoke into his shoulder. 'Maybe she knew what he was doing? It seems they were in contact.'

'I hope you are wrong, but it does make sense.' Faisal remained quiet for a while and then he started the car and pulled out into the traffic.

Over dinner in a small restaurant in a side street the mood was subdued. We didn't talk any more about Asim or Kamila. We didn't really talk about anything. I thought Faisal was still trying to come to terms with her death, and I gave him the space he needed. He'd booked us into a hotel as Mr and Mrs Khan, the most common name in those parts, and we held each other quietly until sleep overcame us. Just before dawn the first azaan woke us. I stretched and stroked Faisal's warm back, kissed the length of his spine. He arched and turned to me, kissed me on the mouth, but then got up.

'We must get back before anyone sees us. I am sorry, Laila. It was not the romantic night we had been looking forward to.'

He was right, but we couldn't ignore the fact of Kamila's death. To have spent the night making love would have seemed a betrayal of her memory somehow.

'It's okay. Just being with you is enough.' I yawned and pulled on my clothes.

As we got to the outskirts of Peshawar, Faisal became wary.

'Drop me here, I'll get a bus the rest of the way. I don't want you worrying about being seen with me.'

'It is not for myself I worry, but for you. In the dark, in the evenings, it is easier, but in daylight, not so. I am sorry it is like this.' He had stopped by the side of the road next to a low stone wall.

I smiled, stroked the side of his face, gave him a kiss and got out. He pulled into the traffic and was gone.

The sun shone weakly over the old city, making the angles appear softer, the buildings cleaner, as if sapped of the grime of years of pollution. The sweepers were out removing the evidence of life lived on the streets – of buying and selling, brokering deals and sealing contracts. Sitting on the wall, waiting for the bus, I thought of the times I'd watched Thirsk from the safety of the flat, seeing the town slowly wake up and come to life in all its familiarity. Here, I was a stranger, the city and the culture confronting. I had a sense that this was a place where I might never feel I belonged, and yet, might live with Faisal for years.

Horns blaring and a scooter screeching within a breath of me brought me back to the present. In the cool of the morning without a bus in sight, I decided to walk back to the Welcome.

As I entered the hotel foyer, Khalid, who never seemed to sleep, smiled at me and winked.

I peered at him. 'Did you just wink at me?'

'Yes, madam, I did. It is what people do when they are having a secret together, isn't it.'

'And what secret would that be?' I asked.

'That would be the person who came to inquire after your good self last evening, and me myself telling him that I had no idea where you were or who you were with. Like your friend suggested,' he said.

'Oh, I see.' My stomach sank. 'A man?'

'Yes, the very same.'

'Did he leave a name?'

'No. I asked if he wanted to leave a message, but he said no.'

'What did he look like – was he wearing a uniform?'

'He was ordinary man, no uniform, big moustache, like this,' and he twirled an imaginary moustache in his fingers.

Pakistani Intelligence, I wondered, or plain-clothes police? My stomach sank further. I clutched the reception desk. Why couldn't they leave us alone?

'You are well, madam?'

'Yes, thanks, Khalid.'

'I did the right thing?'

'Yes, you did very well.'

I went up the stairs on shaky legs.

Outside my room I looked up and down the hall half expecting to see a sinister stranger lurking, but of course, there was nobody there. Once inside, I leaned against the door as I surveyed my little space, checking that no one had snuck in while I was out. The bag containing the silk for Gran and the vase for Mum was still by my bed, my clothes were still dangling half out of my case, the underwear I'd washed was hanging over the towel rail. The window was ajar, and a light breeze ruffled the edge of my sheet. My room was just as I'd left it.

I sat on the bed and started writing in my journal, the words flowing out of me. I was scared. Things were going on around me that I didn't understand – people following us, a strange man turning up at the hotel, a Smugglers' Bazaar. It was like living in a spy novel.

That evening, Faisal and I went again to the farmhouse. I fantasised that it was our home and our nights there rehearsals for our life together.

After he'd left in the morning and I was waiting for Saleem and his taxi, I decided to go for a walk. I had a sense that Sajjad was watching me, so I kept walking, past the barn, round the small hut where he lived, and into an orchard, the branches of the trees bowing under the weight of peaches and apricots. Further on there were apple and pear trees, the fruit still ripening. I picked a soft, plump peach, hoping that Sajjad didn't see. I'd never eaten fruit so fresh, still sun-warmed. One wasn't enough. After three peaches and a couple of apricots, I started heading back. As I passed the barn it seemed to draw me to it, inviting me to peer inside. I couldn't see Sajjad anywhere, so I crept towards it. The door was ajar, but it was so dark inside that I could see nothing except the strip of floor illuminated by the bright sunlight. Pulling the door wider, I stepped into the musty space and stood to let my eyes adjust. And then a shock wave tore through my body: it was an Aladdin's cave of weapons and ammunition. A noise from outside made me shrink back into the shadows. I stayed there, heart thumping, for several minutes, but no one came in. Slowly, I crept to the door and looked out. Sajjad was sweeping the front step of the house with his back to me. As quietly as I could, I slipped out and ran round the side of the barn, then walked back towards him making plenty of noise. He turned, nodded at me, and got back to his task.

Back at the hotel, I stood under the shower as the tepid water trickled over me. A loud noise in the courtyard made me jump and grab my towel. Showers were one of the places I still got scared. As my heart rate returned to normal, I leant against the wall and cried. When was I going to get over all that had happened? When would I be able to take a shower without imagining Jabba rubbing herself against me, or Spud 'checking for contraband'? Those bastards had left deeper scars on me than any of my self-inflicted wounds. And they weren't being held to account. They could, at that very moment, be doing exactly the same to someone else. I buried my face in my towel and screamed.

It was so hot outside that all I could do was lie on my bed under the fan. I read and wrote in my journal until I felt calmer. Someone dropped a plate or a cup in the courtyard, shattering the quiet. And then I noticed the noise of horns honking, and occasionally someone shouting to be heard over the traffic, but it seemed a long way away. I dozed on and off and somehow the day passed. I hated that I lacked motivation to do anything. When I was in prison, I'd have given anything for a day of freedom to do exactly as I pleased, and here I was squandering that very opportunity. As the afternoon wore on, I became more and more angry. With Pakistan for being too hot. With Mum for not being home when I tried to call her. With the British government for locking me up. With Spud and his fingers that forced their way into me, and Jabba with her frantic desire. When would I leave those memories behind, when would I feel clean? And finally, I was furious with Khalid who didn't seem to be able to keep the electricity working, so that the fan stopped and I started sweating immediately.

In the evening I told Faisal about my day, but didn't mention to him what I had seen in the barn. I wouldn't let it spoil our time together, or give him something more to worry about. Instead, I asked him about when we might visit his parents in Karachi, and the next day I emailed Mum and Gran and told them to expect a wedding. I was happy and would allow no space for doubt, no room for obstacles. Faisal and I were together, and always would be. We'd even been choosing names for the children we would have.

A couple of days later, collecting me from the farmhouse,

Saleem drove me not to the hotel, but to a KFC on the outskirts of town.

'Mahmoud will meet us here,' he said as we parked.

My heart skipped a beat. 'He has some news?'

'He has said me nothing. Sorry – told me nothing, but I think so.'

A few minutes later, sitting in the glare of neon lighting in a booth which Mahmoud just managed to squeeze his bulk into, I sat sweating in spite of the air conditioning belching out an icy breeze.

'I have found your father. He was not so difficult to find. He is a farmer who is also a teacher of farming. I have written his address for you.' He slid a piece of paper across the table.

'Thank you,' I said, picking it up and trying to decipher his handwriting.

'I know where this place is, I can take you there no problem,' said Saleem, smiling at me. 'It is good, yes? I think he is a rich man. We go now?'

He rose to his feet.

'No!' I held up a hand to stop him and took a calming breath, except it didn't really do much to relax me. 'Not quite yet, Saleem. I have to think about the best way to go about this – he doesn't even know I exist, remember. I don't want to give him a heart attack.'

'Why would he have a heart attack when he sees you? He will be very pleased to meet you. That is how it is here. I was very pleased to meet you, and he will be too.'

'Thanks, but you're not my father whose unknown daughter is suddenly going to turn up.'

'Maybe I should go and see him and tell him about you.'

'No, I think not. I'll work something out.'

Mahmoud, who had been picking at his teeth said, 'He stays in the city one or two nights a week when he is teaching.

Otherwise he is at his farm with his family. You should take Saleem and go and see him at the university. That is the address I have given you.'

'I don't know how to thank you, Mahmoud.'

He grunted, shook his head, and slid out of the booth.

'At least let me buy you breakfast,' I said.

He nodded and ordered himself an enormous amount of food which he took to another table, leaving Saleem and I sitting on our own with our coffees.

Saleem waited expectantly.

'I think I'll write him a note first. Would you take it to his address?'

'Of course.'

We went back to the Welcome and he waited while I went up to my room and tried to compose a letter to my father. What to say? I'd been thinking about meeting him for years, but not how I'd go about it. In my daydreams we were just together, and he accepted me immediately. The reality, I realised, may be quite different, and it all hinged on the first contact. In the end I wrote a brief note.

Dear Mr Afridi,
Lynette Seaver asked me to look you up since I was coming to Peshawar. I hope we may meet, at your convenience. I am staying at the Welcome Hotel.
Best Regards,

What should I sign it? If I used my first name he'd guess who I was straight away, as I shared his mother's name. And the Seaver would obviously be a giveaway. There were no untruths in the letter itself so I allowed myself a small one in my name. When I was little, my gran had made up a song about her and me. One line was *Little Lily-Laila loved her lively nana*, so I signed myself Lily. With a shaking hand, I sealed the note into an envelope and gave it to Saleem.

I couldn't settle to anything. I was half hoping that Saleem would bring my father back with him. My phone rang and I grabbed it before the second ring.

'It is me, Saleem. I am with your... with Mr Afridi. I was pushing the note under his door when he came out. It is like magic, no? So he is here, and he would like to talk to you.'

I couldn't catch my breath. This was too soon, and not at all the scene I'd pictured.

'Are you there, Madam Laila?'

'Yes, I'm here.'

'So I will pass the phone to Mr Afridi?'

'Is he right there, Saleem?' Had he heard him calling me Laila?

'He is in the next room only.'

'Right, that's good. Did he ask anything about me?'

'Of course. He wanted to know how you knew where to find him. I was able to tell him that I had helped with that task. That is all.'

Thank God. 'All right, I'll talk to him. And Saleem – thanks.'

'You do not need to thank me, Madam Laila. I am your good friend.'

I listened to his footsteps, and a knock on a door.

'Mr Afridi, sir, here she is on the phone.'

I wiped my sweating palms on my skirt, took a deep breath and waited. I was going to hear my father's voice for the first time.

'Miss Lily, welcome to Peshawar. I trust you are enjoying your stay?'

I don't know why, but it had never occurred to me that he would have anything but an English accent, and here he was, sounding like an older version of Saleem.

'Yes, thank you, very much.' An awkward silence followed while I tried to think what to say next.

'Mr Afridi, I don't know if you remember Lynette Seaver at all?'

'But of course I remember her. She was a dear friend and made my stay in England so much more pleasant than it might otherwise have been.'

I'll bet, I thought. 'Oh, that's good. Well, when I said I was coming to Pakistan, she suggested I look you up.'

'May I ask how you know Miss Seaver? Are you a friend? Is she well?'

'She is very well, and no, I'm not a friend, I'm a relative.' Still no lies. 'Could I take you out for dinner perhaps?'

'I would be honoured to have dinner with you, but I must insist on being the host. I cannot have you coming all the way to my country and then having to pay for dinner as well.'

I laughed, a high-pitched giggle. My father had agreed to meet me. It was really going to happen.

'Shall I pick you up at your hotel at seven this evening?'

'Thank you, yes.' I hung up. My mouth was dry and my hands were shaking.

I thought of the photo Mum had of him, the serious young man, and wondered how much he'd changed over the years. It was twenty-eight years since it had been taken. He'd lived more than half his life since then, and I'd lived all mine.

My phone ringing again made me jump.

'Saleem here.'

'Thanks, Saleem, you're a star. What's he like? Will I like him?'

'How can I know if you will like him? He is polite and kind, that is all I can say. I am only a taxi driver, and he gave me tea. He is a good man.'

A kind, polite man. It wasn't much to go on. What else was

he, I wondered? And would he still be kind and polite when I told him I was his daughter? I might need a few glasses of wine to get me through the night, but I guessed that no alcohol would be served.

~

By half past six I was an emotional mess. I still had no idea how I was going to broach the topic of my parenthood with my father, and now whenever I thought of it a wall of panic made any coherent thought impossible. I hoped that the ability to fly by the seat of my pants that I'd developed as a teacher would come to my rescue.

I paced my room, smoothing my dress over my thighs and stomach every few steps, checking in the mirror each time I passed that my features were still in place and that my make-up wasn't overdone.

As I entered the hotel foyer, a man rose and smiled across the large room at me. He had a lived-in face, with laughter lines around his green eyes. He had darker skin than mine, perhaps from working outdoors, but there was no mistaking who he was. He was me in twenty-five or so years.

'Miss Lily, so pleased to meet you,' he said and bowed. He didn't stare, he hardly even looked at me, as was the custom, but I felt seen anyway. I wondered what he was thinking. Gone were my fantasies of him knowing immediately who I was and accepting me into his family and his heart without me having to say a word.

'Shall we walk? I know a good place to eat near here.'

I nodded, unable to form any words.

'So, what brings you to Peshawar?' he asked as we strolled along a side street.

'I came to see a friend who moved back here a while ago.'

'She must be a good friend for you to come all this way.'

'Yes, a very good friend.' I didn't see the need to correct him.

'And are you enjoying your stay? What have you seen so far?'

'It's very nice here.' Oh, God. I felt like a teenager on her first date. 'The museum is very interesting, and the bazaars are great.'

He laughed. 'Is shopping a particular hobby of yours?'

'No, not really.' Was he making fun of me? I felt so embarrassed I wanted to cry.

'I am sorry, Miss Lily, I did not mean to make you uncomfortable. Here we are. We can sit and order, and then perhaps you can tell me about Lynette, and how she came to send you on this mission.'

The menu was written in Urdu.

'Perhaps you could order for me,' I said, and received one of his smiles again, friendly and warm.

'Of course.' He called the waiter over and spoke to him at some length, which gave me the opportunity to have a look around. The other diners were mainly men in twos and threes, although I was comforted to see a couple of other women. The furnishings were what I thought of as Indian restaurant kitsch back home – high-backed, uncomfortable wooden chairs, heavy tables with white tablecloths, and a lot of red on the walls.

'So, how is Lynette?' He smiled, again hardly looking at me. Instead, he looked into the distance as if seeing her there, her blonde hair blowing around her face, blue eyes sparkling.

'She's very well, and sends warm regards. How did you meet?' I asked.

He sighed. 'I was a student of agriculture at Nottingham University, and she worked in the canteen where I used to have lunch every day. She was always cheerful with a smile for everyone. I was very shy, and I think she made it her personal project to bring me out of my shell. Anyway, it wasn't long before she asked me to go on a picnic with her. I had never been on a picnic, and didn't really know what it was, but it sounded important, so I dressed carefully in my one and only suit and tie and met her by the canteen.'

I laughed. I could imagine him, gawky and shy, trussed up in a suit, and Mum coming along in a flimsy dress or shorts and a T-shirt, hardly able to hide her amusement.

'Yes, I suppose I was an odd sight, but Lynette didn't laugh or even say anything about my inappropriate attire. Instead, she took my hand, led me to the park, set out a blanket and invited me to sit. Only then, as she started to get food out of her bag, did it dawn on me that this was meant to be an informal occasion.' He smiled again and shrugged his shoulders. 'She made me feel at ease. It was a gift she had. Probably still has.' He looked at me, the question on his lips.

'Yes, I suppose she does.'

The waiter arrived with our starters, giving me time to think of what to say next.

As my father raised a samosa to his mouth, I said, as casually as I could, 'Lynette told me that you were good friends.'

My heart flipped in my ribcage as he slowly finished his mouthful, wiped his lips with a crisp white serviette, and took a sip of water.

'We were good friends. I should say, very good friends.'

Did I detect a blush? It was hard to tell in the garish lighting.

He looked uncomfortable.

'I'm sorry,' I said. 'I shouldn't have mentioned it. I keep putting my foot in it here, not knowing what's okay to talk about and what isn't.'

'No, it is all right. We were close.' There was definitely a blush, and he looked towards the kitchen as if hoping that the waiter would appear with the next course and save him from having to say any more.

'She was very fond of you,' I said. Had I gone too far?

He swung back to me, eyebrows raised.

'She talked to you about me?'

'Of course. Well, actually, not that much, but she did tell me that she missed you very much when you had to leave.'

He looked at his plate. 'Try the samosas, they really are very good here. I hope they are not too spicy for you.'

I took a bite – the flavours were sensational – and then steered the conversation back to more general topics.

'So, you are a teacher at the university, I understand.'

'That is correct. I had to leave England because my father died, and I was needed back here, but I managed to finish my degree here in Pakistan, and I've been teaching and working on my own farm ever since. I would be honoured if you would visit.'

'I'd love to. What do you grow?'

He leant forward, this was a subject he was comfortable with.

'I use it as a bit of an experimental farm. At the university we have plots and compare strains of crops. We have been growing sunflowers most recently with some good results. I am in the fortunate position of not having to make a living from the farm because I have my teaching, so apart from growing enough vegetables and some fruit to feed the family, I can plant whatever crop I like and see how it does. With the success of sunflowers at the university, I am now growing them on my farm. Otherwise some maize, wheat, lentils, that sort of thing.' As he spoke, he gestured with his hands, the shape of the sunflowers, the fullness of the maize. They were working hands, strong, the skin a little rough.

He smiled. 'I'm sorry. I get carried away. What do you do, Miss Lily?'

'I'm a teacher. Primary school.'

'Also a teacher. That is good. To teach is a great thing, I think. To impart a love of learning, that is a gift.'

'Oh, well, I don't know if I do that,' I said, reddening. It was as if he could read me, knew that my passion as a teacher had been to encourage the children to be curious and extend their learning beyond the classroom.

He smiled again. 'I am sure you do.'

The main course arrived, and for a while we ate in silence. He ate neatly. I would almost say respectfully, as if the food was a gift that deserved his full attention. I liked him. He was gentle and kind, as Saleem had said, and intelligent and courteous. And I was still miles away from getting to the point.

I was torn though. He clearly loved Mum, but had a strong sense of duty to his family. I couldn't tell him that I was his daughter, not now. I wanted to get to know him better, for him to get to know me. I suppose I still wanted the knowledge to dawn on him without me having to declare it, as if that would make it easier for him to accept. Because I really wanted him to accept it. I wanted him to be proud that I was his daughter, as I already felt proud that he was my father.

'Where is your farm?' I asked.

'It is some miles away from here. Perhaps you would be kind enough to visit on Saturday, if you're not busy. I could send a driver to collect you?'

'That would be lovely,' I said. 'Will your family be there?'

'Sadly, my mother passed away three years ago, and my wife not long after. My elder son is at university in Lahore, but my younger son, Zahir, will be there.'

Two sons. Two brothers. Mr Smith had only mentioned one.

'I'm sorry about your wife and mother.'

'Thank you. They are at peace.'

'How old are your sons?'

'Zahir is seventeen and already a good farmer. He

understands the land and coaxes it to yield more than I ever could. Jawad is twenty, and a hothead who wants to change the world. He is doing a degree in IT.'

'You must be proud of them both.'

'Yes, I am.'

We left the restaurant. My father walked me home, and we said goodbye in front of the hotel. I watched him walk away, already looking forward to seeing him again.

Back in my hotel room, I tried to Skype Mum but she wasn't at her computer. I so wanted to talk to her about my father, and how much I liked him, that I understood why she loved him. In the end, all I could do was send her an email and write in my journal.

In the morning, Faisal rang.

'How did it go, my love?'

I told him a little about the evening and arranged to see him later, then spent the day wandering the bazaars. I was becoming more familiar with the place, more comfortable.

At six fifteen, I started getting ready for my evening with Faisal. By the time he rang to say he was downstairs, I had showered, dressed and pulled a brush through my hair. Throwing my toiletries and burqa into my bag I took the stairs two at a time and stopped just short of him. I had been going to throw myself into his arms, and remembered where I was just in time.

'Well hello,' he said, smiling at me.

'Why's it still so damned hot?' I asked.

'It is hotter than usual, even for Pakistan,' Faisal agreed. He peered out of the hotel door, ushered me quickly into the car and eased into the chaos of traffic.

He asked about my day, and I told him I'd not done much.

'Are you okay?' I asked. He looked a little distracted.

'Sorry. It's been a difficult day.'

'What happened?'

'What? Oh – just some small problems.'

'What kind of problems?'

He sighed, waved a hand in the air as if to dismiss the conversation.

'Faisal, tell me, please. Talking helps, you know.'

'It is nothing, really. Let's not let it spoil the evening.'

Over dinner, Faisal tried to be as loving and attentive as always but he was distracted. He asked me more about my evening with my father but didn't seem to be listening to the answers.

Later, I offered him a massage. He lay on the bed as I kneaded the muscles in his neck and shoulders, and I felt him relax under my touch. He sighed as I massaged down either side of his spine in firm, circular movements. Suddenly he turned over, caught my hands and kissed them.

When we made love, he was so tender. His fingertips felt like soft breath on my skin.

In the morning, we had a hurried breakfast of almonds and apricots.

'I'll call you later,' he said as he readied himself to leave. He cupped my face in his hands and looked into my eyes. 'I love you, Laila Farida.'

'And I you,' I said.

10

I watched the dust cloud until he turned onto the paved road towards the city. I felt a deep contentment, and hugged myself to try and contain the feeling.

The phone in the hall rang. I heard Sajjad pick it up and imagined him listening, perhaps nodding at what was being said and then I heard the click as he replaced the receiver in its cradle.

Showered and dressed, I called Saleem and sat cutting the lattice eye covering out of my burqa. I was sick and tired of the world being carved up into tiny squares when I wore it. I was just neatening the edges when I heard a car pull up. Peering out the window I saw a Land Cruiser. I stepped back behind the curtain and watched. Two men got out, and Sajjad ran over to them shaking his head and trying to usher them back to their car. The taller man shoved him away, and Sajjad fell to his knees. Then they strode towards the house.

There were footsteps on the stairs. I froze, one hand on the windowsill, the other covering my mouth. What was happening? They couldn't know I was there. But what had they said to Sajjad, and why had he tried to make them go away?

The door burst open. I clutched the curtain tightly, pulling it across my body.

One man had a loosely tied white turban on his head and pointed a gun at me. A trickle of urine ran down my thigh.

'Move,' he said, motioning towards the door.

I couldn't do as he asked. I couldn't even breathe. My eyes were fixed on the gun and my legs wouldn't respond to his command.

The second man came in. Both were wearing beige perahan tunban, the Pashtun version of kurta pyjama, but instead of a turban, this one was wearing a pakol, the Afghani beret, on his head.

'Move,' the first man said again, and this time stepped towards me. I let go of the curtain and stumbled forward. He took my arm, Pakol grabbed my bag and emptied the contents on the bed. He took the money, my passports, tucked my burqa under his arm and they marched me out the door. Sajjad was in the hall as we descended the stairs. He put his hands together in supplication, but they ignored him and shoved me down the front step.

Thoughts crowded one another in my head. What were they going to do with me? I wouldn't survive more of what went on in prison. Images of that time crowded into my head and I forced them away. I had to think clearly. Could I escape? Should I try and make a run for it? Would I make it to the road? If I did get away from the men, would Sajjad help me? Would Saleem get here soon?

I was sweating, heart racing.

I had to do something. Anything.

I swung around and kicked out as hard as I could. Pakol grunted in pain as my foot made contact with his thigh. He shouted something and grabbed my arm. I lashed out again with feet and free hand, swinging again and again, hitting and kicking whatever I could reach.

Turban said something and laughed. Still I kept going. If they thought I was amusing, so be it. If I could keep going long enough, Saleem might arrive and help. Then I heard a shot and stopped dead. Turban had fired into the air. He came over and pulled me away, one arm twisted painfully behind my back.

'No,' he hissed in my ear. When I looked up Pakol had his gun aimed at me. He sneered at me, victorious, and then turned to bark some orders at Sajjad who rushed towards the barn and came out moments later dragging a large crate. Pakol lowered his gun and went to help. Together they loaded four crates into the back of the car, and then pushed me towards it. It was my last chance. I turned to start kicking again, but this time my captor was ready. He slapped me hard on the cheek. I gasped, my free hand going to my face. He laughed, manhandled me into the back seat and Pakol got into the passenger seat. I lunged for the other door, but it was locked.

The last thing I saw as we screeched away from the house was Sajjad standing with his hands raised, palms up, as if asking for help from God.

We turned away from the town and sped along the road that Saleem had told me led towards one of the many unofficial crossings into Afghanistan.

'Who are you?' My voice quavered.

Silence.

'Are you Taliban? Al-Qaeda? Where are you taking me?' The tears started.

No answer. Both men stared straight ahead. Turban was driving, a foul-smelling cigarette clamped between his lips.

'Why am I here? What do you want with me?' I wiped angrily at the tears – I needed to be strong, to think.

If they wanted to kill me they could have done it at the farm.

Did that mean they needed me for something? Or perhaps they wanted to make my death look like an accident? And how had they known I was there?

The only people other than Faisal who knew where I was were Sajjad and Saleem. It looked like Sajjad had been trying to send them away.

My heart sank.

It had to be Saleem. I'd been so naive, trusting him even when that time at the camp my instincts had warned me not to. He had probably been discussing the plan with that man in the shop. He was to befriend me, pretend to be looking after me, and then hand me over to these men. Warning me off the farm had been a ploy too – a kind of reverse psychology that made it seem more intriguing. And I'd fallen for it. Now these men had caught me and I had no idea what was going to happen. It felt all too familiar. This time, though, I was in a car full of weapons with men who had guns. In reality, I'd probably been safer in solitary. The thought almost made me laugh.

We drove for a long time on the main road and then pulled off in the middle of nowhere onto a dirt track that started rising towards the foothills. It was deeply rutted and I was thrown around every time the car hit a bump. The discomfort didn't help my mood. I was so furious with Saleem that I could hardly think straight, so ashamed that I had fallen for his, 'I am your good friend' routine.

And I was terrified.

When the sun was high above us creating a heat haze that made the scorched earth shimmer and shift, we stopped at a hut with a low stone wall around it.

'Put on,' said the driver, turning towards me and passing me my burqa. I didn't even take it from him.

He shook it at me. 'On,' he repeated.

Pakol pointed a gun at me. 'On,' he said, and flicked the safety catch.

I struggled to pull the yards of fabric over my head in the confines of the car.

'Out,' he said once it was in place.

Was this where I was going to die, in the middle of nowhere? It seemed not. The men left their weapons in the car, but I noticed with a sinking heart that they took the keys out and locked it. They lit cigarettes and leaned against the wall.

I was desperate for a pee, but how was I meant to make them understand?

'Toilet?' I said, gesturing to the hut.

They both laughed. So they did speak more English than the few words they'd uttered so far. Pakol pointed to the other side of the wall.

'Toilet,' he said.

I walked over to the wall stumbling on the uneven ground that I couldn't see because of my burqa, and realised that the toilet was a field, although there was nothing growing in it, just dirt and rocks all round. Squatting down, once again I gave thanks for the privacy my personal tent offered.

When I got back the two men were performing their prayers on small rugs on the ground. I watched as they stood and knelt and touched their foreheads to the ground. It was the perfect time to make a run for it, but as I looked around, I knew the reason they weren't keeping a tight hold of me was because they knew that there was nowhere to go – the barren landscape was harsh and brutal and I'd be dead before I found the road again. When they'd finished, they rolled up their carpets and Turban leaned against the hut and lit another cigarette. Pakol paced by the car shouting into his phone, spit flying. I was given a bottle of water and a stale bit of naan.

'Where are we?' I asked. No answer.

'Why me?'

Turban shrugged.

'Are you going to kill me?'

Turban looked almost at me and said, 'No.'

Relief made my knees buckle, until I remembered that there are worse things than death. Sour bile rose in my throat.

'What are you going to do with me?'

Instead of answering me, the men started talking to each other. I looked around. There were rocky, barren-looking fields and then mountains as far as the eye could see. Steep, craggy mountains that folded on themselves like the rock had melted and then suddenly frozen in jagged angles. Deep, dark gullies alternated with sharp bright ridges. They looked impenetrable. And we were headed into them.

We spent the afternoon bumping towards the mountains, my anger at Saleem keeping anxiety at bay. How long had he been planning this? What was in it for him – was this how he had bought his taxi, by getting a kickback from terrorists? I had let my judgement be clouded by loneliness and fear in this new place, and had been so grateful for a friendly greeting, a familiar face.

We paused again for prayers during the afternoon, the men peering at the sky to determine the correct direction before they knelt. As the sun lowered behind us, we laboured up the foothills on a track that was barely distinguishable from the rocks on either side of it. How Turban knew where we were going I had no idea, but he drove with confidence, and as night fell, the headlights picked out a small village teetering on the edge of a precipice, and we stopped.

'Stay,' said Pakol as if he was talking to a dog. He and Turban got out of the car and disappeared into a building set a little way back from the track.

I didn't care what they'd said, I couldn't stay in the car any longer. Holding my burqa tightly around me, I got out and leaned against the door, looking around. It was dark, but I made out several stone huts with dim lights in some of the windows. The mountains rose ominously behind, huge against the navy sky. To my left, deep black nothing.

Pakol shouted something at me and then motioned me into a house and gestured for me to sit on the floor. It was covered by carpets and big cushions, but I wasn't offered one. An oil lamp standing on a low platform at one end of the room gave out a warm but piteous light. It hissed and sputtered, casting strange shadows over the walls. In one corner was a stack of bedding. Pakol left and came back moments later with another man, older, with a weathered face, who carried his authority naturally in spite of the empty trouser leg pinned up on itself and the crutches he used.

'Welcome to my home,' he said, jamming his crutches into his armpits and spreading his arms wide. 'I am Jamshid. I hope you have been treated well.'

It was such a surprise to hear him speaking English that I didn't respond immediately. He continued without waiting for an answer.

'It is unfortunate for all of us that you are here. It is unfortunate for you because you have been taken against your will, and it is unfortunate for us that we have to do such things.'

'Unfortunate? What are you going to do with me? Why am I here?' I tried to get to my feet, but Pakol stood over me.

'Let her up, Abdul-Bari,' said the older man.

I glared at Abdul-Bari as he backed away, and rose to my feet. I was the same height as the older man, and stared him in the eye. He looked away, refusing to meet my gaze.

'You are upset, but please be assured that you will not be harmed here. We think of you as our guest.'

'Is this how you people treat guests? Kidnap them, bring them to... to medieval villages in remote mountains?' I gestured with my hands, making my burqa balloon around me. 'I'm a prisoner.' Now my hands were tight fists. I wanted to hit someone.

A noise from outside made him turn.

'Ah,' he said, 'I believe dinner is on its way. Please, sit.'

For a few moments I continued to glare at him, but when I smelled the food, I sank to my knees, suddenly hungry.

A young girl in a grubby shalwar kameez came in carrying a tray with a large plate of meat and another of bread. She wore a scarf pulled loosely over her head, but her face was uncovered. She smiled shyly at me and backed out of the room again. What was the etiquette here? Should I remove my burqa? I certainly couldn't eat with it on.

'Eat,' said Jamshid, and he sat down on the other side of the tray. Abdul-Bari went to the door and called someone.

'Come, Tariq, sit,' said Jamshid as Turban entered.

I pulled my burqa up and threw the front over my head so that it sat like a long veil down my back. Half of me waited for the blow and the order to cover again, the other half couldn't have given a damn what they thought, these terrorists, these kidnappers. None of the men reacted.

I could breathe freely again, and even though the lamp was filling the room with pungent fumes I took a deep lungful of air. The food smelled good too. The men tucked in quickly, eating with their hands, deftly picking up the meat in the bread and tossing it into their mouths, chewing noisily, mouths open. I took a piece of bread and dipped it in the gravy. The young girl and two other women in drab kameezes and scarves crept into the room and sat quietly against the wall, watching. When the men had eaten, they left and I heard the click of a lighter as they lit their after-dinner cigarettes, and then the scent of tobacco wafted into the room.

My guts churned, not from the food but from fear. My whole body was shaking as I sat wondering if they were out there deciding what they were going to do to me.

The women edged towards the plate and ate the leftovers in silence, shovelling the food into their mouths and mopping up the gravy with the bread until the plate was clean.

I watched, pitying them eating only leftovers.

'Thank you for the meal. Do any of you speak English?' I asked as they started to clear away. My voice was tight, high-pitched.

The youngest smiled at me again, but said nothing, and the other two bolted for the door.

Not wanting to be left alone, I followed them out into the courtyard. I saw the women disappear into another hut, and turned to see where the men were. I heard the jabbing speech of Abdul-Bari, and Jamshid replying softly, but I didn't understand a word.

The night sky was a huge black canvas for thousands of stars and a sliver of moon, bordered by the denser bulk of the jagged mountains at the bottom, but reaching up to infinity. I'd never seen anything like it. Looking up, I turned a full 360 degrees, almost overbalancing as the sheer scale disorientated me.

'It is magnificent, yes?' Jamshid had appeared by my side.

'Amazing,' I agreed. I wanted answers from this kidnapper, so had to be civil.

'I never tire of it.'

'How did you learn to speak English so well?'

He looked at me and then away again. 'So many questions. But I owe it to you to answer them, to help you understand. And I enjoy conversing in English, it is a fine language. I went to school in Lahore, English medium, as was common then and on to university in London in the days when scholarships were still handed out like sweets to ex-colonials. I think Britain felt a sense of guilt for leaving the subcontinent and felt she should still educate us. I do not know if that is true, but I benefited from your government's largesse.'

'What made you come back here?'

'My family is from here. My father thought to better himself by leaving and seeking work elsewhere. He died a rich man but a lonely one. I think it is better to live poorly among family than to live richly among strangers. And, as you say, this place is amazing. It is the gift of Allah.'

His mention of Allah caused my guts to sink.

'Are you with the Taliban?'

'No, we are not.'

'Who then – some other terrorist organisation?'

Jamshid chuckled.

'You think it's funny? I'm funny? I haven't done anything to you or your people, but if you're going to kill me, why don't you just do it now, get it out of the way.' It was more of a whimper than a challenge.

Jamshid looked at me and there was compassion in his eyes. Another trick.

'We are not going to kill you. You are worth more to us alive. Probably in your country you believe that all who live here are religious extremists who fight in the name of Allah, and who want to return society in Afghanistan back to the days of the Prophet, but you must not trust everything you read in your newspapers. We are all Muslim, but we are not all, how do you say it? – cut from the same cloth.'

'Are we in Afghanistan then?'

I caught the hint of his smile in the starlight. 'The people who live here acknowledge no border. We are all of one tribe,

Pashtuns, and there is neither need nor desire for a border that keeps us apart from our brothers. No one bothers us here. The area, as you no doubt experienced today, is difficult to access, impossible to police, and that is the way we like it. Not that we are bad people, but we have our own laws and we live by them.'

'Pashtunwali,' I said.

'Yes, you've heard of it. Then you know that as our guest, we will not harm you. It is one of the pillars of our lives that we look after those who come to us, by whatever means.'

I could feel myself getting angry again. By whatever means. Kidnapping.

Taking a couple of deep breaths, I said, 'So even if an enemy came to you, you'd have to look after them?'

'Yes. It is so. If anyone asks for our protection, we have to give it. When they leave we can kill them.'

'What?'

'Do not worry, I was only joking with you.'

'Well don't. It wasn't funny.'

'Apologies.' He made an awkward bow. 'I know that in your country, we who live on the border are said to be lawless and violent. I hope that you will learn that this is not the truth. You foreigners have no idea of how we live our lives, nor any right to tell us what to do, as we do not presume to tell you how to run your country.'

He spoke with such authority.

'Are Tariq and Abdul-Bari your sons?'

'No, they are the sons of my cousin. They are like sons to me, and they are my blood. They also want only what is best for all concerned. Like all of us, they want to be left alone to live their lives peacefully.'

I let the irony of his statement go. 'How does gun smuggling and kidnapping people help with that?' I asked, trying to keep my voice even in spite of the fact that my fists were clenched and my heart was thudding.

Jamshid looked up at the sky, the thousands of stars twinkling overhead, and stroked his beard. 'There are many ways to peace. We fight for it. Talk is not the way of the Pashtun. We believe in an eye for an eye. It is badal, vengeance, that is our code and our honour.'

'Doesn't bode well for peace then,' I said.

'Perhaps you are right.' He nodded, still looking up at the sky. 'Allah will decide.'

'Why am I here?'

He glanced at me and then away again, adjusted his crutches and folded his arms over his chest.

I waited.

'The mujahideen always need money to continue their fight.'

'Will you please stop talking in riddles and just answer my question – what am I here for?'

He sighed. 'For a ransom. That is all.'

'That's all? It may be all to you, but what about me? What about the others you've taken? What if no one pays the ransom? I'm not rich, I don't know wealthy people.'

Then I thought. I had been kidnapped just after finding my father. Was that it? He wasn't rich by Western standards, as far as I could tell, but Saleem thought he was.

'You must find Dr Faisal Choudhry and ask him for the ransom. He will pay.'

Jamshid nodded and gave a small smile. 'All will be well.'

I could only hope so. I looked around at the dark outlines of the mountains, at the plains I knew were down below even though I couldn't see them. I shuddered. It would be so easy to 'lose' someone here.

'Until then, I give you my word as a Pashtun that no harm

will come to you.' He placed a hand over his heart, but didn't look at me.

The night seemed to be drawing in. The stars didn't seem so bright, and the moon was hidden behind a cloud. I pulled my burqa, still draped round my shoulders like a cloak, closer around me. I was this man's captive – could I trust his words?

He looked at me, and then gestured toward the smaller building that the women had disappeared into earlier. 'I think we should retire. You have a long day of travelling ahead of you.'

'A long day? Aren't I staying here, in this village?'

'No, you must go with Abdul-Bari. You are his responsibility now.'

'But this is closer to Peshawar...'

'I am sorry, but it is not possible.'

'Do any of the others speak English?' I asked, trying to delay our parting further. Perhaps if I could keep him talking I could somehow persuade him to let me stay there.

He looked surprised at the question. 'Of course. All of them. I believe it is important so I have taught my whole family, and Tariq and Abdul-Bari also. They lived with me for some time when they were young, when their father couldn't feed them because of the fighting. Now, you really must get some sleep.'

My spirits fell at the thought of leaving, of being even further away from Peshawar and any sense of safety.

I crept into the women's hut. The lamp was still lit, but the two older women were already asleep. Only the girl was awake.

'Hello,' I whispered. 'I'm Laila. What's your name?'

'Jawana,' she answered shyly.

'What a beautiful name. How old are you?'

'Thirteen. How old are you?' She giggled and covered her mouth with her hand.

'I'm twenty-seven. Is that funny?'

'No, but it was not polite to ask. I am sorry.'

'I don't mind at all. Are the others your sisters?' I nodded towards the sleeping women.

Jawana almost woke them up with her laughter, only stifling it when one of them sighed and turned over in her sleep.

'No, Shahnaz is my mother.' She pointed to the woman closest to her. 'And Narges is my father's sister.'

It was my turn to laugh. 'Oops. They don't look that old. Do you have brothers and uncles?'

'Yes, but the older ones are fighting. My father is only here because he can't fight anymore.'

'What happened?'

'He stepped on a mine and his leg was blown off. It happened three years ago. He was very angry for a long time, but now he is happy again.'

'How so?'

'He found his purpose. Alhamdullilah.' She yawned and stretched.

I wanted to ask what sort of purpose it was that allowed for kidnapping, but it wasn't her fault, not her decision. She yawned again.

'Time for sleep,' I said, and she smiled, turned over and her breath settled almost immediately into a gentle snore.

I turned the lamp off but lay awake for a long time. Would Faisal pay the ransom? Would he have enough money? How much was I worth to these people anyway? A thousand pounds, ten thousand, a million? My chest contracted when I thought of him. He would have tried to call, and got no answer. He would be worried. I thought of his face at our last farewell, his words of love but instead of being comforted, I only felt further away, more desolate.

Would they also contact Mum for money? I couldn't bear the thought of her hearing about it, being asked to pay money she didn't have, could never get, to rescue me from these people. Did the British government pay ransoms? Not for me, that was for sure.

I must have slept, because I was awoken before dawn by the call to prayer. 'Allahu Akbar' sung by a solitary voice which became multiple voices as it echoed around the mountains. It was beautiful, haunting, menacing.

I was alone in the hut, so I went to the door, and saw Jamshid, Tariq, Abdul-Bari and some young boys performing their prayers in the courtyard. The women were praying in the opposite corner. My body ached from the travel the day before and from sleeping on a rope cot with only a blanket to stop the strings digging into me. I wanted a shower, a proper toilet and food I recognised. I wanted to be in familiar places where people did normal things. I wanted to be home.

Wiping away tears, I went out to join the others. The men had finished their prayers and were chatting over their first cigarette of the day. Jawana was skipping down the hill with the water pots. The women I'd shared a hut with were heating tea in a pan over an open fire, headscarves on and faces covered. Both looked away when I squatted next to them so I got up again and walked to the edge of the building.

There I stopped. What I had failed to see in the dark was a steep drop to a wide plain beneath the village, and then wave after wave of mountains, fading in pastel shades into the distance. I gaped, open-mouthed.

Already at this hour, young boys were herding goats down the hill and women were toiling up with water, or descending with baskets on their backs and scythes in their hands to go and work in the fields that formed verdant terraces down that side of the mountain. I walked to a rocky outcrop and sat watching until someone called.

Back at the compound, I ate naan and drank tea. Several

mules had appeared and were tethered in one corner, watching us with sad eyes and twitching ears.

'So, here is your transport,' said Jamshid, gesturing at the animals.

'What? Those?'

'Indeed. Actually, they will be carrying the cargo. You will be leading them. Where you are going there are no roads, only narrow tracks.' He spoke rapidly to Tariq who had come out of the house carrying blankets, and then called for Narges. 'You must borrow some clothes. My sister will give you something. Walking in a burqa is impossible in these mountains, but you must be dressed to blend in to the scenery. Keep your burqa at hand, however. You may need it if you meet others.'

Narges appeared, looking acutely uncomfortable, listened to Jamshid as he spoke to her, neither making eye contact, and then gestured for me to follow her. In the women's hut, she opened a chest and took out a plain brown shalwar kameez in coarse, heavy cotton, and a large beige scarf, then she left me to change.

The clothes smelled of dung and sweat. Once again I yearned for home, clean clothes, washing powder. Once again, I pulled myself together and got on with what had to be done. Leaving behind the pretty shalwar kameez I'd bought in Peshawar, I changed into my 'camouflage costume'. I was at the mercy of these people, and if I ever wanted to see home again, my only choice was to go along with whatever they wanted.

By the end of the day, my feet were bloody, I was exhausted and ached all over, but I was still alive. We'd walked miles along narrow ledges leading the sure-footed donkeys and their cargo of weapons wrapped in blankets and tied on securely. Twice,

Abdul-Bari had ordered me to put on my burqa when he saw people approaching, and each time I'd played the voiceless, subservient woman, keeping my head down and waiting patiently while they had long conversations I couldn't understand, wishing at the same time that I could beg them to take me back to Peshawar and safety.

On the positive side, Jamshid had told Tariq and Abdul-Bari to practise their English on me, and although they didn't answer my questions about what they were going to do with me, they did tell me a bit about the area we were in and that it would take three days in all to get to their village from Peshawar.

The mountains, which looked barren from afar actually had a spattering of juniper and stunted birch trees. The scenery from high up in the mountains was heart-stopping, and I found it difficult to remain angry surrounded by such beauty. The reality, when we descended to the plains was a different matter. The brown mountains gave way to valleys where twisted fruit trees and shrivelled crops struggled to grow in parched soil. Willow-lined streams that might sometimes have been full were now turgid, sludge-filled ponds, and when I slipped my sandals off to soothe my feet, the water was warm and offered little relief.

'Drought,' said Tariq, shaking his head sadly. 'Usually at this time of year this is like – how you say it? Fruit basket.'

'How long's it been like this?' I asked.

'Since some years.'

Abdul-Bari looked to the sky. 'And no rain coming.'

We carried on, across the valley, approaching a village only to find that the whole place was deserted. Several houses had been bombed.

'Americans,' he said, filling his water bottle at the well. He spat on the ground.

'Recently?' I asked.

'Since last time we came through – a few days before.'

'Where is everyone?' I didn't dare look around in case I was confronted with dead bodies lying in the rubble. Fear made me tremble.

Tariq looked towards the mountains. 'In the caves, up there.'

I followed his gaze towards the mountains, imagining people cowering in the caves having lost their homes and I didn't care. It was war and British lives were also being lost.

'What will they do now?' I asked.

'They will rebuild. They have done it before, they will do it again.'

'And they will keep fighting?' Hadn't they learned anything?

'Of course. Now, we will go.'

As we went, we picked a few hard apricots and peaches from the trees in the orchard and munched on them as we climbed back up into the mountains.

That night, we stayed in another village, high up, overlooking their terraces of vegetables and corn. Tariq and Abdul-Bari disappeared to talk to the men as soon as we got there, and I was left to the mercy of the women, who spoke no English and were far bolder that Jamshid's family, staring at me and making comments to each other. I may not have spoken the language but it was clear what they thought of me. I was pushed into a corner in the small, windowless room with chicken and goat shit all over the floor, and a fire in one corner over which they cooked naan and a chicken stew. When it was ready, one of the young girls took it to the men, and half an hour later, we got the leftovers, which included the head and gizzard of the chicken, a few vegetables, and not much else. I scraped the gravy off my plate with half a naan and lay on a blanket on the floor to sleep still feeling hungry. I was too tired to think of anything but my stomach, which was a relief, since I'd spent a lot of the day fantasising about Faisal paying my ransom so I could get back to Peshawar, and what I'd do to Saleem if ever I saw him again.

With my feet bound in scraps of fabric and my sandals tied on with string, we set off just after morning prayers. Every muscle ached, my hips hurt from sleeping on the hard earthen floor, and the stench of chicken shit was still in my nostrils. This was a village that could do with bombing.

'We must make our village by nightfall. We have far to go today,' said Abdul-Bari as soon as we were out of earshot.

'How far?' I asked, my feet already bleeding through the binding.

'Ten hours, maybe more.'

I groaned, feeling beaten already.

We trudged down into the valley along rock ledges that threatened to spill us over the edge at any moment. One false step and we would have plummeted to our deaths. The mules were calm, but I was terrified.

'Are you all right?' Tariq asked after I stumbled and let out a shriek.

'I'm okay,' I said, holding on tightly to the donkey I was leading.

But I wasn't okay. How could I be?

'We take five minutes.' Abdul-Bari crouched on the ground. Somehow we'd reached the valley safely. Tariq helped himself to some fruit and I drank from a trickling spring.

We sat on the dry grass at the edge of a field of stunted corn. I wanted to lie down and close my eyes, but the men seemed tense and alert.

Tariq looked up into the sun, squinting.

I looked at him, wondering what he thought, what those dark-blue, deep-set eyes had seen. He had an aquiline nose and a straggly beard. I guessed he was about my age, but it was hard to tell, his skin was leathery from being outdoors most of his life. Before he started fighting, and smuggling weapons over the border, he would have farmed the family plot like the young boys did now. I got the impression he'd rather be there still. He lacked the harshness of his brother – I could imagine him whiling away the hours under a tree reading a book. He'd had some schooling, mostly when he was living with Jamshid. Then his father had decided that getting an education wasn't important for a mujahid and his father's word was law. Being a mujahid was his duty and his honour, he'd said.

Abdul-Bari said something in Pashtun, and Tariq sprang up.

'Come – we have to go. Quick.'

I struggled to my feet, grabbed the two mules that I was leading, and stumbled after the men who were heading for some large boulders at the edge of the dusty fields. As I wedged myself in between them, and pulled the mules as far out of sight as I could, I heard the chop-chop-chop of a helicopter. It sounded like it was right over us already, but Tariq whispered that it was still some distance away and that the mountains made the sound carry.

'You must stay very still. One movement and they will know where we are and they will kill us. They do not wait to see who is there.'

I kept as still as I could. I was so scared I could hardly breathe. The helicopters got louder and louder until I could feel the thwump of the rotor blades in my whole body. And then all seven levels of hell erupted around us. The mules got spooked, and one broke free and cantered out of the shelter of the rocks. The terrified beast wove an erratic path through the field, and in a matter of seconds, there was an almighty crack and there was a crater the size of a tennis court where the mule had been. After that, the mayhem lasted for what seemed like hours as the field and the rocks where we were hiding were strafed with round after round of gunfire, and the ground seemed to bounce and shake around us, pouring dirt and dust into every orifice. Shards of rock flew past my face as one of the boulders was pulverised.

And then it was all over. The helicopters turned and flew off.

We left our shelter on shaky legs. I couldn't hear anything and my ears felt like they were pulsing in time with the gunshots. The air was brown with dust and debris. The remaining mules were flaring their nostrils and pulling at their leads, eyes rolling in fear. Looking at the devastation, I felt angry and scared.

'Are you well?' asked Tariq, not quite looking at me. My hearing was coming back, but his voice sounded like it was coming from far away.

'I'm okay,' I replied, 'But you are not – there's blood–'

'It is nothing.' He tried to move his arm and winced.

'It's not nothing. Let me have a look.'

Tariq looked at his brother who nodded, then he sat on the dirt and pulled his sleeve up. There was a deep cut on his upper arm, still oozing blood.

I gazed around for something to bind it with.

'Can you cut a bit off one of the blankets?' I asked Abdul-Bari.

Minutes later, when Tariq's arm was bandaged as well as I could manage, I asked how the Americans knew we were there.

'They fly sorties all the time. When they saw the animal they knew there would be people close. They are afraid so they try to show that they are mightier than us, but they are not, and they do not know our land. They will not beat us. They are looking for bin Laden. Many people are killed,' he said.

'And what do you think of him? Bin Laden, I mean.'

Tariq didn't answer. Abdul-Bari said, 'He is rich. He has big ideas, but he is not an Afghan.'

'What's that meant to mean?'

Abdul-Bari turned away, finished with the conversation. I looked at Tariq for clarification, but he just shrugged.

'So you'll win this war? Make the Americans and their allies leave? How will you do that when they have helicopters and bombs and you have little guns?'

'Do not underestimate the power of the little gun when Allah is guiding our hands. We will win. Come, we must go – we cannot stay here longer. And we will have to keep to the hills now where the cover is better,' said Abdul-Bari, tugging on the reins of his two mules.

He strode off. I grabbed the mules and had to jog to keep up, wincing at every step.

I have no idea how we made it – as the afternoon wore on I was almost delirious with tiredness and my feet felt as if they'd been shredded. I would happily have walked off the path into thin air, but as the light began to fade, we reached the men's village. It hung halfway up a mountain, above a wide plain, as so many villages seemed to. It was safer, they said, and having seen the valley being destroyed earlier, I could see why. Plus, the houses blended so well with the mountain backdrop, being made of baked mud bricks, I hadn't actually noticed the village until we were almost in it.

11

It was late afternoon, the shadows deep and dark. Night fell quickly in the mountains, and it wasn't far off. Men and children rushed out to greet us when they heard us coming, and Tariq and an old man greeted each other.

'Assalamu alaikum.'

'Wa alaikum assalam.'

I stood near a wall watching. It seemed that in this village there were no women. Not one had come out when we arrived and I didn't see any watching us from the shadows or the doorways. It felt strange and frightening. I pulled my burqa out of my bag and put it on as quickly and quietly as I could.

The older man looked in my direction and gestured for me to come over.

'This is my father, Izat Ali Mohmand. He says thank you for binding my arm.' Tariq translated.

'Tell him that's okay,' I said, but kept my head down, making no eye contact.

Izat said something else.

'He says that you will not be locked up but if you try to leave you will be beaten, but it is better to stay because if you escape you will die in the mountains. He also says you are foreign so do not have to wear the cover,' Tariq said.

'I'll keep the burqa on for now.' I felt safer under the veil. In prison I'd been too visible, my every movement watched. I couldn't take a deep breath without the guards knowing about it. Here I would be invisible. They would know nothing about me I didn't want them to know. Being open and trusting had got me into this situation. At the thought of Saleem, I wanted to scream in anger.

'Tariq – where are the women?' I asked, to distract myself.

'They are doing their work in the fields or in the house. I must go to see my uncle now. Stay here.' Tariq, his father and Abdu-Bari headed down the dusty track.

I sank to a squat in the shade of one of the houses. Some of the older boys had taken the mules and were unloading the weapons carefully. The younger children had all run after Abdul-Bari and Tariq, pulling on their clothes and chattering loudly to get attention. I was hot, tired, thirsty and filthy, daydreaming about brushing my teeth when a little girl approached shyly. She stopped about two metres away.

'Hello,' I said.

She stared.

'Assalamu alaikum,' I tried.

She giggled, perhaps at my accent.

She was about six, small, with dusty, knotted hair and blue eyes. I tried one of my schoolteacher tactics – when I wanted the children to pay attention to something, I would pretend to be totally absorbed by whatever I was looking at. I lifted the burqa slightly, picked up a pebble and got focused. Sure enough, within a few minutes, the girl was right beside me, trying to see what was so interesting.

'My name is Laila,' I said quietly. I raised the burqa over my head so that she could see me and repeated my name, pointing at myself.

'What is your name?' I pointed to her. She kept looking at the pebble and said nothing.

'Laila,' I tried again, a hand on my chest, 'and–' I touched her on the shoulder. She pulled away as if I'd hit her. Was touch not allowed even between females?

When Tariq and Abdul-Bari came back a few minutes later, I asked them what the girl's name was.

'She is Farida, the daughter of my sister,' said Abdul-Bari.

'That is my middle name. Can you teach me some words in Pashto so that I can speak to her?' I asked.

Tariq laughed. 'First you kick us and try to run away, and now you want to learn our language so that you can talk to the children?'

'I'm a teacher,' I said, 'and they have nothing to do with kidnapping and fighting. Do they go to school?'

'Some of them. The boys. They go to the school in another village an hour from here.'

'What about the girls?'

'They do not need school,' said Abdul-Bari.

I bit back my response.

Abdul-Bari laughed and spat in the dirt.

The men disappeared into a hut and I was left with the women who had returned from the fields. At dinner I tried to speak to the young woman next to me, but she turned away, as did all the others. It was as if I didn't exist to them.

I could hear the murmur of voices from the men's hut, and wondered if they were talking about what to do with me. And I thought about Faisal and how long it would take him to gather my ransom, or if he had called the police and was even now trying to find me. He must be frantic with worry. Perhaps he had found

Saleem and taken him to the police and they were interrogating him. For the first time I wished I'd travelled on my own passport and Interpol or some other international agency were trying to find me. There was no use dwelling on it though. I closed my eyes and imagined my reunion with Faisal, and found myself smiling.

The night wore on and still the men talked.

I was almost asleep sitting up before an old woman showed me to the women's quarters and pointed to the corner. I crept over to the thin mattress and pulled the stinking blanket over me.

In the morning, I woke to find Farida curled up against me. It seemed I'd made a friend after all.

As I got up she awoke, smiled, and put her hand on her own chest.

'Farida,' she said in a huskier voice than I would have expected.

'Farida,' I repeated and smiled. My first student.

We went out into the courtyard together. I pointed upward. 'Sky,' I said.

'Sky,' she said.

I pointed down. 'Ground.'

Everything I said, she repeated.

After breakfast of bread, nuts and something that looked like lumpy yoghurt but tasted sour, Tariq came to find me.

'My father sent me. He says that you will teach the boys in the evenings when they have done their work. Their school was bombed some days ago, so you can teach them here.'

'Bombing? Will this village be bombed?' I looked up into the sky half expecting to see the planes approaching. Fear clamped my chest tight.

'They look for Osama. They bomb the villages that do not help. We will go to the caves when the time comes.' He turned and pointed up the mountain.

It was hardly reassuring, but Tariq carried on as if he'd allayed my fears. 'My father says it is good for the boys to learn some English so that they can understand what the Americans say if me and Abdul-Bari are killed. We do not have time to teach them.'

'Only the boys?'

'Only the boys.'

My spirits dropped further. I wanted to teach the girls too, and I didn't want to teach at all just for them to be able to kill more people. I didn't want to be a part of their war.

I also had to admit that my sinking spirits might have had a tiny bit to do with the idea of Tariq being killed. I'd only known him a few days, but I'd come to appreciate his quietness, the way he played with the children, his respect for the elders in the village, men and women, and the fact that he actually spoke to me so that I didn't feel so alone and afraid. Abdul-Bari had clearly decided to leave the communication to his brother, and hardly said a word to me. Tariq was a killer, a smuggler and a kidnapper – he wasn't a friend, but he was the closest thing to it in my situation.

'I'm sure my ransom will be paid soon so there may not be time for too much English, but please tell your father I'll do what I can. Can I just ask one more question?'

'Ask.'

'Why do the women here wear only a scarf?'

'Only Taliban say cover the whole body but now they have gone.' He walked away, and I was left standing in the courtyard.

If I wasn't to teach until the evening, I had the whole day to fill. The children had all disappeared to do whatever work they had to do, and the men had left the village with their Kalashnikovs and ammunition slung over their shoulders, rocket launchers too. I tried not to think of people being killed.

A noise came from below that sounded like humming. I

walked over to a spot between two boulders from where I could see down into the valley. The women were cutting grass with scythes and had started singing. One woman would sing a few lines, then the others would take up the song, the swinging of the scythes keeping the rhythm going. Farida and some of the other young children were with them, gathering the cut grass into bundles and tying them with more grass. The sun shone hotly, and it must have been back-breaking work, but they kept going, wiping the sweat with their headscarves as it dripped into their eyes. With nothing else to do, I decided to go and offer my help – it was either that or go mad doing nothing. I made my way down the stony path, sliding as much as walking, and arrived, panting slightly, wiping my hands on my kameez.

'Assalamu alaikum,' I said.

The singing stopped. Most of the women didn't even acknowledge my presence, but one of the older ones looked up, eyes narrowed, her mouth a thin line of contempt.

I tried to mime cutting the grass, and pointed to myself but the woman shook her head and got back to her cutting, so I went over to Farida to see if I could help there. I was amazed that a child as young as her was so dexterous. As I watched her gather and tie the grass, I thought of the children I'd taught in England who, at her age, would be out playing. I bent to help sweep the grass into a pile.

Farida and the other children immediately straightened and looked at me. And then she came over to me and took the stalks out of my hands. One of the women said something to her without looking up from her work and Farida took hold of the hem of my kameez and led me away, back towards the village. I wasn't allowed to help, that was clear.

Farida left me to go back down to the valley and I sat in the shade of a scrawny bush wondering what to do. In the end I planned what I'd teach the children and how to go about a lesson with no books and no paper to write on. Our classroom would be the mountainside, and sticks and dirt would be our tools.

By the time the women and children came back up the hill, I was ready.

On that first day, only a young boy called Zalmay turned up, but Farida and another girl, Latifa, sat listening a few yards away. It was a start. I taught Zalmay how to say 'My name is...' and count to ten.

When the men came back, muddy, dishevelled, their cartridge belts empty, Farida ran to them.

'Hello, my name is Farida,' she said, and burst into giggles. Tariq lifted her onto his shoulders, ruffled Zalmay's hair and smiled at Latifa. His bandage was bloody, but he seemed not to notice his injury.

'My name is Tariq,' he said, and then added something in their language, and she smiled.

'I didn't ask the girls to come. They just listened.'

Tariq didn't respond.

'What did you do today?' I asked, shielding my eyes from the setting sun. I just needed to talk to someone and he was the only person who was prepared to speak to me.

'We destroyed a roadblock and some vehicles.'

He smiled, proud of what he'd done, while I wondered how many men had been hurt, and what for – a point made, an upper hand, a yard of ground gained?

Over the next few days, I observed the pattern of life in the village. Knowing that there was some routine made me feel less afraid somehow. The men fought in shifts. Just after dawn prayer, some would go off and only return for dinner and evening prayers. Others left after dinner and returned at sunrise. Some returned wounded, but I didn't care. They chose to fight, they took the consequences.

I was woken one night by gunfire in the distance and leapt up ready to wake the other women who were all still sleeping. Farida opened her eyes, and I pointed outside and mimed shooting a gun. She pointed into the distance, reassuring me that the fighting was far away, that the sound carried on the still air and ricocheted off the mountains. Then she pulled me onto the mattress again and stroked my back. I didn't sleep again that night.

Time passed, I don't know how long, but I became anxious about the ransom. Surely someone should've paid by now? Or were they asking so much that nobody could afford to free me? At least I wasn't being hurt, I was largely being ignored, and I was still alive. I was being fed, and came to believe that these people weren't going to kill me after all. I got through the days, each one feeling longer than the last.

The children came for their lesson after work, a few more each day, until even the older boys were attending. Sometimes Tariq would come and see how the English lessons were progressing, speaking a few words with the children and praising their skills. The reality was that Farida, even at her young age, was by far the brightest. She was like a sponge that soaked everything up so easily, even though she sat listening on the periphery pretending to draw in the dirt and I wasn't officially teaching her. Soon, some of the older boys realised that she knew more than them and started complaining. After that I had to be careful not to be seen to give her any attention, but it was hard – all teachers love a bright student, and Farida was so engaging. Sleeping next to me, curled around my body had become her habit, so I started and ended each day with her smile. It was the only comfort in a harsh life.

. . .

One morning Tariq and Abdul-Bari didn't go off with the other men. Instead, they fetched the mules from where they were tethered in the shade of some juniper bushes and readied themselves to leave.

'Are you going to Peshawar?' I asked.

'Yes,' said Abdul-Bari.

'How long will you be gone?'

'Several days. Maybe two weeks.'

'Has anyone paid my ransom?' It was clear that no one had, otherwise I'd be going back with them, but I had to ask.

'We will see,' said Tariq.

'What do you mean?'

Neither of them answered. Maybe they didn't know.

'Have you asked Dr Faisal Choudhry yet, like I told you? Go to him at the Nasir Teaching Hospital. He will pay for my release. Please, go and talk to him.'

The brothers looked at each other, and Abdul-Bari said something to Tariq.

'We will talk to him,' he said.

'Thank you. He'll find the money, I'm sure of it.'

Abdul-Bari and Tariq led the mules past me on their way out of the village.

With them gone, I was cut off from the rest of the villagers with no one to talk to or translate for me. None of the adults spoke to me, and the children had only told me a few words, mainly useless for conversation unless I wanted to say hello and goodbye, count to ten or name animals and plants. I was glad to teach my lessons in the afternoons, but still the days dragged. All I had to fill them was fantasies of Faisal handing over the money and me leaving this place forever.

I retreated under my burqa, sitting under a tree at the edge of the village for hours at a time. Bored beyond tears, I had to find something to fill my time, to make this waiting bearable. One day, when the women were in the fields below, I rolled my sleeves up and started cleaning the kitchen hut. I found a broom made of coarse dried grass, tied a rag over my face to stop myself gagging at the smell, and swept out all the chicken and goat shit, piling it in a corner of the yard to use on the vegetable garden where corn, onions, cauliflowers and peppers were trying to grow. Then, using as little water as possible, I dampened down the earthen floor to reduce the dust while I stacked the bags of flour, lentils and dried beans neatly in the corner. I looked around. What next? There was nothing else in the kitchen, so I went on to the next job. The manure was steaming in the hot sun. I found a shard of pottery to carry it in, scooped it up and took it to the garden, spreading it carefully around the plants and then trickling some precious water on top.

I was sweating when I'd finished, and went back into the courtyard to find some shade. It had been at least an hour since I had thought about Faisal and freedom. Sitting against the wall of the main house, I heard a faint moan. And then a louder one. Following the sound, I went round the back of the kitchen to a smaller hut, and there, lying on a thin mattress on the floor, was a young woman I'd seen around the village. She had a hand over her face and her knees drawn up to her very pregnant belly.

'Assalamu alaikum,' I said quietly, not wanting to frighten her. She groaned in response, and tried to roll onto her side. It was then that I noticed that the mattress was wet. I knew nothing about childbirth, but I knelt beside her, and wiped the sweat from her forehead with the bottom of my kameez. Suddenly she shrieked, her eyes wide with fear, and started breathing fast. What should I do? I reckoned the baby was on its way, and I didn't have time to go and get anyone, even if I could have explained what was happening. The woman looked young and strong, so I had to trust that she'd be okay. I rushed out to fill a small pot with water, and found a blanket which I tried to push under her so that she wasn't lying in the wet, and then washed her face and hands, and gave her a sip of water. Another contraction swept through her and she gripped my hand so tightly I could hardly feel my fingers when she let go. And then another and another, closer and closer together. With the next, her knees parted and without thinking, I looked over. There was something between her thighs, lots of blood and a black thing: the head. I felt the panic rise. The place was filthy, how on earth would a healthy baby be born in these conditions? And then there was no more time to think, because with the next contraction, out came the shoulders and a minute later, the rest of the body slid out onto the blanket. It was a girl, with lots of dark hair and a scrunched-up little face. She looked so fragile I was scared to pick her up, but I had to. I almost dropped her she was so slippery from the blood and odd whitish substance that covered her, but I managed to place her on her exhausted mother's chest where she held her, counting her fingers and toes as I suspect every mother the world over does when they first meet their child. There was a lump in my throat as I watched them, but then she turned her head away and pushed the baby from her. I was too busy to think much of it as I saw that my work wasn't over yet. Something had to be done about the cord – wasn't it meant to be clamped and tied? What with? There was nothing in the room that would do, so I drew out the string that kept my shalwar up and tied it as tightly as I could round the slimy cord. Then what? I had nothing to cut it with. I was just trying to work out what to do when Ulicha arrived. She took one look at the situation, bent down beside the new mother, and cut through the cord with the scythe she'd been using down in the fields. Then she started rubbing the mother's belly hard, and the placenta, a red bloody shock of a thing, came out. She looked at me and nodded, which I took to mean that I'd done a good enough job, but was now dismissed.

Feeling emotional, I went outside and took some deep breaths. I'd just helped deliver a baby, a real live baby. Tears slid down my cheeks, and I found myself wishing that I could tell Faisal about it. He'd be so proud of me.

Nothing was made of the birth. No celebration, nobody even went to see the mother and baby. It may have been that childbirth was so run-of-the-mill here that it didn't warrant any special attention, but I felt sad – a new life had entered the world completely unacknowledged.

The days were long. I was lonelier amongst all these people whose customs I didn't understand than I had been in solitary confinement. It had been made clear to me that my efforts in the kitchen were unwelcome, and that I wasn't to interfere again. I ended up talking to the goats when they were in the yard, telling them about Faisal, and what our reunion would be like, although most of the time I didn't even have them for company as the younger boys took them to find grazing. The only time I felt useful was when I was teaching the children. I was a shwooneky (at least that's how it sounded). Teacher.

One day I was talking to myself, trying to remember the street names in Thirsk just to give myself something to do, when I heard an engine far away. For a moment I thought it was a car, and that I was home, safe in Yorkshire, but one look around me put paid to that fantasy. It was a plane. I started scanning the sky, remembering Tariq's warning about a bombing. There was no one around, they were all working away from the village. I looked up the mountain, searching the steep slopes for the caves we were to hide in, expecting the villagers to appear at any moment, running for their lives. Minutes went by and nothing happened. The plane flew over the village, dipped, turned, flew back again. I pulled myself out of sight, holding my breath, waiting for the carnage. Nothing. The plane flew away, heading into the sun. I started breathing again.

Then, several days after Tariq and Abdul-Bari had left, just as evening prayers were being performed, the whomp of helicopters reached us in the evening stillness. The men, several of whom were visitors wearing black turbans, stopped mid chant and looked at the skies. I followed their gaze but in the darkening sky, could see nothing. I wasn't too worried. Planes, drones and helicopters had buzzed the village every day since that first time and done nothing. But now the men grabbed their Kalashnikovs from the ground beside them, and shouldered them as they took cover behind walls and boulders. Several readied rocket launchers.

Izat shouted something, and the women and children started running. Farida took my hand, speaking urgently, and pulled me after the others, heading up the mountain. I stumbled after her, losing my sandals. We carried nothing, the only thought was to get to higher ground away from the village.

Someone shouted 'Allahu Akbar' and there was a sound like a hundred firecrackers igniting as they let off a round from a rocket launcher.

And then the hillside exploded in a deafening roar, the ground fracturing around us, trees splintering and uprooting with loud groans, branches and rocks and people flying through the air. I was thrown several feet to the side of the path we'd been following. Stunned, with blood dripping from cuts on my head and arms, I sat up and looked around, trying to breathe without choking on the dust-filled air while my eyes began to adjust to the gloaming again after the flares and flashes of the bombs. The helicopters were circling. Farida lay a few feet away, next to Izat's brother, Daoud who was groaning. On my other side were some women and children who were sitting looking dazed. I went to Farida. She was bleeding from a gash in her abdomen and was unconscious.

'Farida, keep breathing little one, just keep breathing.' I'd had my burqa round me like a cape and now took it off and pressed its folds into the wound, praying for the bleeding to stop. Daoud groaned again and vomited blood. When he tried to roll over, I saw that the back of his head was missing. He took another breath and then fell back onto the ground, eyes staring at the sky as if in disbelief.

I looked around again for any help that might be coming, but I was the only one who seemed able to move. I kept up a steady stream of desperate prayers to a god I didn't even believe in, and pressed the blood-soaked cloth more firmly to Farida's belly. Looking towards the village, I saw another bomb drop, felt its violence throughout my body as, lower down, the hillside starting slipping into the valley, taking with it more buildings, the vegetable garden, flattening the trees and bushes, leaving destruction where moments before there had been life. I clutched hold of a tree to prevent myself from being taken with it. Smoke from the burning trees, dust and dirt thrown high into the air forced their way into lungs and eyes and mouths.

'Come on, Farida, wake up,' I croaked.

A hand touched me on the shoulder. Ulicha was standing over me, her kameez bloodied, one side of her face red and swollen. She knelt beside Farida and put her ear to the little girl's mouth, then she straightened up and shook her head. At first I didn't register what she meant, but slowly it dawned on me.

'No,' I screamed. 'No, she can't be dead.' I picked up the inert little body, her head lolling on her neck and cradled her to me. 'No-no-no-no-no, please, no,' I croaked through sobs.

Ulicha tugged on my arm and gestured up the hill. We had to get to safety, and there were others to help, but I couldn't leave Farida there on her own. Gulping back tears of rage and grief, I put her down next to Daoud and placed his arm over her as if he was protecting her. Only then did I turn and as another bomb fell, followed Ulicha blindly up, up, up.

The next few days blurred into each other. I tried to clamp my mind and heart shut and get on with the business of looking after the injured. I was allowed to help only because there were so few who could. Ulicha directed us to wash and bandage wounds, offer food to those who could eat, and water to those who couldn't. Day by day, there were more deaths from the initial injuries or from the infections that set in. Izat was in a terrible condition, Sayyed, Ulicha's husband, died two days after the bombs fell. Latifa had lost an arm, and when an infection set in, it took only a few days to claim her. I lost count of the number of deaths.

Those men capable of wielding a shovel had dug shallow graves for the dead, or just piled the loosened earth on top of the bodies. Prayers were said, tears wept. Every time I stopped, I thought of Farida who had taken my hand to save me, and whom I hadn't been able to protect.

I was isolated in my grief. I couldn't tell anyone how sad I was, and I felt almost as if I had no right to feel so deeply when I had known her for such a short time, but Farida had worked her way into my heart. I was so angry at the senselessness of the attack, the waste of lives, the destruction of the village. The other survivors went about their work with a stoicism I tried to emulate. They had all lost family members, most of them more than one. It wasn't that they didn't feel anything, but rather that for those still living, staying alive was the priority. So we tended to the sick, went to the village to see what could be salvaged, lugged sacks of wheat and vegetables up the mountain to the caves where we had made our home. All hands were required, and finally I felt useful. We were joined in the harsh reality of getting on with life. And something had changed in the way the women treated me – a smile here and there, more space made for me when we ate, so that I was part of the circle rather than sitting outside it.

One evening, sitting by Farida's grave in the dark, I cried until I had no more tears and then sat talking to her. I told her how clever she'd been and the hopes I'd had for her, the love I'd felt for her.

'I don't know what's happened to me, Little One, but I hate the Americans who did this. It can't be right.'

I stopped, surprised by my own thoughts. How could I think such a thing? Looking about me, how could I not?

I climbed back up to the cave, crawled into a corner, and slept properly for the first time since the bombing.

The men and women who were able returned to work. The men started to rebuild the houses, making bricks out of mud, leaving them to dry in the sun, and the women went back into the valley to tend to the crops that were left and look for the animals that had fled. In the evenings, I was allowed to help get the fire lit for the meal, although I wasn't permitted to help prepare the food. I wondered if it was because I wasn't a Muslim – that non-believers touching the food was haram. It didn't matter. I was included to a greater extent than I had been, and that was fine by me.

I had washed Farida's blood out of my burqa after she was buried, but barely wore it anymore. Instead, I covered my head with a scarf like the other women, and pulled it across my face when there were men around. It was easier to look after the injured, but more than that, I no longer felt the need to hide.

Six days after the bombing I was bathing Izat's wounds when I heard someone behind me. Tariq and Abdul-Bari were back.

Abdul-Bari greeted his father and said something to him. Izat tried to talk, but his voice came out as a harsh wheeze.

'We heard that there had been bombing and came as quickly as we could. How is our father?' asked Tariq, 'and the others?'

'Your father will be all right but it will take some time. He was wounded in the chest and the stomach. He also has a broken leg. But he is strong. I think he'll make it. Others were not so lucky, as you will hear.'

'We will avenge these murders,' said Abdul-Bari, his jaw and fists tightly clenched.

I didn't respond, but innocent people had been killed and I began to understand the need for justice by whatever means.

'Thank you for what you are doing,' said Tariq, and then he and Abdul-Bari left to go and talk to the other men and assess the destruction in the village.

Later that night, after a meagre dinner, I went to find Tariq.

He was sitting on a rock near the mouth of the cave where his father lay sleeping on a blanket. I watched him for a moment before he saw me. There was a curl of hair on the nape of his neck. He turned and motioned for me to step a little closer.

'We brought with us what medical supplies we could, but I think they will not be enough.'

I nodded. I'd seen some of them – rolls of bandages with Russian writing on them and pictures of bloody wounds, bottles of drugs of uncertain origin, the script Arabic and Chinese.

He nodded towards his father and spoke in a whisper. 'He has been a fighter for so long. When he was young, he fought the Russians, and when they left, Afghan fought Afghan, then the Taliban and now the Americans. Never was he so badly hurt. He will recover entirely?'

'I think so, yes, but it will take a long time. I'm so sorry this happened.' I also spoke quietly. It gave our exchange a certain intimacy and I wondered if Tariq also noticed.

He looked at me, eyebrows raised.

'You are sorry? Did you order the attack, or drive the planes that dropped the bombs?'

'Of course not, but so many people were killed. It makes me sad and angry.'

'You do not have to be sorry. They are not your people.' He sounded surprised that I would feel anything for them.

'No, but I have been here for some time now, and I...' I couldn't explain it to myself, let alone Tariq.

'I like the children,' was all I said, and squeezed my eyes shut against the tears that waited to fall.

'Yes, the children,' he said. 'Inna lillahi wa inna ilaihi raji'un.'

'What does that mean?' It was what Faisal had said when I told him about Kamila.

'Surely we belong to Allah and to Him we shall return.'

'Amen,' I said, hoping that Kamila, Farida and the others were being looked after wherever they were. I thought that having a faith at a time like this would be a comfort, but I was just angry with any god that would allow innocent people to be slaughtered.

'So, what happens now?' I asked.

'What do you mean?'

'Well, you're back, the village has been destroyed, what do we do now?'

'We? You wish to help?'

'Of course. My father is Pashtun, did you know?'

'But you are British. Passport says so.'

'Is that important? Anyway, I'm stuck here – unless Dr Choudhry paid the ransom?'

He shook his head. 'Not yet.' He paused. 'But not long, I am sure of it.'

'Have you ever kidnapped anyone before? Do you know how the ransom thing works? You have to ask, you have to demand.'

'I have not.' Tariq remained calm.

My anger bubbled to the surface again, but it wasn't him I was angry with. It was Saleem, the smiling shit of a taxi driver who had said he was my friend and who had sold me out. I'd never trust my judgement of people again.

'It was wrong of those men to come to our village,' said Tariq, changing the subject.

'What? What are you talking about?'

'Sometimes when they have lost many men, the Taliban take refuge in the villages. They believe they will not be shot at because the Americans are not meant to bomb villages. Sometimes it works, other times, not. My father says that the night our village was bombed there were Talib here. It is they the bombs were for.'

I couldn't get any words out. Those bastards must have known that they were putting everyone in danger, and yet they sat there as calm as anything and ate dinner with Izat and the other men. And Izat must have known why they were there, and because of his principles, fed them anyway.

'Pashtunwali,' I muttered eventually.

'Yes,' said Tariq.

'None of them were among the injured. They must have just slithered away leaving the villagers to face the bombs.'

'It is their way,' said Tariq.

The final death toll from the bombing was thirty-six. Those left standing, eighty-seven, including me.

Every night when I crept into my corner of the cave to sleep on the dirt floor, I thought of Farida, and every morning I missed her smiling face. Yet in between, my dreams were filled with violence.

12

One day, I was down in the village tending the vegetables I'd planted after the bombing and I saw a tall, rangy man approach with a group of bedraggled men, Kalashnikovs and ammo belts slung over their shoulders. As they came closer, I covered my face with my scarf and stared.

'Asim? Asim Malik?'

He turned to see who had called him, and peered at me, trying to see the face behind the scarf.

'The only person here who would know my real name is Laila. So you are still here,' he said.

'What? How did you know I was here at all?'

He smiled. 'How do you think?'

'Saleem.'

He smiled. 'How are you, Laila? Do you still desperately want to understand your 'Pakistani side'? Do you wander round asking obvious questions of your fascinating Pakistani friends? "Oh, Kamila, what's that? Oh, Mrs Malik, this is so good, how do you make it?"' He spoke in a childish sing-song voice.

I reddened and my hands curled into fists. He hadn't changed at all, he was still a bully.

'Do you even know what happened to Kamila or how worried your parents are about you?' I asked.

He nodded. 'It is a shame about my sister, I thought she was... stronger.'

'You don't even sound sad!'

'There is no point in being sad. What has happened has happened.'

'She idolised you.'

'Yes, but now she is gone and I have work to do.'

'You're a psychopath.'

He looked up at the sky and scratched at his beard. 'Not true. Who was it that wrote and told you where to find your lover? That was kind, wasn't it?'

I gasped. 'You?'

He laughed. 'I knew you'd come running, you're so predictable. I told you just enough to get you interested. A little mystery is such good bait, don't you think? So you found him, and then it was all too easy for us.'

I wanted to cover my ears and beat Asim to a pulp at the same time.

He smiled. Abdul-Bari appeared and greeted him like an old friend.

I marched back up to the caves with hatred in my heart. Asim had got me into this. Saleem must have been working for him. And I hated Asim for another reason – he was right about me playing at being Pakistani in England, wanting to be like them, accepted by them. I had felt an empty space in my life then that I thought could be filled by putting the two halves of me together and making a whole.

~

Asim and his men stayed in a bombed-out house in the village for two days, resting up and talking to Izat and Abdul-Bari. I noticed that Tariq wasn't included in the talks, and although I didn't understand why he was excluded, I was glad he had nothing to do with Asim.

On the day they left, Asim came looking for me.

'If you make it back to England, tell my parents I am well.'

What did he mean, *if* I got home? I'd thought the ransom would be paid and I'd be released – was there a different plan now? I felt my heart beating in my throat.

'I said–'

'You should go and see them yourself. They're heartbroken about Kamila. Your mother hasn't worked since her death, and your father drifts about with no sense of purpose. Do you honestly think they'd be proud of you, rejoice in your victories in your little war over here that they don't understand or support? They just want their daughter back. I don't suppose you even care though.'

He took a step back as if he'd been slapped. His mouth opened, and then shut.

'You haven't given them a thought until now, have you?' I said.

'I have been called to the fight. My family would understand.'

'You don't believe that, or you wouldn't have told them that you work in Quetta.'

'I said that to protect them from the truth.'

'No. You said that because you're a coward. I will deliver no message from you. You have ruined their lives, and mine. Now fuck off.' I turned and walked away but he called after me.

'Your fate is in my hands. I told Izat he should sell you to the Taliban. He'd make more money that way.'

I felt the blood drain from my face and ice coiled round my insides.

'What–'

But Asim, having delivered his blow, laughed and walked away.

Later, Tariq stopped by as I sat by a scrubby bush trying to calm myself down.

'You knew that man?'

'Yes, from England.'

'But you did not like him.'

'No. He is the reason his own sister is dead.'

'It is sometimes the way that the outsiders are the most fanatical.'

'He said he told your father to sell me to the Taliban.' I wanted to cry and had to bite my lip.

'It is true. They have money and need women.'

I gasped and felt the blood drain from my face. An image of the black-turbaned men who had visited the village came to me. So pious, so sanctimonious. Such hypocrites.

'What did your father say?' My heart was pounding.

'He said no. That man, you call him Asim, but we know him as Mohammed, has respect for my father and he said he needs you here. I do not know if he will come back and try to change my father's mind, but for now you are safe.'

'Safe? Bombs fall, men want to sell me to the Taliban, and you say I'm safe?'

He smiled. 'Yes. We will keep you safe.'

I wanted to believe him, but it was hard. I didn't trust Asim as far as I could have thrown him. If he wanted something, he'd find a way to get it, respect or no respect. I was only safe until he worked out how to get what he wanted or until Izat and the others were better and no longer needed my nursing skills.

A sex slave for the Taliban or a womb to breed their children. I couldn't imagine anything more horrific.

From that day on I kept a lookout for Asim's return and wondered where I could hide if he came. I couldn't sleep, I hardly ate. I only felt safe when Tariq was around, even though I knew that he would not be a part of any decision that was made about me, and that ultimately, he would have to go along with whatever Izat decided.

And then Tariq and Abdul-Bari left again for Peshawar to stock up on medical supplies and weapons since so many had been lost in the bombing. I was again plunged into silence and left with my own circular thoughts.

Abdul-Bari and Tariq were gone only a week and arrived back exhausted. I had just taken Izat's dinner to him when Tariq came and pulled the curtain aside. When he saw me he smiled, but knelt by his father to greet him first. I waited outside the cave to speak to him.

'How are you?' I asked as he passed me.

He paused mid-stride. 'I am well.'

'How was the journey?'

'It was what it was. Tomorrow we take the weapons to the outpost to restock.'

'Outpost?'

He bit his bottom lip and said no more.

'I thought you just went out and hoped to find Americans to kill.'

I was shocked. I'd imagined the men hiding behind boulders and picking off anyone in uniform that went past. The idea of an outpost made it sound too organised, too planned. I'd started seeing the villagers as the victims, the poor people who were only trying to protect their own. In spite of all the evidence before me, I had closed my eyes to the fact that they were ruthless killers. Willing participants in the game.

The next day started off the same as all the others. Dawn prayers over, the women and children went to the fields, exhausted-looking men came back from fighting. Tariq, Abdul-Bari and several others were laden down under the weight of weapons and ammunition as they left the village. When the sun was high in the sky I heard bombs dropping somewhere in the distance. It was difficult, in the mountains, to tell which direction the sound was coming from, and there was no one else around to ask, so I got on with mending my kameez, which was already patched to within an inch of its life. Flies buzzed about lazily in the hot sun. The air was still.

I was wondering what to do next to fill my time when a young man ran into the village and dropped to his knees before Izat. He spoke to him urgently, and Izat tried to get up, falling back onto his blanket with a frustrated growl. Then he barked some orders, and the young man went to wake up the night fighters who appeared, bleary-eyed, pulling their pakols onto their heads.

The men left and I sat staring after them. From far off I heard gunfire, bombs dropping. The day was punctuated with the sounds of war.

Hours later, Abdul-Bari returned and went straight to Izat. He spent some time with him, and then he spoke to Ulicha who started wailing.

He passed me on his way to his cave.

'Where's Tariq?' I asked.

'Dead.' He didn't stop.

My guts twisted. Tariq had been the closest thing I had to a friend in this nightmare. I walked a little way from the caves and found a tree to sit under, and gave myself up to thoughts of the people I had lost.

Abdul-Bari and all the other men who were able left the cave after Fajr prayer the next morning looking grim.

I continued helping with the injured in the caves. Izat seemed to have shrunk in on himself, his grief for his son evident in his body as well as in the tears that wet his cheeks. I wanted to tell him how sad I was that Tariq had died, that I had liked and respected him, but all I could do was wipe his face and help him drink some goat's milk.

Life went on. When I could, I held lessons for the children, and in the evenings, some of the younger women also sat nearby, but without Farida's husky voice repeating my words, and Tariq listening in, the lessons seemed pointless.

Some days passed with no missions. The men finished rebuilding the houses, and at the end of the week, we were able to move back down the mountain into the village. Izat was the only person who had to be carried, although some were still using my home-made crutches.

One day after morning prayers, Izat took a few tentative steps outside his house and sat on a stool in the sun. The men seemed restless, pacing and drawing hard on their cigarettes. Most of the women went, as usual, to the fields. The children who were too young to work were meant to be indoors, but a few ran outside to see what was happening. Ulicha, who had hurt her foot and couldn't work in the fields, herded them into a room in the house next to Izat's, motioned for me to join them and closed the door. I was unnerved by this change in routine and put my burqa on, then positioned myself near a window, heart thumping. There was obviously a meeting of some sort about to take place, and I wanted to make sure it wasn't with Asim.

The men formed a circle around Izat, squatting or sitting on the ground, listening intently as he started speaking in a low voice. Within minutes, I heard the sound of footsteps, and four American soldiers appeared.

My heart started galloping – had they come for me? How did they know I was there? I felt flushed and was suddenly hot. When I put my hand on the windowsill to steady myself, it was shaking so much that it made the fabric of my burqa flutter.

The men around Izat stood, hands on their guns as one of the soldiers approached him.

Abdul-Bari stepped forward.

'I will translate. What is it you want?'

'Thank you. Our translator left us, and my Pashto still isn't great.'

Izat said something.

'My father greets you, Captain Davies, and says sit and say what you came for.'

'Thank you.' The captain told his men to sit and he took a patch of ground in front of Izat.

'The last few days have seen a series of unfortunate incidents. I'm sure that you don't want any more of that. Too many men have been killed on both sides.' He paused for Abdul-Bari to translate. Izat said nothing.

'As I said in our last meeting, we want to work with you not against you. We agreed then that our aims were the same. To get rid of the insurgents, Al-Qaeda, the Taliban and their supporters, and build infrastructure.'

I was shocked. They'd met before like this, quite civilly, and they still went and killed each other later. Maybe I was naïve, but I really didn't understand this war.

Izat said something and Abdul-Bari translated; 'There are no foreigners here.'

'As you say, but there were some here recently.'

As Abdul-Bari repeated what the captain said, Izat became angry. He spoke heatedly, looking at the captain as he did so.

'He say you want to build a clinic and a road in the valley, but only if we tell you where the insurgents are. You tell us that we know where they are, and yet, we don't.'

The captain smiled. 'Look, Mr Mohmand, I know how tricky the Taliban can be. They're very good at melting away, but don't you have any idea where they might be holed up? You know these mountains so well, probably better than them. Where would you go?'

There was another exchange between Izat and Abdul-Bari.

'They come, they go. They tell us nothing. They wanted food. We gave them food, they left when you attacked. Captain Davies, you have been here long enough to know Pashtun custom. You yourselves have eaten with us. We do not ask questions. Maybe they hide in caves, maybe they go over border to Pakistan.'

'Well, you know that without intel I can't authorise the money for your clinic.' He looked around at Izat's men. 'Sure looks like you could do with one right about now.'

Izat shifted on his stool. He was obviously in a lot of discomfort.

My attention was caught by movement to my right. One of the children was running out of the house holding something in his hand. The American soldiers snatched up their weapons and took aim. Without thinking, I followed him and shouted, 'No!'

The next few minutes seemed to happen in slow motion. The soldiers turned their weapons on me. Captain Davies turned to his men. 'Put your weapons down. At ease.'

It occurred to me that I could leave with these Americans,

that all I had to do was take my burqa off and start speaking to them in English. Without thinking, I took a step towards them.

Abdul-Bari leapt up. He started yelling at me in Pashto. All eyes followed. He was at my side in a second, hissing at me to get back into the house and say nothing more.

Hands grabbed me, and pulled me roughly to one side. I fell, landing heavily on my hip and shoulder, unable to put my hands out to break the fall. Ulicha's voice was in my ear, saying words I didn't understand, but making herself clear anyway: she was angry, and I was to go with her.

As we reached the house, I heard Captain Davies call his men together.

'Looks like they've got themselves a little domestic here, boys. Time to leave. Mr Mohmand, we'll see you real soon. I'm sure we can reach an arrangement that is mutually beneficial.'

Captain Davies led his men out of the village and down the hill without a backward glance.

There was a vein throbbing in Abdul-Bari's neck when he spoke to me.

'Do you know what you did? If the Americans knew that you were English they would have taken you away and killed us all.'

'I thought they were going to shoot Zalmay.'

'You stay away from what you don't understand.' He spat on the ground then turned and left.

'You brought me here you fucking hypocrite,' I shouted after him. His step didn't falter.

Some days later Abdul-Bari came to find me.

'We leave tomorrow,' he said.

'Where are we going?'

He waved a satellite phone at me. 'Money has been paid.' He turned and walked away.

'Who by, the Taliban? I won't go,' I called after him.

He swung round.

'Not Taliban.'

Relief swept over me. I was going back to Peshawar, to freedom. To Faisal. Alone in the village later, I hummed as I sat in the dirt, drawing pictures with a stick.

I had nothing to pack, no preparations to make, so the day dragged on and on. In a few days I would see Faisal. My world would feel right again.

The children had not been allowed to come to me for lessons once I'd made the faux pas in front of the Americans, so I didn't even have that distraction to look forward to when they came back from the fields.

As the sun sank behind the mountains I was surprised to feel sadness as well as relief. This was my last night in the village, and I'd become familiar with the place, the lifestyle. I'd been bored a lot of the time but I had a grudging respect for these people.

After Fajr the following morning, I went to say goodbye to Izat. He was almost completely recovered, although he would never have the strength to fight again.

I knelt in front of him and apologised for my behaviour in front of the Americans. Abdul-Bari translated.

He waved a hand as if to discard my apology. 'You have helped us,' he said.

I didn't know if he meant that the ransom money was useful, or that my nursing skills were appreciated, and I didn't really care. 'I will remember you all,' I said, and got up to leave.

While the mules were being loaded with the few vegetables

the villagers could spare, the women and children appeared. They were carrying their scythes ready for a day's work, but they stopped and smiled, some even touched me on the arm. In leaving, I was forgiven. Zalmay ran up to me and hugged me round the waist.

'Goodbye, teacher,' he said.

'Goodbye, student,' I said. 'Keep practising your English, okay?'

He pulled away. 'Okay,' he said, and gave me a thumbs up.

And then we were off. Abdul-Bari and another man, quiet Pohand who was barely more than a boy, would be accompanying me and collecting more weapons for the return journey. I thought of Tariq and the ways in which he had subtly made life easier for me both on the way to the village, and once we got there.

On the third night, we arrived in Jamshid's village. Jawana ran out to greet me.

'It has been a long time,' she said.

'Yes, it has.'

'How are you, Jawana? Are you well?'

'I am well, Alhamdulillah.'

'I'm glad.'

'Thank you. And now, my father is waiting to greet you.'

Jamshid was sitting in the main room of his house on a cushion.

'Forgive me if I don't get up,' he said as I entered.

'Of course,' I said.

'Please, sit. I hear that times have been hard since last we met.'

I bowed my head.

'I admire you. You didn't have to help, and yet you did. May I ask why?'

I took a deep breath. It still hurt to think of Farida's death. And Tariq's too.

'It's complicated. The attacks, the suffering. I understood then the desire for vengeance. But when the Americans came into the village and were welcomed, given tea, I was confused. I don't understand this place. I thought I could, but now I know I never will. It's all so senseless, this fighting, killing...'

'I understand.' Jamshid was quiet for a few moments. 'But you know how we feel. We cannot do nothing. You know that?'

'Yes, but I can't agree with it.'

The next morning Pohand and Abdul-Bari loaded up the Land Cruiser with produce from the village to sell in the markets in Peshawar.

'We must go,' he said.

Jamshid came out to say goodbye.

'Keep us in your thoughts,' he said. 'As you will be in ours.'

'I will. I hope this war will be over one day.'

'Insha'allah.'

With that, we were on our way. The track was every bit as bumpy and alarming as I'd remembered it, but by mid-afternoon we were driving along a sealed road, travelling fast. And every heartbeat was taking me closer to my love.

Abdul-Bari eventually broke the silence I'd grown accustomed to.

'My brother, may he rest in peace, admired you greatly. I thought you should know.'

I was taken aback and took a while to respond.

'Thank you. I had great respect for him too,' I said.

'That is all we will say.' Abdul-Bari flashed me a stern look in the rear-view mirror.

'That is all that needs to be said,' I agreed.

'Will you be taking me to the city?' I asked a while later.

'No. To the place we picked you up, the farm near Pir Qala. It has been arranged,' said Abdul-Bari. He turned and handed me back my passports that he'd taken when all this started.

As we approached the farmhouse, Sajjad rushed out to meet us and bowed low to Abdul-Bari as he got out of the Land Cruiser. I looked around for Faisal.

And then everything was chaos. My door was yanked open and I half fell out. Hands helped me regain my balance.

'Saleem – what the–'

'It is good to see you Madam Laila,' he said, almost bouncing with excitement. So he hadn't been the one to betray me after all. I felt guilty for blaming him.

I saw my father standing by the steps to the front door of the house. 'Mr Afridi – what are you doing here?'

His face was one huge smile and light danced in his green eyes.

'I came to welcome you home.' He came over and took my hand. 'I am proud to call you my daughter. I should have known right from the first moment of our meeting. Please forgive me.'

I couldn't answer, there was a knot in my throat.

I looked around. 'Where is Faisal?'

Saleem had started bouncing again and my father turned to me with a puzzled look on his face.

'We know nothing of a Faisal. Who is he?'

'My friend. Faisal Choudhry.'

'I did not know his name, Madam Laila. I have not seen him,' said Saleem.

Of course he didn't know him. They'd never met, I'd never mentioned his name. He must even now be searching for me, wondering what on earth had happened. Or maybe he thought I'd suddenly left him and gone back to England. I had to see him as soon as possible. 'I thought he must have paid the ransom,' was all I said aloud.

'Your mother and grandmother paid most of it. A friend of yours paid some, and I made up the rest,' said my father.

Saleem was still bouncing up and down like a kid in a sweet shop.

'Tell her, Saleem. Tell her what you did,' said my father.

He turned to me, his grin almost as wide as his face.

'I had to think what to do, but then I thought of your father. I told him that his fair daughter had been kidnapped and that he should do whatever a father could to have you returned. It was a good idea, I think so.' Saleem ran a hand through his hair and smiled at me.

I must have looked confused. Saleem faltered and my father stepped in.

'I'm afraid I didn't believe him at first. You had said nothing when we met, and I am afraid I was blind. I thought that maybe he was trying to trick me out of some money.'

'Yes, it was too frustrating. I had to practically tell him twenty times before he believed me!'

'And then, of course, Saleem brought me here to find out what we could. Sajjad was here, but no one else. I left a note with him demanding the kidnappers contact me and only me. Sajjad also had your handbag with your address book in it, so I contacted your mother' –he reddened but carried on – 'since then we have been in constant contact.' He looked away, blushing deeply.

'Mum? On Skype? You've seen her?'

'Yes. She is still the same, still beautiful.'

I took a deep breath. 'I must let her know I'm okay. And I need a shower and some clean clothes,' I said. 'I haven't washed properly for – how long have I been gone exactly?'

'Almost eight weeks,' said my father. 'I am so sorry it took so long to gather the ransom.'

'It's all over now. Thank you. And now, that shower.'

Saleem looked embarrassed, but my father laughed. 'Quite so. I brought some of your clothes from the hotel.'

Standing under the hot water I tried to think about what had happened. Why hadn't Tariq and Abdul-Bari contacted Faisal? Why hadn't they found him? I needed to go to the hospital as soon as possible.

Clean and feeling more relaxed than I had in months, I sat with my father and Saleem.

'I can't thank you enough for masterminding my release, Saleem. I owe you, big time.'

'But I am your good friend. I was only worried that we might not find a way to get you back from those kidnappers.'

'But you did.'

'Did you like my country?'

I thought for a moment and answered as honestly as I could.

'It is harsh but beautiful,' I said.

He seemed content with that.

I turned to my father.

'I'll pay you back the ransom money when I can, but thank you.'

'You will do no such thing. It is an honour to be able to help and would bring me great shame if you would not allow me to do as I see fit. It is over. We will talk of it no more.'

I started to remonstrate, but he raised an eyebrow that said very clearly that that was the end of the matter.

Who was the friend who had helped? Pete? Jeanette? Had Bindhi asked her wealthy family?

~

'I booked a room for you again at the hotel. I would invite you to stay, but it would not be proper...' said my father.

I smiled. 'I understand, it's fine.'

In truth, I would have felt awkward staying with him. He was my father, but he was also still a stranger, and all I wanted to do was find Faisal. I craved his touch after all this time.

When we got to the hotel I thanked Saleem yet again.

'It is nothing. I will see you soon, Madam Laila. I am your good friend. I will look after you.'

I watched him drive off, honking his horn at a truck that swerved to avoid him, and entered the hotel, overjoyed to be out of the din and crush of traffic, the heavy, polluted air and the press of people on the streets.

Khalid grinned and rushed out from behind the desk. He shook my hand firmly.

'I am very glad to see you, Miss Laila. Welcome back to the Welcome.'

'Thanks, Khalid. It's good to be back.' And also very strange. The last few weeks already felt remote, so far removed was the experience from life in the city with its noise and bustle, running water and the promise of a soft bed.

'I asked my sister to put your belongings in your room, the same one you had before.'

'Great, thanks again.' I needed to lie down.

But back in my room, I sat on the edge of the bed trying to think. Saleem hadn't betrayed me to the kidnappers. I should have trusted him. Asim was the snake. I couldn't believe a man like him could be related to the rest of the Maliks. Or that Kamila had loved him so much.

I tried to get through to Faisal, but his phone was turned off. He was probably in surgery.

I plugged my computer in and Skyped home.

Mum, Gran and I cried and talked over the top of each other.

'I can't believe you disappeared again. We were beside ourselves,' said Mum through tears.

'Thank God you're all right, pet – we were so worried,' said Gran, wiping her eyes.

They asked about my "ordeal", and I tried to tell them, but I still hadn't found the words to describe it to myself, let alone anyone else. In the end, I said, 'I'll see you soon, okay?'

'I can't wait, pet, I can't wait,' they said in unison.

I was about to put my laptop away, but thought I'd check my emails first. I decided I should probably let my friends know I was safe and sound.

There were hundreds of emails in my inbox. I scrolled through them. The oldest ones were from Mum and friends, wondering how I was and what Pakistan was like. I'd told them all I'd found Faisal, and they asked how it was going with him, and had I tracked my father down?

There were four messages from Jake, all short.

```
Aired this morning. Getting a few calls to the
station. J xx.
Being picked up by bigger stations. Good news.
J xx.
Are you there? This is getting BIG! J.
Fuck, Laila. This is huge. Get back to me. J.
```

I stared at the screen. I'd forgotten the radio interview, the fear I'd felt before I left. But now I punched the air. It had worked. All these other emails were from people who had similar stories, who had come forward because they'd heard me speak out.

There was also a message from Taban Malik.

Salam Laila, I hope you are well and enjoying Pakistan.
I had to write to you to thank you for your radio interview. I recorded it and have played it to many people. You spoke well, with not too much emotion, and I think you will be believed. I hope it is heard in the right places. I have contacted Jake – his number was in Kam's address book. I think it is time I took some action. You have been an inspiration to me, and, I'm sure, to others. Jake and I will continue to tell whoever will listen what happened to you and Kamila, may she rest in eternal peace.
My mother and father listened to the broadcast together and shed some tears. You are in their prayers.
Taban.

I skimmed through a few of the emails from strangers thanking me for having the courage to do the radio interview, telling their stories of detention, abuse and denial. Some of them were just glad to get out, others were still traumatised by their time in prison. They had been held for anything from a few days to several months. I shook my head as I read them.

13

The next morning, after a troubled sleep and still no word from Faisal, I was sitting in the courtyard with a pot of kahwa and an omelette when Khalid ran in, waving his arms and calling my name. There was a look of alarm on his face, and I understood why when I noticed two policemen following him. My hands shook as I put my cup down. I stood up, I don't know how, and turned to face the men, aware of all eyes on me. A hush had fallen over the dining area.

'Miss Laila Seaver?'

I swallowed hard and nodded.

'You must come with us. Immediately.'

Khalid stood behind the policemen shaking his head and wringing his hands. 'It is all a mistake,' he said. The police brushed him aside.

'It's okay, Khalid,' I said, surprised that my voice sounded normal. A feeling of dread flowed through my veins.

Picking up my bag and burqa, I followed the police out to their waiting car. After the initial shock, I had been overtaken by an almost surreal calm. Of course this was a mistake. There was nothing they could hold me for. I had done nothing wrong. A little voice in my head said, *I've heard that one before.*

In the police car I opened my mouth to tell them that this was ridiculous, but the policeman who was sitting in the back with me put up a hand before I could say anything.

'Not for talking now. All questions will be put at the HQ.'

I took a deep breath, readying my string of questions, but again he held up his hand.

'No talking. It will be better for you if you do not speak.'

His tone wasn't menacing exactly, but it held authority, so I shut my mouth and remained silent throughout the drive, fearful of making things worse for myself.

It got hotter and hotter in the back of the car, and at one point, when the driver lit a cigarette, I thought I might pass out, but he opened the window to flick the ash out and the cooler air revived me.

We stopped outside a grimy, run-down-looking building in the old part of the city. A sign in Urdu and English above the door announced that it was Police HQ. I was pulled out of the car and across the potholed pavement, causing a group of young men who were passing to stop.

'Help me!' I wanted to shout at them, but their stares were not curious, not the looks of men who would stand up for a woman in the hands of the police. They had stopped merely because we were in their way.

Buoyed by the emails I'd read the night before, I remembered I had a voice, rights.

'What are you charging me with?' I asked as I was bustled through the entrance and into a small hot foyer that smelled of overly sweet air freshener on top of years of sweat and stale cigarette smoke.

'Not being charged. Just answering questions,' said a short

round man with a stout stick tucked into his waistband and boots so old the leather was cracking along the creases.

'I haven't done anything wrong. I want a lawyer. I won't answer any questions otherwise.'

I got no response. Instead, I was shown into an interview room and told to wait.

'I will get tea, then we will talk,' said the short man, and left.

I looked around the small, shabby room. There was a camera in one corner, hanging useless on its bracket. The window was so dirty there was no seeing out, the walls needed a coat of paint and had insects smeared all over them. The formica-topped table was pitted with cigarette burns and the plastic chairs had seen better days.

Left alone, my confidence failed me. I didn't know how long I could control my feelings so I put my burqa on. I would not give the police the satisfaction of seeing my fear. I paced the room, heart pounding.

After a while, the portly policeman came back with tea in a chipped cup, a paratha and a man who introduced himself as Mr Khan.

I laughed bitterly. Khan is the equivalent of Smith in Pakistan, and the reminder of my time in solitary was only too stark.

'Are you quite well, Miss Laila?' he asked.

I nodded.

He seemed relieved. I suppose a hysterical woman in the lock-up would have been inconvenient.

'I am the lawyer assigned to your case.' He looked at me over black-rimmed glasses and smiled, showing paan-stained teeth.

I didn't feel reassured. 'Has the high commission been informed I'm here?'

He looked to the policeman who shook his head.

Mr Khan gestured for me to sit and he took the seat next to

me. He leant in and whispered, 'It might be better not to demand a high commission representative at this point in the proceedings. They will know soon enough about your return, but hopefully not quite yet.' His breath was sour.

I drew away. 'Why not?'

Mr Khan turned to the policeman again. 'Please be so good as to fetch Miss Laila another cup of tea – this one is cold.'

When he'd gone, sighing and muttering as he went, my lawyer looked at me.

'Please, do you wear the burqa for religious reasons?'

'No.'

'Then please take it off. It will do your case no good to wear it.'

'What do you mean?'

'Are you a Muslim?'

'No.'

'So, you are an English national who has come to Pakistan and now you are wearing a Muslim covering. What will the police deduce from that?'

My heart sank as I understood his words. I pulled it over my head quickly, shook my hair round my face and took a deep breath. It had been airless under there but I had felt protected. Now, if Mr Khan was right, wearing it would have the opposite effect. I stuffed it into my bag which I then kept on my lap.

Mr Khan looked in the file that the policeman had placed on the table. As he read, he raised his eyebrows.

'What is it, what does it say?' I asked, craning to try and see the words.

'There is a letter in here from a man who says he saw you leaving a known training camp in the mountains. He believed it to be his duty to inform the police.'

'What? That's a lie! I was kidnapped!'

'Yes, just so. I recognise the name. He has informed on other people in this way. Such is the way of things in Pakistan that usually the charges come to nothing. You will be questioned and released. If you insist on having representation by the British high commission, this case will automatically become more complex.'

My heart was thudding. 'How do you mean, more complex?'

'I mean,' he said, leaning in again as the policeman entered the room with my tea, 'that it will be more thoroughly investigated and the police may find some evidence to keep you here. You will be made an example of.' He straightened up and addressed the policeman in Urdu.

I didn't know whether to trust him or not. What was he saying? The policeman spoke English, so why switch to Urdu? Was he trying to keep the British government out so that they could keep me in a Pakistani prison as long as they liked? Did I have any option but to go along with him? My insides churned as I sat twisting the strap of my bag in my hands.

In the end I stood and drew myself up to my full height.

'Speak in English so that I can understand what you're saying,' I said.

The men stopped and turned to me. I was taller than the policeman, and about the same height as Mr Khan.

'I want it to go on the record that I am innocent of whatever you have brought me here for. I was kidnapped and held hostage in a village in Afghanistan. A ransom was paid for my release and I was returned to Peshawar. That is all.' I looked from one to the other, eyes narrowed, daring them to dispute my story.

Mr Khan spoke first. 'That is what I have already asserted to Sub-Inspector Marwat.' He nodded at the policeman. 'I am asking him to dismiss your case.'

'Ask him to speak to my father, Mr Afridi, and my friend, Saleem. They will vouch for me. My father paid the ransom.'

'Just so. We will speak to them also, rest assured,' said the sub-inspector with a thin smile, and I wondered if I'd just got them into a whole lot of trouble too.

With Mr Khan by my side I endured the questions, most of which I couldn't answer – where was the camp I'd trained at?

I wasn't at a camp.

How many other foreign nationals were there?

I wasn't at a camp and I was the only foreigner kidnapped and held captive in the village.

Who had recruited me?

I wasn't recruited. I was kidnapped.

And finally, after what seemed like hours, 'And how long have you been working with Faisal Choudhry? We have reports of you meeting. Photographs even.'

I gasped. 'Working with Faisal Choudhry?' My stomach had hit my feet. I could hardly hold myself upright. Faisal.

'I didn't work with him.'

I had a lump in my throat but I was suddenly angry. So angry.

'So you say, but he is well known to us. You look quite friendly here.' He tossed a photo onto the table.

'Well known? What do you mean?'

'He is a member of a group we are keeping a close eye on.'

'I don't believe it. You're lying.'

'And yet, here you are. And where is he now?' He smiled and waited.

I looked at the photo. It had been taken outside the Welcome as he guided me to the car, holding my elbow and whispering something in my ear. Something that had made me laugh. It didn't look like he was going to hand me over to kidnappers.

'And this one.'

How the hell did they get that? It was of us kissing on the

rooftop of the farm, Faisal's hands in my hair. I remembered the moment, the love I'd felt. And then I realised what he'd done.

'I thought he loved me,' I said icily. Ice was better than tears. It kept me going. 'And where were these photographers when I was being kidnapped, eh? When I was being hauled into a car and driven away against my will?'

SI Marwat shrugged.

Mr Khan interjected. 'Enough. My client has told you that she was not working with anyone, that she has not been involved in any illegal activities. In fact, it is she who has had a crime committed against her. Enough questions. She has been as helpful as she can. It is not her duty to prove her innocence. It is your job to prove her guilt, which you are unable to do. You must release her.' He added something in Urdu.

SI Marwat looked at him with loathing.

'We will keep your client in for a few days while we gather information.'

'You have no authority to do so. Charge her or let her leave.'

I held my breath. What was Mr Khan doing, playing with my life like that?

Words were exchanged in Urdu again, SI Marwat getting angrier and angrier as Mr Khan responded reasonably to everything he said, a smile on his face.

Finally, he turned to me. 'All right, so now we go,' he said, gesturing to the door.

Clutching my bag, I practically ran out before SI Marwat could change his mind.

Mr Khan called for me to slow down, and caught up with me.

'There is no need to rush,' he said, puffing slightly.

'Okay. What did you say to Marwat to make him let me go?'

Mr Khan smiled. 'I reminded him that I knew the name of his informant and suspected that he was a relative of his. Many police have informants, of course, and there can be a lot of money in it.'

'What do you mean?'

'It is a corruption in our system. An informant gives information and the suspect is arrested. The police look good because they are putting people in prison. The more convictions, the higher the promotion, the bigger the pay. So the informant also gets more money. It is simple, but it is wrong.'

'So much for justice,' I said.

Mr Khan nodded. 'Indeed.'

We'd got to the packed foyer and I spotted Saleem leaning over the counter and remonstrating with the police officer on duty.

'Saleem!' I shouted above the din of dozens of men waving their arms around, demanding to be heard.

He turned and came over. I introduced him to Mr Khan who apologised and said he had to go to another case. I shook his hand and thanked him for all he'd done.

'It was nothing. I will send the bill to your hotel,' he said, and rushed off.

'Come, Madam Laila. We will go,' said Saleem, leading the way.

'How did you find me?' I asked as we sped away.

'I went to the hotel this morning to see if you needed anything and was told what had happened.'

'Once more, I'm in your debt, Saleem. I don't know how I'm ever going to thank you.'

He grinned. 'One day you can write me a reference for being a good taxi driver and a good English speaker!'

'I'll write you a hundred references.' I laughed. And then burst into tears.

How could Faisal betray me? The question circled in my head until I thought I would go mad.

~

The next day I had a visit from two men from the British high commission, Mr Nesbitt and Mr Richardson. I sensed SI Marwat's hand – if he couldn't get me, maybe they could. We sat in the courtyard, the sun filtered by the potted palms. They had a file on me. They asked the same questions that Marwat had the day before but with kind smiles on their faces hiding their disbelief, their already made-up minds. Then they changed tack.

'Tell us about the radio interview that aired in the UK on...' Mr Nesbitt looked at his notes. 'Third of July this year? What prompted you to tell a story like that?'

'Everything I said was true.' I lifted my chin and looked him in the eye. It was entirely possible that he really didn't know that his own government was throwing people into jail for indefinite periods. I suddenly saw him and his crony for what they were – small cogs in a very large wheel, not important enough to be trusted with the truth.

Mr Nesbitt changed tack again.

'What were you doing with Faisal Choudhry?'

'He was my boyfriend. We were together in England. I came out here to be with him.' I thought for a moment. Rage pulsed under my skin. 'It seems he's been radicalised. Apparently it was him who organised my kidnapping.'

The two men glanced at each other and then nodded.

'Just as we thought. Thank you,' said Mr Richards. 'Any other names you can give us?'

I thought of Jamshid and Izat, Abdul-Bari and the others in the village. And I thought of Asim.

'One other,' I said. 'Asim Malik. He's British but based in Quetta, I think. He's in all this up to his eyeballs.'

'Oh, yes, we've been watching him for some time.'

'What about me? I want to go home.'

They looked at each other again.

'We think that's a good idea.'

I had dinner with my father at the hotel that night. Mr Nesbitt and Mr Richardson had also spoken to him.

I apologised for getting him caught up in my life.

'You have nothing to apologise for. But what will you do now, Laila?' he asked, concern written on his features.

'I think it's time to go home. No one's taken my passport away again and said I can't travel, so maybe I should leave before they do.'

'You will be safe there?'

I shook my head and shrugged. 'I don't know. I have no idea what's waiting for me, to be honest.' Fear clenched my stomach.

My father frowned. 'If there's anything I can do, just tell me and it will be done.'

I was close to tears. 'Thank you. I'd love you to come and see us.' I wanted to hug him but knew how inappropriate it would be in public. Instead, I wrote my email address and mobile number on a napkin and gave them to him, letting my hand brush against his as I did. It was the first time we'd ever touched.

The next day I booked my ticket home. I had two more days left in Pakistan. I spent one of them with Saleem. He introduced me to his younger sister, who was beautiful and as intelligent as her brother, and the other with my father at his farm. I met my brothers, Zahir, a quiet, shy young man with a wide smile, and Jawad, who had returned from university especially to meet me.

He looked like a younger version of our father, and welcomed me as if we had known each other all our lives. We talked about our childhoods. Our upbringings couldn't have been more different, and yet there were so many things we agreed on, opinions we shared.

'You even have the mannerisms of our father,' said Jawad, laughing.

I raised an eyebrow.

He laughed, pointing. 'That's it, exactly. And the way you turn your head to the side when you don't understand something, as if you haven't quite heard it. He does that, too, you watch!'

My father smiled. 'I think he is right.'

I did watch, but not only my father. I observed my brothers, committing as much as possible to memory. And then we took photos of each other. Lots of photos.

I wanted to leave quietly, to slip out of the country unnoticed and free of drama. I had said my tearful farewells, but as Khalid dragged my suitcase out onto the pavement, there they all were – Saleem, my father and brothers. Khalid laughed, and heaved my case into the boot of Saleem's taxi.

'We planned and plotted this big surprise for you! You will come again, Miss Laila. I know it. It is not goodbye, only 'See you later!''

'I hope you're right, Khalid. Thanks for everything.'

I laughed, although tears also sprang to my eyes. I looked at the bright faces of the men who were looking at me – my family, my friends. I would miss them all.

Khalid stood in the road as we drove off, waving.

Airport farewells have to be the saddest of partings. We sat around stiffly, filling in the time with idle chatter, not wanting to start conversations we wouldn't be able to finish. In the end, I stood up and declared that it was time to go to the departure gate.

'Can I give you a hug?' I asked.

My father smiled. 'We are family, it is permitted. Even Saleem is your brother for today.'

'I am your brother always,' he said.

14

October 2006
England

I entered England on my own passport. I'd torn up the fake one before I left Peshawar. I half expected to be met by police or government officials but no one stopped me. I breathed a sigh of relief and let the tension in my shoulders release.

As I entered the arrivals hall I saw Mum jumping up and down, waving madly. We fell into each other's arms and held onto each other while people flowed around us. Finally, Mum stood back, holding my face in her hands.

'Let me look at you.'

I smiled as she peered at me.

'I have to say, that in spite of everything, you look well, pet.'

'So do you,' I said. She didn't. She'd lost weight. Her face was gaunt.

'I want to know everything, but I'm not going to ask now and make you tell it twice. Your gran made me promise I'd wait till we get home. Just tell me one thing. Were you hurt in any way?'

I thought about that. The truth was, it wasn't the kidnapping that had been the worst thing, but how to tell her that? She was searching my face, waiting for an answer. 'I was treated quite reasonably. It was primitive, I was scared, but I wasn't hurt. Not by the villagers.'

Mum looked at me, the tension leaving her face. 'But?'

I sighed. All the sadness and anger I felt about Faisal hit me like a fist. I felt winded, crushed.

'I thought Faisal loved me.' Tears spilled and I grabbed hold of her and held on for dear life. She rubbed my back and uttered soothing noises until I pulled away, blew my nose and smiled apologetically to the woman who was trying to wheel her heavily-laden trolley past us. Mum was about to say something, but I didn't want to talk about him, not then.

'Dad says hello,' I said, and watched her blush.

'Car's not far away,' she said, and grabbed my case.

It was a cool day, the clouds hanging low in the sky. Such different light to the mountains I'd left behind. Mum manoeuvred the car out of the multistorey car park and headed east along the M4.

'Don't we need to go the other way?' I asked.

Mum smiled. 'We've got a little visit to make first. Won't take long.'

I was tired, and had been more anxious than I wanted to admit about my return to England. All I wanted to do was see Gran, eat some home-cooked food and go to bed. Instead, Mum was taking me on a magical mystery tour.

I huffed. She put her hand on my thigh and said, 'We won't stay long, promise.'

After a few miles she turned off the motorway and minutes later we pulled up in front of the Maliks' house.

'Ayesha and I have been chatting quite often since your interview.'

'Ayesha?'

'Yes. Ayesha Malik. She's desperate to see you, to make sure you're all right.'

Taban opened the front door, a big smile on his face and arms wide in welcome. I'd never noticed before how like Kamila he looked. It took my breath away.

'Let them in, let them in,' said Mrs Malik pushing him aside. She would never be anything but Mrs Malik to me.

'Laila – it is so good to see you. What a terrible time you've had.' She hugged me so tight I could hardly breathe. 'And this is your mother, Lynette,' she said, releasing me and turning to Mum. 'So nice to finally meet you in person.' She took Mum's hands, and then pulled her into a hug too. 'Come, come. Tea is waiting.'

She ushered us into the living room where samosas and chutneys had been laid out on the coffee table.

'Now, sit and eat,' said Mrs Malik. 'Taban, fetch the tea and coffee. It's ready in the kitchen.'

I couldn't believe the change in her. Gone was the thin, practically monosyllabic, grieving mother, only to be replaced by this talkative, rather bossy woman – the Mrs Malik I'd first met years ago.

'It is such a shame we couldn't get hold of Asim. We tried over and over again, but he must have been on one of his sales trips. He would have helped, I'm sure.'

I gulped and dropped the samosa I was eating. The very name Asim made me shudder. Here I was with his family who would likely never see him again because of the choices he'd made, and yet I couldn't tell them, it would break Mrs Malik's heart all over again.

'Laila, are you okay?' Mum was watching me.

'I'm fine. Got a bit of chilli in the samosa.'

Taban came back with a tray of drinks.

The doorbell rang and Taban went off again to answer it. I heard male voices in the hall and then Jake walked in.

'Here she is, the people's heroine,' he said, and pulled me to my feet.

I laughed, glad for the distraction, and surprisingly happy to see Jake.

'Hardly,' I said. 'You did all the work.'

'Me and my mate, Taban here,' said Jake, slapping him on the arm. 'We done another piece, ain't we? Did you tell her, Tab?'

'No, not yet. She only just got here.'

'What is it?' I asked.

Mrs Malik interjected. 'Let the poor girl eat. She has been sitting on a plane for hours.'

Mum smiled at me and raised her eyebrows. 'You okay, pet?'

'Yeah, fine.' I turned back to Jake. 'So, tell me all.'

'Well, we heard that you were kidnapped, and by then you were becoming a rallying point. People who heard you on the radio started news groupings on this new thing called Twitter, as well as MySpace and Facebook. #Lailainsolitary did the rounds. And we set up a Flickr account and shared photos of you, and other people who'd been rounded up and thrown in prison started sharing their photos too. It was like this great community that was growing before our very eyes, wasn't it, Tab?'

Taban nodded. 'It was so fast we could hardly keep up.'

'Yeah. So we did a bit on you being kidnapped, and it was huge. I'm talking thousands of likes and shares. So we started #Lailaiskidnapped. We've had people calling the Home Office demanding they step in to get you freed, and Pete somebody started a collection via Facebook to help pay the ransom.'

I sat listening, my eyes growing wider. I looked at Mum.

'You knew about all this?'

'Yes, pet. Jake even interviewed me over the phone for his second radio piece. Not that I could tell him much, but he thought it would help.'

'Course there were some who thought you'd been radicalised and gone off to join the cause, so we got quite a bit of hate mail too. People can really be nasty. But most of it was really positive. It was so cool.' Jake shifted from one foot to the other in his nervous, hyperactive way, drew his hands through his thin hair and smiled.

I looked at him, awed by all he'd done. To him it was a game, to see what he could come up with next. It was good to have him on my side.

'But how am I going to repay all these people?' I asked.

'Nothing to repay. Not money, anyway. They were happy to give what they could. There is something though – I've promised an interview with you as soon as possible, and some of the folks want to meet you.'

I felt heavy all of a sudden. Exhausted. And yet, I was also more grateful than I could express.

I tried to smile.

'She's been through an ordeal, Jake. She needs to rest,' said Mum. I wanted to hug her.

'Sure, sure,' said Jake. 'Next week'll be fine.'

'Thanks,' I said.

Mum stood and pulled me to my feet, put her arm around my shoulders. 'And now, Laila needs to go home. Thank you for your hospitality, Ayesha. We'll see you all again soon.'

I fell asleep in the car, waking only when we left the motorway and were driving through the outskirts of Thirsk. I sat up, rubbing my eyes, taking in the familiar scenery – St Mary's church, the square, and clock tower, the green hills in the background.

I fell into Gran's embrace as she opened the door and felt Mum's arms wrap around us both. I was home.

Gran had made dinner and I savoured every mouthful as I tried to tell them about my – I didn't know what to call it. Mum referred to it as my ordeal, but only some of it had felt like that. I thought of it more as hollow time, time spent outside of my life. An extension of my time in prison but different. All I could do was assure them that I was okay, that I hadn't been hurt. It seemed so inadequate, but how could I sum up all that had happened, all I had felt, all I had done?

'The mountains are incredible. They stretch so far and change with every shade of light.' And they hide so much, I added to myself. 'I really like my father,' I said, 'And my brothers.'

Mum took my hand and squeezed it. 'I'm glad you met him.'

I smiled. 'He'd like to see you again.'

She blushed and played with her hair.

Gran made a great show of collecting the plates and taking them to the sink. Too much emotion for her.

I lay in my bed that night but couldn't sleep. There was too much going through my mind. The excitement of learning that there were others speaking out, the idea of meeting some of them and sharing our stories. I was also worried that there would be more questioning. Just because I hadn't been detained at the airport didn't mean I was in the clear. No doubt I was on some sort of watch list, my movements being monitored. Things had gone too smoothly since my 'interview' with Mr Nesbitt and Mr Richardson in Pakistan. I had been watched almost constantly since I was first detained and now I couldn't trust that I was finally free. I fell asleep thinking of Mum and Gran, and that I was lucky to be so loved.

The next day I called Jake. If he was surprised to hear from me so soon, he hid it well. He said he was at my disposal, and so we did the interview there and then, over the phone. I told him everything and was exhausted by the end. I hadn't spoken in such detail about these things to anyone. Now everyone who was interested would know.

'Okay. I'll get it out as is. No need to edit it. It'll air tonight.'

'Thanks, you've been great.'

'So, can I set up a meeting with some of your supporters soon?'

'How about next week?'

'Sure, I'll let you know when. Hang in there, babe.'

I smiled as I hung up. Babe indeed.

EPILOGUE

So that's my story.

I've been home for a year now. I still talk to groups occasionally about my time in detention, and I lobby the government to treat detainees better, but I have moved beyond the raw anger, the desire for revenge.

As well as Mum and Gran, the Maliks and Jake, Pete has been my steadfast companion and my rock. He moved up to York for work and I now teach in my old primary school in Thirsk.

Last weekend, when we were up on the moors on a cold blustery day, he proposed. I said yes, and we ran, whooping with joy, to the nearest pub to celebrate. My father and brothers, who I talk to weekly, have promised to come to the wedding and bring Saleem with them.

All is well in my world.

THE END

ACKNOWLEDGEMENTS

I am indebted, as always, to many people who provided support and encouragement along the journey of this book from initial idea to publication.

To my Writers Group at Writing NSW who gave helpful feedback, and to my first readers who were quite a cheer squad, which was encouraging.

I would go mad without all my friends – you know who you are – so big thanks to you for keeping me sane(ish).

Michael Cybulski, Sue Anderson and the team at NAC have always believed in my work and helped me bash it into shape and find it a home... with the fabulous Bloodhound Books. Thanks to Betsy, Fred, Tara, Maria and my wonderful editor, Ian Skewis.

And finally, to my family near and far – we're spread around the world these days – huge love and thanks.

A NOTE FROM THE PUBLISHER

Thank you for reading this book. If you enjoyed it please do consider leaving a review on Amazon to help others find it too.

We hate typos. All of our books have been rigorously edited and proofread, but sometimes mistakes do slip through. If you have spotted a typo, please do let us know and we can get it amended within hours.

info@bloodhoundbooks.com

Printed in Great Britain
by Amazon

67091032R00190